VANGIE'S GHOSTS

BOOKS BY PAUL DI FILIPPO

PAUL DI FILIPPO
VANGIE'S GHOSTS

BLACK
STONE
PUBLISHING

Printed in the United States of America

First edition: 2024
ISBN 979-8-212-17527-2
Fiction / Science Fiction / General

Version 1

Blackstone Publishing
31 Mistletoe Rd.
Ashland, OR 97520

www.BlackstonePublishing.com

To all the Deborah Newtons of creation

PROLOGUE

The man and the woman spoke of the girl child as if she weren't there.

And truthfully, she really wasn't.

She was everywhere and nowhere at once.

The rusting, shabby car—a lumbering 1980 Electra Park Avenue now some fifteen years past its showroom glory, its formerly bronze paint faded to unlovely taupe—sped too fast through the winter's early dusk. A dreary country road, palisaded by bare spectral identical trees, hosted little additional traffic. The newly sunken sun had left an umber smudge across a low band of dull platinum clouds.

The man drove. Wiry and compact, he wore a beaten yet defiant look on his unpleasant narrow face, a look that seemed to hint at a capacity for violence should he be pushed too hard. The woman sat as far away from him as the bench seat allowed, pressed against the passenger door's seepage of intrusive chill, for the car's heater hardly worked. Dark-haired, she showed once-elegant lines of face and form ground down and coarsened by travails.

Intermittent slashes of tree-shadow whipped across their nighted faces. From the lowered radio came a jarring musical complaint: "The world is a vampire . . ."

In the rear seat, a scuffed child-carrier pasted with peeling fairytale decals was strapped into position, offering its backward-facing, blank-eyed rider a view of seat cushion fabric and, through the gloom-filled rear window, of all the skies being left behind.

The child in the carrier was of average size for her age, some three years old, neither spindly nor hefty. Her cheap outerwear, a dirty white sweater under a half-zipped black nylon shell, was insufficient for the temperature, and she seemed to shrink into herself for heat. Pink wool leggings and little sneakers adorned with the Magic School Bus completed her outfit. Her features were coarse and slack, not alert or engaged like those of a normal toddler—almost smeared into indistinctiveness. A paintbrush's worth of lusterless straw-colored hair protruded from beneath the rim of her too-tightly cinched cloth cap.

The car's wheels ate up another mile before the man spoke.

"I hate this fucking kid. She's killing me. Look at all this driving we had to do today, just to get her to the clinic and back."

The woman's expression registered a sharp instinctive protest against the harshness of the complaint, but a moment's quick reflection upon the consequences of any hasty words from her quashed any verbal rejoinder. After some further thought, she said only, "We adopted her. We have to take care of her. It's our duty now. Our obligation."

Her words seemed designed to convince not only her partner, but herself. They emerged with little conviction or force, in a kind of quietly desperate tone.

"They stuck us with a feeb on purpose."

"Steve, you know that's not true. Nobody had any idea

Vangie would turn out like she has. She was only six months old when we got her. She seemed normal. A mostly happy baby. We both wanted her. You remember? We agreed right away. After so long trying to have one ourselves . . . There was no way to tell how she'd develop. This autism thing doesn't come out till they're older. It's just a chance any parents take."

"Oh, shit, that's funny, really funny, Becky. Parents! We ain't no parents. I didn't knock you up because you can't get knocked up. If things were different, if she'd been really our flesh and blood, then we'd be parents. The way it is, we're just like—I don't know. Caretakers, zookeepers. Shit, they couldn't even tell us where she came from, who her mother was, never mind her father. How'd we know she wasn't born to some other dimwit, and she's got the same damn sick genes?"

"Don't be cruel, Steve. Please."

"It's just the goddamn truth. Feeding time at the monkey house. Stick a banana in her mouth and turn out the lights."

Becky began to weep softly. Steve pressed harder on the accelerator, and the Buick's surly V8 engine surged.

Twenty silent minutes later, the car turned off the road at the entrance to a trailer park, past staked-open sagging wire gates. The peeling plastic letters of the wanly illuminated sign read Many Mansions RV and Trailer Court. Packed cheek by jowl, the dozen sessile habitable hulks situated across the gravel grounds resembled a herd of large sleeping animals.

Steve parked the car adjacent to one sloping trailer set atop a cinderblock foundation, then emerged with a jagged hurry and swept inside, leaving Becky to retrieve the girl. The woman exited, opened the rear door with a weary sigh. Leaning into the back seat to unlatch the belts securing the girl, Becky crooned softly.

"Vangie, Vangie, my little Evangeline. Come to Mama."

But when the child, Vangie, evinced no change of expression, no stirring of emotional response, no reaching out, Becky's voice soured, altering in tone and tenor.

"Oh, Christ, you little freak, why can't you just show me *some*thing human?"

She set Vangie on her feet. "You'll walk now, I'm not gonna carry you no more."

With the impetus and guidance of Becky's hand in hers, Vangie toddled in a stiff-legged, half-oblivious manner after her mother. Up the unpainted, canted wooden steps of the trailer and inside, where several bare, low-watt bulbs dispensed a stingy radiance.

A foldable futon frame bearing a thin mattress, angled upright to serve as a couch, pressed against one wall. The stained futon was partially covered with an acrylic afghan of colorful knitted squares. An oval faux-wood coffee table showed scars where cigarettes had extinguished themselves. A smell of disinfectant and boiled vegetables permeated the cabin's interior.

Steve sat in a tattered recliner in front of the blaring television, a giant Magnavox hosted in a particleboard cabinet, with a half-full bottle of Smirnoff Ice vodka and a paper cup in hand.

"No, Professor Arturo," said the young man on the flickering screen. "It's not another planet. It's our world. The same planet, but a different *dimension!*"

Becky shut and locked the trailer door, kicked off her snow boots. "You're not gonna start drinking without something in your stomach, are you?"

"Maybe. Maybe not. Depends if you heat something up fast enough for us. Don't we have a frozen pizza left?"

"I'll see. Just give me a minute to feed the kid and get her to bed."

"Why bother? She won't complain or know the difference if she has to wait. She wouldn't bitch if she didn't eat till breakfast."

"Do you want her to get sick and die?"

Steve said nothing.

Vangie remained planted upright exactly where she had been halted by her mother. Her eyes seemed to be tracking the darting flight of a swarm of invisible midges. Occasionally her lips would move, almost imperceptibly, as if attempting to form all the words she had never yet uttered.

"Steve, look at her. She's having one of those spells again."

"So what? She's just seen a doctor, and they said there's nothing wrong with her body. It's all in her head. Bad wiring. Nothing we can do about that."

"I guess. But it still creeps me out."

Becky hastily stripped the child down to her underwear. "You could use a bath, I guess, but not tonight. It's too late, and I'm tired."

Stuffed into cotton pajamas more suited for summer than the damp chill in the trailer, Vangie was lifted and placed in a high chair that was a tight fit for a child her age. Becky set before her a white-bread peanut butter sandwich and a sipping cup of milk. The eating and drinking process had to be initiated—food emplaced in hand, hand carried to mouth—but then Vangie carried on autonomously, in a robotic fashion.

"Thank Christ you can do that much," Becky said to no one special before moving off to attend to the meal for her and her husband. She found a tub of coleslaw to accompany the pizza, and some Oreos for dessert. When the microwave dinged, Steve got up boozily and came to the table. The level in the vodka bottle had sunk by two inches. The television continued to play to no audience.

Vangie finished eating, carrying nonexistent food and drink to her mouth for a few passes before the absence of objects penetrated her dulled awareness, whereupon she stopped.

Observing this empty ritual, Steve let disgust wash over his face. "Jesus, what a goddamn farce! Get her outta here, right now!"

Becky pulled Vangie roughly up and out of the chair. In the bathroom she passed a wet cloth roughly across the girl's dirty face. She yanked down Vangie's bottoms and undies and set her on the toilet, then left the room. The girl used the pot with no evident consciousness, just an animal habitualness. Becky returned, satisfied herself about the elimination, and took a disposable diaper out of a pack on the floor. She crammed Vangie into the diaper, yanked the pajama bottoms on, then hustled her to the tiny room at the farthest end of the trailer.

Here Vangie had a crib, a small chair, a few stuffed toys. Otherwise, the room was undecorated and colorless.

Becky arranged her adopted daughter on her back under a white fleecy blanket, head pillowed. Vangie's gaze sought the featureless ceiling.

Becky bent halfway down, intending a kiss. But she stopped before completing the gesture, straightened up with a sigh, and left the room.

The mostly closed door brought a darkness lanced by a tranche of light and television laugh track and the voices of her parents arguing—but no immediate sleep for the child.

There remained too much to see.

The ghosts swarmed everywhere, all the time, omnidirectionally present, no matter where she aimed her gaze. A full-color theater of alternatives, an endlessly exfoliated cinema of possibilities.

And all the most prominent ghosts, the salient actors, the foregrounded figures, were her.

Other familiar figures, and many strangers, were represented in her field of vision as well—so long as they were in proximity to the many Vangies: so long as they shared some connection to her life.

To the billions of lives she simultaneously led.

The other spectral Vangies—she knew her own doughy face from multiple mirrors' surfaces, from cognition tests in the offices of a dozen doctors, therapists, and clinicians—were not opaque, not solid like Steve and Becky and the bed in which she tautly rested. They exhibited varying degrees of lifelike polychromatic translucency. Some seemed *almost* tangible, more prominent and privileged; others were nearly transparent, just faint adumbrations of form and silhouette. They were stacked behind and around each other, inhabitants of myriad floating windows or ethereal television screens, arrayed at all angles to each other: an infinite corridor of worlds receding into infinity, interlaced, interleafed, each ever-traveling pane featuring actors in full motion, as these Vangies went about their lives.

Some of the lives in these incessant animations—those somehow "closest" to her—were identical to what she experienced minute by minute—so far as she could discern with a mind not trained in logic or rationality or linear thought, a mind barely sentient but nonetheless sharpened with three-plus years of acute observation, of continuous sensory acquaintance with these ghosts, of empathizing with and internalizing their existences. These nearest Vangies mimicked exactly whatever was happening to her. There seemed to be an infinite number of this type of ghost, each pointlessly replicating Vangie's sad existence.

Then, there were an equally inordinate number of ghost Vangies at one further metaphysical remove, who might differ from her in the slightest, the most minute and almost imperceptible points: a sweater buttoned one button different, a fingernail chewed down to the quick where hers was unbitten, a blanket pulled up just a fraction of an inch closer to her chin.

And beyond these slightly divergent Vangies the spectrum of differences continued, extending in limitless variability almost beyond reason or perception or prediction. Vangies who looked more and more unlike her the further they receded. Vangies with different parents, living in different houses. Vangies in worlds where alien flora and fauna proliferated. Vangies amidst scenes of desolation or paradise. These wildly disparate incarnations were the most diffuse, the hardest to see or reach, ranked deep behind the more common instances. Although sometimes their panes swam to the forefront of the parade, as if some circumstance in Vangie's own life brought them momentarily closer. Also, by exerting a kind of indescribable focusing of her vision, Vangie could willfully pull these more distant apparitions closer momentarily before they flew away again.

This constantly oscillating visual cacophony was accompanied by an audible roar, although thankfully much less intense in degree than the visions. Regardless, the sonic chaos filled her ears. All the sounds from each living window—gratuitous noises, deliberate speech, natural phenomena—played out at an almost subliminal level. But, combined into a composite hubbub, they mounted to a universal susurration, a perpetual tide of moving air molecules. If she strained, however, Vangie could separate out some of the individual sounds, listening to voices and thunder, meows and surf, sirens and wind from a thousand worlds: a ceaseless, limitless unstructured symphony.

This whirling circus of alternity—imagery, action, and noise—had to some degree been with Vangie since birth, a moment she could keenly remember as if reinforced from a thousand perspectives.

Pushed from her mother's womb (and what face, what name, what history went with that lost maternal figure?), Vangie entered the world in serried fashion, aligned with scores of other

spectral births invisible to all but herself, a crowd of ghost Vangies filling the OR. But in the emotional and physiological crisis
of the moment, the shock and buffeting, those aligned and parallel and orbital Vangies had retreated into a kind of shrouded
presence, easy enough to ignore amidst the dominance of the
new extra-uterine world of novel sensations. And so the specters
had remained, background buzz only, for the next half year or so,
as infant Vangie acquired all the milestone abilities of any child.

But then, at six months, cradled in the arms of her new
mother, Becky, a quantum jump had occurred in her neural
architecture, as new synapses came online and sought mates,
as fresh juices and sparks seeped and crackled. A tipping point,
a cascade, was reached. Walls crumbled. Her perceptions widened, expanded, rushed outward as if to meet and beckon all her
doppelgängers. Like a flock of vampires formerly kept at bay by
ancient wards and now invited in, they swarmed into her sphere
of consciousness, shocking Vangie into a kind of battered stupor.

A state of besieged consciousness, information and fascination overload, which, years later, she had accepted as the norm,
her default condition.

She had learned how to modulate its effects to some small
degree, to pay small necessary attention to her real, immediate
surroundings, such as when set on the toilet. And she could
shift the spotlight of her attention from one iteration of herself
to another. But taken all together, the flock of ghostly Vangies
dominated her life, more so by far than her interactions with
her native continuum.

She was swamped with her selves, almost drowned in duplicates. It took all her energies not to lose the reality of her
individual unique existence, not to simply dissipate and melt
away into the pool of possibilities. Somehow she sensed how
easy it would be to accept such a fate, how likely it was that

many others like herself had already gone down such a path. Nonetheless, day by day, she found ways to keep her toehold in her own reality, to resist the call of all her ghosts. But she did so not by ignoring her alternates—an impossible task—but by keeping a sharp eye on them.

In turn, she felt the ghosts keeping an equally sharp eye on her. In fact, some of the farther-out ones—more advanced, more mature—seemed to be straining to contact her, to reach out across whatever dimensional barriers separated them all.

To say what? To do what?

Lacking an answer, Vangie hesitated to reciprocate. She kept her distance.

But the unceasing vigilance took all her energies, was all-demanding.

There was no time or capacity left for anything else, no space for anything or anyone actually within her immediate grasp.

Lying on her back in her crib, Vangie kept guard against and over all her selves. As night thickened in many of those parallel worlds (but not all of them; in some it was daylight, a noncongruent season, a shifted year), the ghosts dimmed from lack of parallel illumination, just as Vangie's own room darkened. With the lessened distractions, she felt sleep begin to creep over her.

But still she kept up her guard, until the last possible moment of awareness.

Steve and Becky had never made it into their own bedroom. They huddled, still dressed in street clothes, in an unconscious sloppy contorted tangle on the futon. The Smirnoff's bottle was empty. An ashtray held minute twists of dope roaches. The TV played on softly to no audience.

Hours passed.

A siren sounded, faint at first, then cycling into a full-throated peal. No mere vehicle's warning; it was the civic apparatus atop a tower in the nearby town.

An emergency bulletin interrupted the televised late-night talk show.

"Alert! Tornado! All citizens . . ."

The couple stirred but did not overcome the alcohol and pot still in their veins and lungs.

A roaring, whooshing, gleeful cataclysm, a rare winter atmospheric funnel gorged with debris, raced across the flat countryside, bearing down on the Many Mansions RV and Trailer Court.

And then the broad stomping foot of the killer cone of winds hit the trailer where Vangie and her parents slept, crashing into it, kicking it, lofting and hurling it like a missile against its companions, then through a line of trees, and into the steely frozen pastures a quarter of a mile distant.

For the first time in Vangie's life, cruel reality dominated over the virtual. For once the ghosts, still present, could not contend with what truly was. Their numinous allure was diminished. Her immediate circumstances outweighed the panoply of ghostly environments.

The receding express train passage of the twister filled her hearing. On her back amidst the wreckage, she had a view of the starry sky, partially obscured by a scrim of blood across her eyes. Cold radiated into her from beneath and all sides. She inadvertently filled her diaper with pee. Shards of wood and metal creaked and groaned as they settled into new configurations. Water from broken pipes dripped onto her foot. She stirred, and felt something broken in her.

She had no idea of how she had come to be here, under these conditions. (Although . . . had there perhaps been some dim foreshadowing of this, glimpsed in a remote pane, happening to another Vangie in a forward-shifted, time-discordant stream?) But she knew that she was in agony, suffering, even in imminent danger of dying, here and now. Her heart raced, and she tried to move, to push up with weak-muscled arms and legs. But something had her pinned down.

Vangie began to wail. Her cries evoked others. Moans and sobs commenced, familiar voices, a man's, a woman's, although forming no actual speech.

Becky. Steve. Her parents.

Vangie writhed against the materials that trapped her, but to no avail. Her hurting increased.

In her first moment that demanded real application of her will and her senses and her limbs to her surroundings, she met only frustration. Her physical abilities proved insufficient to alter reality.

Fear and anxiety loaned fresh urgency to her efforts—but with no results except to incite further pains.

As if sensing her despair and the limitations that weakened her, her ghosts swelled up again, clustering closer around her in a fog of realities.

While her parents continued to make their pitiful noises, and the warning siren continued to keen, Vangie gave the specters her full attention, resuming her lifetime's habit of observation, but with unprecedented purpose and concentration.

She saw in these apparitions her condition as if from outside herself: enwombed in the cold and darkness in the fractured remnants of the trailer.

Directing her sharpened focus, Vangie began to flip through the successive panes of her many lives, viewing her trapped self over and over, shuffling each unuseful image off to one side to bring another into the spotlight of her attention.

It felt like something . . . something unfamiliar.

Like running, a thing she had only witnessed, but never done. Or had she?

Running across the worlds with her mind.

After innumerable swift flicks of her focus, and miles of psychic travel, the scene started to change.

Here was a Vangie recumbent amidst the warped trailer, but not trapped. Here was a Vangie situated a little further out from the center of the debris field. Here was a Vangie entirely removed from the wreckage, lying on a frosty tussock of grass. Vangie could sense somehow—maybe just by a certain placidity of attitude and expressions—that this avatar had no injuries beyond a few bruises.

With all the powers of her mind, she reached out to this luckier counterpart. She could detect a catenary of affiliation between them, a conduit offering passage across a thinning barrier. She could follow it. She would follow it.

But then she stopped.

Her parents. Where were they in this other, safer place?

Instinctively, Vangie directed her perceptions of this new refuge down different angles of vision, scoping the scene from alternate angles allowed by her entanglement with these significant others.

In this other world, she saw Steve and Becky, dead in the smashed trailer from which little Vangie had been miraculously ejected.

Did they yet live, in other frames? Possibly, even certainly. Could she save all three of them, reunite them as a family?

But why? What family were they, what did they offer?

And the cold and wetness bit deeper into her *now*! Her shattered parts ached *now*! She wanted out *now*!

There was no time to search further, no motivation to do so, no love.

Acting on half-grasped forces, desperately, Vangie hurled some nebulous but essential portion of herself down the open avenue that stretched across unplumbed dimensions to her other form.

Her astral body leaped and ran, her consciousness, the totality of her self, riding with it.

The dry icy grass of the tussock beneath her back crackled as she rocked her small body side to side, delighting in the sensations of wholeness and freedom. Yards distant, the wreckage of the trailer that coffined her parents creaked as it settled.

The ghosts still surrounded her. But now they retreated a bit, as if suddenly placated or satisfied, happy that she had made her maiden journey through their ranks.

Vangie examined her own thoughts and memories.

She remembered awaking here on the grassy pillow, unharmed, after the twister's departure.

And she remembered awaking in the wreckage, dying.

Her mentality from her origin stream had overlapped or merged with the other mind. But the Vangie who had nearly died, the one who had initiated the leap—that was the dominant mind in the blend because it possessed the experiential memories of the other world and of using her power to travel hence.

She had saved herself.

And with that knowledge, both Vangies passed out.

BOOK ONE

PART ONE

PART ONE

In motion, the car, a six-month-old red 1998 Ford Festiva, hosted an eternal fug older than its age, an odorous clime composed of the scents of fast-food french fries, forgotten dirty gym clothes in an unzipped duffel, coffee spills, and a banana mashed underfoot into the carpeting two weeks ago and imperfectly cleansed. Its driver, a young woman, used the car as a traveling office—paperwork jutting from manila folders in a scuffed plastic passenger-seat tub—occupying it for many hours each day as she moved from one assignment to another. Today, at four p.m., with hot July sunlight heating up the un-air-conditioned interior and accentuating the stench, the atmosphere reeked of slovenly desperation, an exitless, endless incarceration.

How had she gotten into this condition? Had it only been three years since she graduated, bright-eyed and eager to help those less fortunate, to do good for society?

Making an effort to shed this recurrent black cloak of despair, the woman chalked up her low feelings to a particularly hard day. Starting at eight a.m., she had visited ten clients across a broad circuit of many tedious miles centered on her small city and extending out to the suburbs, and she still had two more families to see before the shift's end. Prior to the 1997 budget cuts at the Department of Children and Families, she had been responsible for far fewer cases. But now her workload had blossomed beyond any sane capacity. That her coworkers all wallowed through the same conditions afforded no relief. The cumulative griefs and problems and sufferings of her clients, intractable and always in danger of boiling over into a crisis situation—fights, financial losses, illnesses, accidents, foreclosures, familial feuds, evictions, firings, arrests, educational failures—weighed inexorably on her, no matter how often she tried to put aside the frustratingly avoidable yet dire predicaments of the families she serviced, after she finally clocked out at the end of a long day.

A red traffic light halted her progress. She made a quick assessment of herself in the rearview mirror. Her dark bangs clung to her pale sweaty brow. Her blue eyes were hammocked in puffy darkened flesh. Her complexion inexplicably appeared both flushed and sallow. Portrait of someone no one could or ever would love. Her mouth was sour with gas station coffee and factory-wrapped Danish pastries, and she swore that the flesh of her butt bore the impression of her car's fabric seat material. In her light, black, short-sleeved cotton top and khaki pants and comfortable beat-up boat shoes—a kind of uniform she had adopted to minimize any threatening or alluring femininity on her part, reducing her more or less to an office appliance such as a Xerox copier or new Compaq desktop personal computer—she felt dumpy and overweight, all muscle tone fled.

She really should try to get back to Gold's Gym, before or after work. But she had to start so early each morning to meet her quota, and by day's end she had no zip or initiative left. Maybe when this workday was finally over, she could at least pop her Tae Bo tape into the VCR . . .

But then she remembered. Tonight was Friday, and that meant attendance at the Temple.

Thinking back over her initial contact with the Temple and its charismatic leader, Vardis Salthouse, she was surprised to realize that she had been going there every Friday for six months now. That made her one of the longer-term members, part of the hardcore elite, for curious newcomers were always dropping in and out, never hanging in for the promised rewards—just like her girlfriend, Kelly, who had accompanied her to the first meeting on a lark, back in January's chill, when no other Friday night occasion beckoned two single women, and a small ad in the local free weekly had caught their eye while they unwound with a drink.

HAVE YOU EVER FELT EMPTY AND DIRECTIONLESS?

HAVE YOU EVER FELT YOU WERE
NOT LIVING UP TO YOUR POTENTIAL?

HAVE YOU EVER FELT THAT THERE WAS
A BETTER YOU JUST WAITING TO BE BORN?

THE TEMPLE OF HUMAN POTENTIAL KNOWS THESE
FEELINGS AND THE SOURCES OF YOUR DISCONTENTS

AND WE HAVE THE ANSWERS AND SOLUTIONS!!!

VISIT US AND HEAR THE WISDOM
THAT LEADS TO A BETTER YOU

EVERY FRIDAY, EIGHT PM,
310 CHAMPION STREET, FIRST FLOOR

VARDIS SALTHOUSE,

MANY LIVES REIFIER OF THE FIRST DEGREE

And after all these Fridays at the Temple, if one were to judge solely by the externalities of her continuing miserable drudging existence—no steady partner and few enough one-off affairs; compromised health and vitality; student loans still extant; a tedious, demanding job that was relentlessly wearing her down to a nubbin of her younger, more carefree self—then the Temple had done her little if any good. But she sensed otherwise, had an intuition that changes were building within her, even if not obvious or imminent, that all of Salthouse's lofty oratory, whose full meaning and import and redemptive significance continued to tremble tantalizingly on the verge of realization, would very soon result in her metamorphosis.

But all these speculations and desires, always fermenting at the back of her mind, could wait—and would have to wait—until tonight. She still had two clients to deal with.

Her penultimate client was a member of the Burris household. Their neighborhood, within the city limits, was lower middle class, its small individual houses all built in a postwar surge, cheaply and claustrophobically close. Present day, most of them were well-maintained, embellished over the years with additions and often gaudy refinements.

But the Burris home was an exception. Its small front lawn had been trodden to weedy dirt and was littered with toys and car parts. The water in a plastic swimming pool was more mud pit than pond.

She parked on the street rather than in the driveway, facilitating a quick getaway. She had learned this tactic during her first year on the job. Sometimes the seconds spent reversing out of the driveway would allow an irate client to catch up to her and bang on her hood, wrench off an exterior mirror, or—this had never yet happened, although she sensed it easily could—smash in her windshield.

Exiting the car, the woman adjusted the ID holder on its lanyard around her neck so that its transparent front faced outward, revealing her identification. An official badge from the DCF bearing her photo from three years ago—how happy and lively and confident she looked!—and her name: Kris Troy.

At the door Kris was greeted by Mr. Burris, currently unemployed: a skinny, perpetually harassed-looking fellow with thin sandy hair and a sparse beard to match. Barefoot, he wore jeans and a T-shirt advertising a local sandwich shop. He was attended closely by two preschool kids, a boy and a girl, the children of his current marriage. (Mrs. Burris was the family breadwinner, employed at a local muffler-repair shop.) But neither of these two kids were Kris's clients.

"Good afternoon, Mr. Burris. Sally should be home from school, I hope."

Burris streamed his fingers through his scanty hair. He spoke as if preoccupied with many other matters. "Miss Troy, sure. In her room."

"I'll just go in to see her then."

"Sure, fine, whatever."

Having knocked on teenager Sally's bedroom door, Kris received a begrudging invitation to enter. Her client rested on her back on her bed, just staring at the ceiling. A pair of red Doc Martens dirtied the coverlet.

Dressed as if following the point-by-point style guide in some notional goth handbook, Sally Burris, pale, slim, and still basically undeveloped as an adolescent, looked, Kris thought, as unthreateningly silly as a young trick-or-treater emulating some adult pop star.

"Hello, Sally. How was your day? Do you have a few moments for us to talk a little?"

"Okay, I guess. Why not?"

Kris sat on the edge of the mattress and began to inquire gently about homework and friends, diet and afterschool activities, self-cutting behaviors and suicidal ideations, all while trying to focus on keeping Sally's gaze and not letting her professional eyes wander to the girl's many scars.

After the session—which Kris thought went really well—she sat in her car and made her notes while everything was still fresh. Slotting Sally's file into the plastic tub, Kris retrieved the next and final folder, for the Everett family.

Mother Ginny Everett and five foster children: Gavril, Toby, Drew, Blaine—and Vangie.

2

Kris sat idle in her idling car for a moment outside the Everett house on Plank Street. The withering July light had mellowed a little as the sun dropped toward the horizon, but its summertime tenacity still left her eyes slightly road-dazzled and her armpits sweaty. A new favorite song of hers had come on the radio just as she was pulling up to the curb, and she wanted to listen to it all the way through.

"I want something else to get me through this semi-charmed kinda life, baby . . ."

Something else, something unknown and perhaps unobtainable. That was what she needed to revolutionize her stale, semi-charmed kinda life. But what?

As the last notes of the song segued into the disc jockey's glib patter, she switched off the car's engine, radio banter as well, and pulled the key from the ignition. She reached again for the Everett file in the tub, but then stopped. She had studied all her notes for hours, internalized all the facts. What more could be learned at this late date about the very perplexing enigma at the center of the household? What new angles of attack would further study allow her to pursue? No, there was no help in that manila sleeve. She would just have to wing it and hope not to encounter any more inexplicable phenomena that fell totally outside everything she had learned while getting her degree.

The beaten-down Everett house sat with four others on a short dead-end block. This side street terminated at a rusting chain-link fence, gapped at the bottom from various shortcut seekers and trespassers, beyond which roared the freeway that had bisected the old neighborhood decades past. Beyond the freeway, the other half of the old district had faced the incursion of an LNG tank farm and lost. Some remaining houses practically abutted the mammoth tanks. Even with its cracked treeless sidewalks, Plank Street and its surrounding blocks could not be precisely deemed a slum. But the area certainly represented the lowest rung of the ladder that transitioned from dependence— on charities or the government—to the barest minimum-wage self-sufficiency. Most of the residents, Kris knew, were minorities. A white woman, Ginny Everett was an exception, her tenure having been established through marrying a Black man, Walter, now absconded.

It was Walter's departure that had brought Ginny Everett, basically unemployable due to a confluence of poor attitudes, habitual lateness, and stubborn refusal to learn, and yet desperate for money, to foster parenting. The state paid almost three hundred dollars a month per child. Along with food stamps and Medicaid and church grocery donations, Ginny's five wards netted her barely enough to sustain her household, but she managed somehow. Her motivations might have been less than noble, her qualifications dubious, but the state was as desperate for caregivers as she was for cash, and so the bargain had been made.

At the twinned front door of the gray, asbestos-shingled

duplex whose left side housed the Everetts (the screen door sagged from one hinge, its protective mesh ripped), Kris anticipated hearing the usual noise: the back-and-forth tumult of four of the kids, all home from school and afterschool activities by now, supplemented by the coarse bellowing of Ginny Everett herself, whose eternal quest for "just one goddamn minute of peace and quiet" was destined never to be fulfilled.

But instead, total silence. Not even the constant television cacophony.

Kris rang the bell, heard it chime inside. But it still took over a minute for the door to be opened.

Gavril's unconventionally handsome pale face—a small eruption of acne at one corner of his mouth (raspberry maculations against vanilla ice cream)—bore an expression of solemn intensity, as if he had been interrupted while conducting a lab experiment involving high explosives.

Wheaten-haired Gavril had entered the United States from one of the infamous Romanian orphanages during the scandal and wave of pity occasioned in 1990, eight years ago, by the TV news program *20/20*. He had been seven years old then and showed all the seemingly permanent ill effects of malnutrition and lack of affection. A dire future had been predicted for him. But, amazingly, under more nurturing conditions, Gavril had exhibited the resilience of a baby wildcat.

Gavril's English was still a little idiosyncratic. "It is Miss Kris Troy, I see. And this is another official visit?"

"Yes, Gavril. Is Mama Ginny home?"

Gavril looked nervous, shifting from foot to foot in his secondhand Nikes. "Yes, ma'am, she is. But she is not awake."

Kris had often encountered Ginny Everett in drunken afternoon stupor, so she was not surprised. Thank God for Gavril's sense of duty to his quasi-sibs.

Upon his arrival in the USA, the boy's quick assimilation of American culture, and his ability to utilize every rich calorie of his new nation, had left him physically fit, basically upbeat, joyous, and keenly observant. Passing through a succession of foster homes—mainly due to the ineptitude of his sponsors rather than any deficiencies of his own—Gavril, Kris sensed, was patiently abiding his institutionalized time until his release into adulthood. She had had some long conversations with him about his future and had been surprised to discover that he was inclining toward enlistment in the armed services. "I must pay back this fine country," he declared solemnly.

At fifteen, he was the oldest of the fosters and was often left in charge of his "siblings" while Ginny occupied a stool at the nearby Bearsville Tavern. This breach of adult supervision was technically reportable, but Kris had never written up the infraction. Such were the practical ethical compromises every fieldworker learned to fashion. She knew Gavril to be smart and responsible, and in fact probably a better parent than Ginny. Reporting the laxness would have likely resulted in the removal of all five kids, and their reassignment to new homes, maybe no better than this one. And after more than a year together, they had begun to function almost like real siblings.

Except, of course, for Vangie.

Tired, eager for the day to be over, Kris was growing irritable. But she restrained her impatience, realizing the boy was not at fault. "Well, we can wake her up, I suppose. Try to get her coherent. I'm so sorry this falls on you, Gavril. Let me in, and we'll see what we can do."

"Well, Miss Troy, I will reluctantly report this much. It is not the hard spirits that have downed her. I think—"

"What is it, Gavril? Is it a medical emergency? Should I call nine-one-one?"

Gavril studied the uninformative welcome mat on which Kris stood. "I think it is something Vangie did to her."

Kris's brain refused at first to process the statement. She could not reconcile the reality of a semi-catatonic six-year-old who had never exhibited any kind of violence or aggressive behavior somehow rearing up unprecedently and rendering an adult unconscious. But then again, juvenile development went through stages. The girl was fully able in limbs and muscles. With a case as strange as Vangie's, who could say where her neural and physiological maturation would take her—what new plateaus of action she might graduate to?

Three years ago, the girl had been a miracle child, rescued from the aftermath of the twister that had killed her adopted mother and father, a hapless couple leaving no other relatives able to take in the girl. A three-day journalistic sensation, Vangie had not lacked for immediate foster placement, with an eye toward adoption again.

But all of those placements had terminated in one kind of crisis or dissatisfaction or incompatibility between Vangie and her caretakers.

The breadwinner in the first family, the Ralstons, had suddenly received an irresistible new job offer several states distant, and of course Vangie could not accompany the Ralstons out of the state.

The second placement, with the Brents, had ended when Mrs. Brent, after decades of inability to conceive, had suddenly found herself pregnant. Back to the orphanage for Vangie.

With the Bannerjees, Vangie had done well, except when the Bannerjee's dog—an elderly chihuahua who had never previously demonstrated malice toward any humans, fellow animals, or inanimate objects—suddenly attacked the child. Luckily, its feeble constitution forestalled any great damage. Declining to abandon their dog, the Bannerjees had instead surrendered Vangie.

And the most recent family before Ginny Everett, the

Hopps, had seemingly doted on Vangie, despite the child's nonverbal and unresponsive nature, until the day when Mr. Hopp had had a stroke that left him, post-recovery, somehow ill-disposed toward the child.

Only this last case had fallen under Kris's purview, but she knew of all the others, and had been praying fervently that this latest sponsorship by Ginny Everett would break the chain of bad luck.

But now, seemingly not.

Kris said soberly, "This sounds serious, Gavril. I'm coming in."

3

The tiny, antiquated mudroom just off the entrance was piled high with winter's detritus, never properly stored at season's end: boots, coats, scarves, hats, a plastic snow shovel with a busted handle. The odor in the cloistered space featured the main notes of wool and mothballs, with grace notes of the duplex's old plaster and wood, horsehair fibers showing in a rough hole.

The room beyond the entryway was the kitchen, and its countertop and tabletop clutter recorded at least the past several meals: cereal bowls with an ounce of colored sugared milk in the bottom, an open peanut butter jar with knife protruding, a plate lacquered with dried egg yolk, an open loaf of white bread with staling slices spilling out like dominoes, a repurposed jam jar holding two inches of congealed bacon grease . . . The aluminum-legged dinette table with its vinyl-padded chairs reminded Kris of a similar set in her aunt's house, twenty years ago: seventies kitsch.

Gavril led the way through this disreputable mess without apparent guilt or chagrin, although he did look back with concern at Kris every few steps, as if dubious about how she would receive the sights at their ultimate destination.

The parlor presented a similar scene of chaos, with school-books splayed open on the spavined sofa, empty soda cans whimsically stacked three high, and a heap of leaking stuffed toys looking like the fallen combatants of some internecine animal war. Thick dusty curtains of some kind of cheap burlap, drawn together despite the daytime, blocked the hot sunlight as best they could. Dominating the space, a bulky Sony Trinitron a few years old occupied its low table like some alien god on its altar. Sound muted, its active screen showed President Clinton outside the White House on its South Lawn making a speech, with the Marine Corps band ready to play behind him.

Gavril conducted Kris right up to the closed door she knew to be that of Ginny's bedroom. The boy hesitated for a moment with his hand on the knob, then opened the door.

Frilly curtains, a poster from *Lethal Weapon 4* in a flimsy Kmart frame, allowing Mel Gibson to radiate his allure over the sleeper's dreams. Stretched out on her unmade double bed, unconscious and fully clothed in a dirty pink tracksuit, Ginny Everett immediately and spontaneously engendered in Kris the utterly foreign notion of Sleeping Beauty. A petite woman with dyed red hair, skinny save for an alcoholic's potbelly, she generally looked much older than her thirty-five years thanks to her booze and nicotine intake. But now the unconscious Ginny somehow boasted a softer and less stressed appearance than her usual presentation.

Kris took in Ginny's regular breathing, and her fear and anxiety lessened a tad.

Only then was she able to apprehend the other three children sitting quietly around the bed like a squad of professional mourners, or observant surgeons at an unbegun autopsy.

Next oldest at twelve, Toby possessed a wary, chipmunkish face that hid behind oversized secondhand charity eyeglasses.

His white hands cradled and massaged his bare elbows as if something foreign might be growing under the skin.

The two girls, Drew and Blaine, aged five, were twin sisters. Darkly complected despite their arbitrarily assigned Anglo names, with thick black hair and hawkish features, they radiated a kind of Levantine mystery and solemnity, like waifs from some uncharted Greek island. Abandoned outside a fire station shortly after birth and hence of unknown parentage, they might indeed have fallen out of Circe's den, Kris often imagined.

The children regarded their social worker with none of the typically juvenile fidgety or rambunctious attitude they usually manifested during interviews. It was as if they had been stunned into a respectful quietude.

Kris dearly desired not to bring her boss into this, for fear of making endless future work for herself. With some intuition that arose from her three years of hard-fought fieldwork, feeling that it was safe not to immediately call an ambulance, and that proceeding slowly and deliberately would achieve the best results (and hoping fervently to still make her time at the Temple tonight), Kris broke the silence. "Gavril, Drew, Toby, Blaine—I want to hear your own story about what happened to your mom. Gavril, you say it was something Vangie did? Where is she?"

Gavril picked at a spot of acne. "Our strange sister is still where she always maintains herself, when she is not eating or in the bathroom or pursuing allied activities. Right in her chair in her room."

"I'll go check on her then. You four stay right here."

The narrow duplex boasted just two more rooms upstairs. Ideally, the boys would have slept in one room, the girls in another. But all four of the normal kids had to occupy a single room, on bunkbeds, giving Vangie the other, for Drew and Blaine would not share any sleeping quarters with their fellow foster. They could not articulate why, but it was an unswayable position.

Vangie's room showed an absence of any personality other than the generic rudiments of character imposed on her by others. A few toys, a poster of the Powerpuff Girls, some hair ribbons atop a scarred dresser. No books, of course. Aside from the bed, the only other furniture was an adult-sized recliner, black vinyl with imperfections sealed by gray duct tape. In its extended position, the chair seemed almost ready to swallow its small occupant.

Good Lord, Kris thought as she invariably did upon coming into the little girl's presence, *she is the homeliest creature I've ever seen.*

At six years old, Vangie was of average size, anomalously exhibiting good muscle tone and a healthy complexion, although lack of any real regular exercise should have hindered both. But her face had a kind of disconcerting amorphous quality, an imprecision of features as if clay had only been rudimentarily thumbed by the sculptor before being abandoned. Her flickering gaze, always fluttering in saccades as her eyes tracked flitting nothings, added to the impression of nullity. The girl could exhibit certain autonomous actions when prompted: walking, eating, hygiene. But she remained nonverbal and bereft of initiative. The chair was an alternative to letting her lie abed all day and deteriorate. She was supposed to be put through a schedule of physical activities at intervals throughout the day, but Kris suspected that Ginny—and also Vangie's "siblings"— would often just leave her to recline insensate.

How could this lump have done anything to send Ginny Everett into a coma?

Kris stepped to the chair and caused it to fold in on itself. Vangie's shod feet failed to reach the floor.

"Vangie, dear, come with me, please. We need to go see

Mama Ginny and the other children, so we can figure out what happened and what to do next."

Using a hand behind the girl's back, Kris gently brought her to a standing position. Taking the girl's hand and gently tugging her caused the child to accompany Kris out of the room. At the head of the stairs, Vangie stopped. Kris knew that the child could descend on her own, but laboriously. Suddenly begrudging all this extra unanticipated time at the Everett home, Kris just scooped up Vangie and started downstairs with her. The girl smelled like peanut butter and some dowager's powder box.

In Ginny's bedroom, Kris found the tableau unchanged. The arrival of Vangie sent a kind of subliminal shiver through her "siblings." Kris set the girl down on the foot of Ginny's bed. Vangie remained in a sitting position, as if awaiting further commands or programming.

Kris regarded the other four children with what she hoped was a look of affectionate curiosity mingled with no-nonsense authority.

"All right. Who wants to be first to tell me what happened here?"

4

Gavril always made a point of getting home first after school, before any of his siblings. He knew that he often had to be present to act as their guardian, given Mama Ginny's frequent absences or lack of attention. That meant skipping a lot of stuff he would have liked to do, from just chilling with pals to playing sports, or maybe hanging out in the computer lab. But the daily parenting demands did not trouble him very much. After the horrors of his earliest years, nothing seemed a burden. He didn't see his life as unfair; he regarded the domestic necessities not as a duty but as a privilege. Despite any erratic or illogical or selfish or temperamental behavior from Mama Ginny, this was still the best foster home he had ever been sentenced to endure. No hitting, no endless stream of put-downs, no lack of food. A safe, dry, warm place to sleep. He was allowed to go to school and to amuse himself when home. True, Mama Ginny made no pretense about why she was sponsoring the five of them: it was just for the money. But still, she could occasionally exhibit moments of genuine warmth or affection. Once, with some lottery winnings, she had actually bought all the children—except Vangie, of course—a toy apiece on a grocery-shopping trip to the plaza that also featured a KB Toys store. No, her benign neglect—Gavril had gotten that phrase from Miss Troy—was a lot better than the active abuse Gavril had so often encountered in other settings.

And his fellow fosters were all right. Toby was a nervous doofus and couldn't throw a football to save his life, but he liked the same TV shows Gavril favored: *Buffy, 3rd Rock, Unsolved Mysteries* . . . And he could be counted on to stand lookout when penniless Gavril just had to have a Kit Kat bar swiped from the local variety store—especially since Gavril always grabbed a box of Nerds for Toby too.

And Drew and Blaine, the twins, were no hassle. Fiercely dedicated to each other in a self-sufficient and self-involved way, they did not require much prompting to do whatever needed to be done, from making their beds to helping gather up dirty laundry for a trip to the Bubbles 'n' Sudz laundromat using the Radio Flyer red wagon with the one erratic bent wheel. They could even be counted on for a round of such baby board games as Candyland or Sorry! on rainy days when other fun was unobtainable.

So today Gavril was not anticipating any extra demands from his small crew when they arrived home, and was not in fact even giving any real consideration to any topic other than what his fellow ninth-grader Holly Turner might look like under that very tight blouse she had worn to school that day.

The first thing the boy did was to search out Mama Ginny. She was nowhere in the house, and Gavril felt relieved. Easier to manage everything without her. He recalled that they were due for a visit from Miss Troy today, and hopefully their foster mother would return in time for that obligation.

About Vangie, he did not worry. Yes, theoretically, Mama Ginny should not have left the girl alone. What if the house burned down? But other than such an unprecedented disaster, there was little that could befall the totally immobile child in her chair. Lacking the impulses to get up and, say, eat something, she couldn't even choke to death. She was not going to drown in the bathtub either. And she had excellent bladder and bowel control. So Gavril did not even hurry upstairs to see how she was faring.

A two-thirds-emptied liter of Pepsi in the fridge decanted into a full tumbler, quickly downed. Gavril wanted another but, regarding the level in the bottle, decided to save the rest for his sibs. Shoving stuff on the kitchen table to one side, Gavril made four plates of Ritz crackers with peanut butter. He found a slightly withered apple in the back of the lettuce crisper and quartered it. He did not pour the cold soda until he heard the school bus depositing Toby, Blaine, and Drew half a block away.

The three newcomers were greeted with the simple declaration, "Mama Ginny is among the missing." They all reacted with a decided loosening of tension and devoured their snacks.

"Okay," said Gavril when they had finished, "First, we must attend to duties before pleasures. Please give the vegetable girl some exercise, as stipulated. Get her on the toilet. Then walk her around some, massage her arms, you know the drill."

Toby said, "The twins should really sit her on the toilet. It's not right for a boy to do it, and I'm tired of it."

Gavril braced for balkiness or outright refusal from Drew and Blaine. He knew that Vangie creeped out the girls, and they usually shied away from any close interactions, performing only the tasks he assigned, and with the bare minimum of effort. But to his surprise, they readily assented.

The girls slipped eagerly off their seats. One of them— Drew or Blaine, Gavril still often mixed up their peas-in-a-pod faces—said, "That's okay, we'll do everything."

"Sure," said the other, "we're happy to help Vangie. You boys just have fun down here."

Then they sped out of the kitchen and up the stairs before Gavril or Toby could even react.

"They are unusually compliant," Gavril mused. "Any special reason?"

"I don't know," said Toby. "But they were whispering about Vangie on the bus ride home. I couldn't really make anything out except her name. Maybe the potato head smiled at them or something. You ever seen her smile?"

"Sister frozen-face? Never!"

"It sure would be nice if all the girls could be in one room, and you and me got the other. Then we could talk private about stuff that guys talk about."

Gavril poked Toby in the ribs. "Like what? Titties?"

Toby blushed and his reply was flustered. "Naw! I meant cars, boxing—stuff like that."

"Sure you did!"

"Aw, go soak your head!"

With that defiant put-down, Toby headed into the living room to turn on the TV. Gavril put the snack plates and glasses in the sink without washing them. This room was a mess, and he really should try to clean it. But not now. He joined Toby in front of the Trinitron for a rerun of "Miracle at Trapper Creek," an *Afterschool Special* about underprivileged kids at a wilderness camp. Gavril imagined how great that would be. He pictured him and Toby battling a forest fire or rescuing a lost hiker who looked just like classmate Holly Turner. She'd be so grateful she might even take her shirt off. Maybe even the twins could participate in the daydream too in some way or another. Gavril felt generous. But not Vangie. Gavril was not being mean, he felt, just realistic. It didn't matter what her surroundings were, so why bother? She would just be a drag.

When the movie was over, Gavril suddenly realized that

Drew and Blaine had not come down to join them. The twins did often play together in the shared bedroom, but they also could be counted on not to miss any episode of *Afterschool Special.* Gavril's sense of responsibility kicked in. Maybe something bad had happened to the potato head, and the girls were afraid to come down and tell him. She could have fallen in the bathroom and cracked her skull wide open!

"Let's go check on Vangie and the twins. They might need some help from us men."

"Okay!"

The door to Vangie's private bedroom was shut, and Gavril could hear noises from within: not conversation or laughter or cries of alarm coming from the other side, but rather what sounded like exclamations of surprise and awe. Feeling somewhat relieved, he let himself in, Toby right behind.

The July heat and the unopened window had rendered the room stuffy and close. The girls stood on either side of the recliner where Vangie lay, stretched out in her typical insensate fashion. Blaine and Drew each held up one of their Barbie dolls. Purchased from the Salvation Army shop, these dolls had come with one tattered mismatched outfit apiece, and the mannequins themselves were bedraggled, with sparse hair and ink stains on their limbs like random tattoos.

Except now the dolls weren't what Gavril knew them to be. They were gleaming new and perfect, each one attired in a top-of-the-line suit and accessories. Blaine's doll wore a fur coat, while Drew's was clad as Cinderella.

And then, in the blink of an eye, the dolls changed.

Now one sported a cowgirl outfit, while the other exhibited a *Star Trek* minidress and black tights!

Gavril let out an involuntary grunt of surprise, while Toby shouted, "Wow!"

The twins jumped away from the recliner, and their dolls suddenly reverted to their drab and damaged natural condition.

Blaine started to sniffle, prior to full-blown weeping, and Drew yelled. "Now see what you did! You made her stop! We were all just having fun. Nobody was doing nothing wrong!" Her voice suddenly took on some uncertainty. "Were we doing something wrong? I didn't think we were. It seemed okay."

Gavril went up to the girls, gave them awkward hugs and patted their shoulders reassuringly. "Sisters, buck up! No crying, if you please, for all is okay. Nobody has done wrong. However, Toby and I were definitely shocked. Upon entrance, we could not figure out what was going on. And by the way—what *was* going on? Did our dear potato head teach you some kind of magic trick? Or have you merely stolen some more dolls, and learned a sly way of displaying them? Any such theft, I fear, is greater offense than my occasional five-finger-discount candy bar!"

"No, nothing like that. It's all Vangie's doing. Somehow she can change things. You just have to ask her nice."

"She understands our talk?"

"Yes, she does. We found out a few days ago. We got tired of putting her socks and shoes on, so we just said, 'Vangie, you do it,' and she did."

Gavril studied the blank-faced creature for a few moments, then said, "Vangie, I apologize for all the names I have called you. Please understand, our belief in your low-grade intelligence was predetermined by the authorities. But now the truth is obvious. You have something going on that keeps you satisfied with your limited circumstances. Maybe it is something even better than what the real world can offer. Or maybe you cannot be anything but what we see. Whatever it is, we accept."

There was no reaction from Vangie, but Gavril somehow felt

a sense of atonement accepted with queenly pride. He turned back to the twins.

"Okay, so frozen sister grasps everything we say. How does that lead to magic toy changes?"

"Well, yesterday we were in here with our dolls and I said, 'Gee, I wish we had nicer Barbies,' and all of a sudden we did! We knew then it had to be something Vangie pulled off, because it wasn't me nor Drew did anything, even if we coulda."

Gavril looked down at his crummy old Nikes. "Might Vangie bring me better sneakers?"

Suddenly his feet were encompassed with the sweetest pair of Air Jordans he had ever seen. But the shoes departed slightly, in almost subliminal ways, from the style Gavril knew intimately from much study, as if hailing from some source stranger than the corner store.

"Uncanny!"

"Me next!" Toby hollered. "I just want some better eyeglasses, cool ones like Will Smith wears. You know, *Men in Black*!"

Instantly, Toby's plump immature face radiated supreme suavity with his new shades.

"They're my exact prescription too!"

"Vangie, please," said one of the twins, "can we have our nice dollies back too?"

As the four children exclaimed and marveled at their new acquisitions—and as Vangie continued to lie torpidly supine, manifesting no exterior changes—the children were loudly interrupted, causing them all to jump.

"You devils!" Mama Ginny hollered. "You monstrous goddamn little freaks! What unnatural, horrible things are you doing!"

5

The hot and stuffy bedroom made Kris long for a drink of cool water. This day seemed endless. Gavril paused in his narrative of what had preceded Mama Ginny's catatonia, eying the social worker like a nervous singer sizing up the judges at a talent contest, and Kris tried to let her mind catch up to and assess the reality of the events the boy had described. Vangie conscious of her surroundings, responsive, aware? Okay, maybe that much she could buy. But having the ability to magically transform items at will, by request? To summon mundane things like new sneakers out of nowhere? This had to be some kind of consensual delusion at best, or a deliberate lie at worst. But Gavril had never indulged in such fantasies or fibs before. And his co-fosters were seemingly all onboard. But if he and the others had somehow been responsible for Mama Ginny's knocked-out condition, then there'd be reason to lie . . .

Unable to make up her mind, Kris said, "So Mama Ginny had been standing at the door for a while before she butted in, and she saw and heard everything that happened?"

Gavril nodded eagerly. "Indeed. Her assertions of evil

deeds and devil worship must have come from just a long-enough spying."

"All right, what happened next?"

"Well, first off," Gavril continued, "all our new stuff vanished. My speculation? Vangie became scared at her perceived wrongdoing and undid everything. But this reversion did not stop Mama Ginny. Her rant continued. 'You knew this creature could do this kind of thing all along, didn't you! How long have you been hiding it? All of you little bastards are like poison in my heart. This is the work of Satan.'"

Kris knew that Mama Ginny had occasional bouts of religious fervor, when she would attend a local evangelical church almost daily, trying to cure herself of her "sins." There on the dresser stood a botánica candle bearing imagery of the Virgin of Guadalupe to complement the secular saintly portrait of Mel Gibson. But such self-improving holy intervals quickly faded, and generally she evinced no more piety or superstition than the average person. But if she had arrived home after a long stint at the barroom, her drunkenness might have left her susceptible to such an outburst.

Gavril continued, "So now the girls are crying, and I began to fear that brother Toby will wet his pants. As for myself, I am trying to figure out what to say to calm Mama Ginny down. But then she goes off on a new angle. Suddenly, we are not devils, we are just not practical enough! 'You children are idiots! Babies! Getting the demon seed to summon up toys! She can make us rich! She can solve all our problems! We just have to force her to obey. She's helpless. She'll have to do it—or else!' And then Mama Ginny rushes past us all and snatches up Vangie from the chair—and boom, down Mama Ginny goes, out like a light, like someone has administered a huge blow to her skull. Yes, it may sound odd, but as soon as she picked up Vangie, she was gone."

Squirming, Toby seemed compelled to buttress the account. Kris tried to picture the nerdy boy sporting slick Will Smith shades, and the image caused her to smile.

"That's just the way it happened," Toby said. "As soon as Mama Ginny grabbed Vangie, she went unconscious. It was lucky Vangie landed right on top of her. She wasn't hurt at all."

Drew and Blaine nodded their own mute confirmation.

"So," said Gavril, "we put Vangie back in her chair where you found her, and I carried Mama Ginny down to her own bed." Gavril seemed to want to proudly flex a bicep but, considering the gravity of the situation, refrained. "Amazing to recount, but she did not even weigh as much as me. At school I wrestle kids bigger than her all the time. And we were just figuring out what to do when you rang the bell."

Kris digested the full tale. Suppose the events were as stated. They still need not be supernatural. Incredible as they sounded, they must have some logical explanation. First, a kid's game spun into a willful fantasy, some kind of shared self-hypnosis. Then, a disorienting break that cemented the fantasy in place. The surprise arrival of a greedy, hateful drunken woman, herself taken in by the gameplaying charade. She had plainly worked herself up into a lather and fainted. Maybe a drop in blood pressure? But surely she should have recovered from a simple faint by now.

"Did Mama Ginny hit her head when she fell?"

"No, ma'am. Her precipitous action was as if she folded up in slow motion and lay down."

Chiding herself for not investigating sooner, Kris went over to the woman and palpated her head for a lump—nothing—then felt her pulse. Strong and regular.

Standing next to Mama Ginny, Kris felt the mute, undemanding, but implacable presence of Vangie like heat from an oven. Simply by holding herself upright just as Kris had initially posed her, the expressionless lump of a girl child seemed to dominate the room. The other children were focused more on her than on their comatose foster parent.

Could Vangie understand what everyone said? Unable to be tested, her intelligence levels remained unknown. What kind of comprehension of the universe could a child have who was immured in a chair twenty-four seven—a child whose knowledge of reality had been shaped mainly (exclusively?) by whatever unknowable universe was unspooling in her head?

And yet what if somehow everything that Gavril had related were true? The manifestations, the possibility that Vangie, feeling attacked, had somehow lashed out invisibly, causing Ginny's condition? Then only Vangie could change the current situation.

Kris spoke almost as if musing aloud, speculating, trying hard not to sound as if she were issuing a directive or even making a wish.

"Well, I don't know what to do next. If Mama Ginny doesn't wake up, then I'll have to call an ambulance and you kids are all going to have to come with me back to the office and we'll make arrangements for new placements—just temporary, I hope. And of course you'll probably all get split up. No one's going to take all five of you. No discredit to you, Gavril, but you all can't stay here without adult supervision."

Beaten, acknowledging the sad reality of their plight, the children remained silent. They began to fidget, Gavril really digging at his blemishes, and the three younger ones seemingly ready to tear up. Vangie, of course, was the exception, just maintaining her Easter Island moai imperturbability.

And then Mama Ginny groaned and stirred.

The kids were a flurry of activity. Gavril helped the woman sit up, propping pillows behind her. Toby ran for a glass of water, returning swiftly and losing half the glass's contents on the way. The twins each held one of the woman's hands, using both of their own. As the mattress shifted and rocked under all this fussing, Vangie maintained her balance and did not tumble backward or fall forward off the bed.

Kris allowed Ginny Everett some time to become fully aware. The foster mother's demeanor was one of baffled calmness. If she had been drunk just an hour ago, no traces of intoxication remained. Her current affect showed none of the reported verbal aggressiveness and impulsive assault on Vangie. In fact, Mama Ginny's gaze passed right over Vangie as if the girl were an innocuous chair or lamp.

"How are you feeling, Ginny?" Kris asked.

"Kris? What are you doing here? Is it time for our appointment already? It can't be that late in the day."

"It is, though. You've had some kind of fainting spell. What do you remember?"

"I was just— I mean, I came home— But where was I before that? The bar, I think . . . I didn't drink all that much. Did something happen to me when I got home?"

Ginny Everett's usual mix of put-upon self-pity, of abrasive snark, of cruel candor and dismissive cynicism seemed nowhere to be found. This change was somewhat scary to Kris, even if not unwelcome.

"You had a spell and passed out. The kids all witnessed it. It was a little scary. Isn't that right, guys?"

Gavril, Toby, Blaine, and Drew all made various sounds of affirmation.

"And Vangie? Why is she here?"

"We just didn't want to leave her alone upstairs. Especially because we didn't know what we were going to have to do if you didn't recover quickly. Do you want to go to the ER?"

Ginny pivoted and swung her legs off the bed. Some of her

old feistiness and habitual rancor began to return. "Hell, no! I can't afford a medical bill like that. I feel fine."

"Well, I can't make you go to the hospital, but I think that tomorrow you should visit the free clinic for a checkup at least."

"Yeah, yeah, all right, Doctor Kris. Just let me splash some water on my face, and we can do the visit. I know the place is a mess, but you should be used to that. You're not gonna mark me up for trivial shit like some dirty dishes, are you?"

"You know I'm just concerned with the children's welfare, Ginny. They have to have a safe and nurturing home."

"Yeah, sure, they got all that. Gavril! Go see what kind of food you can rustle up for us outta the freezer. I think there's some hot dogs in there. Beans in the cupboard. I'm goddamn starving! And the rest of you go wash up for supper."

"I'll bring Vangie back to her chair," Kris said. "That'll give you a minute to get settled."

Cradling the inert girl and ascending the stairs, Kris tried to pierce Vangie's barrier of indifference and unawareness. But the girl's flickering gaze permitted no breaches or contact. Still, some kind of vague resonance seemed to fluctuate between the child and the social worker, an almost subliminal and wordless sensation, not like information being transmitted, but more like stepping into a warm ocean.

Setting the child into her chair, Kris experienced a moment of timeless disorientation, somehow briefly losing cognizance of who she was and what she was doing here. The spell passed, and she went downstairs.

Kris conducted a hasty, abridged edition of the standard interview. Ginny Everett seemed fully competent and healthy, as unlikely to have another unprecedented spell as she had been for all the prior untroubled portion of her life. There was no practical or ethical compulsion to take the children away. Kris felt she was not betraying the department or her own standards.

Finally Kris left, saying goodbye to the children seated obediently around the slightly decluttered kitchen table. Gavril cast her a knowing look, as if to say, *This weird stuff has yet to play out fully!*

In her despair-redolent car, the fierce sun westering behind the tank farm, Kris realized just how late it was. There'd be no time to go home and freshen up. Straight to the Temple of Human Potential she must go.

6

As usual on a Friday night, Kris had to contend for parking with the boozy patrons of Bryce's Bad Boy BBQ. She pulled into the lot slowly, so as not to hit any pedestrians. The men and women, no kids, tumbled from their cars and made heedless haste across the asphalt, eager to enjoy the tasty fare, the low-priced pitchers of beer, and the live music, all obtainable not just inside the low-slung, false-timbered restaurant building but on the open patio, strung with fairy lights in the shape of chili peppers, its picnic tables already filling up. At seven thirty, with twilight coming on, the band was still setting up outside, and the trial notes from keyboard, guitar, and drums randomly spattered the air.

The whole scene, for a moment, looked infinitely appealing to Kris. Just to kick back with someone—her girlfriend Kelly, say, whom she hardly saw anymore, what with work and the Temple taking up all her time—and to enjoy a frosty mug of beer and a succulent plate of ribs, maybe dance a little, meet a handsome screwable stranger. It seemed for a second like absolute heaven. Why had she deprived herself of these simple pleasures? What did she hope to gain or achieve with her over-work and her loyalty to the Temple of Human Potential? Wasn't she wasting her life instead of maximizing it?

But as she contemplated the choices she had made that had led her here, the remembrance resurfaced of the strange feelings she had experienced when carrying Vangie up to her room—feelings more imbued with sheer numinous potential, of expansiveness, rather than any glimmerings of uncompli-cated happiness or instant fulfillment—and she sensed some kind of connection between the mute child and the teachings of Vardis Salthouse.

The lot associated with the restaurant provided the closest space to stash her car, since the Temple itself afforded no park-ing, save for a curbside space or three right outside the building, always taken by the cars of the Temple's neighbors. The owner of Bryce's Bad Boy BBQ didn't mind the Templegoers occupy-ing a few spots, even on a busy Friday night. There were few enough of the noncustomers, and apparently Salthouse had sweet-talked the owner into it somehow. Another tribute to the preacher's persuasiveness.

Preacher or teacher, guru or seeker, messiah or madman, roughneck or saint—Kris had alternated among these assess-ments of Vardis Salthouse ever since she had known him, unable to settle on any definitive interpretation of his multifaceted per-sonality. Ultimately, she had chosen not to choose, but rather just to accept and evaluate what he had to offer, day by day and word by word.

She slid her car into a slot, rolled up the windows, exited, and locked it. The band had begun to play, rather proficiently, an old Steely Dan tune, "Any World (That I'm Welcome To)." The delicious smell of charred meats and the sounds of festive enjoyment—laughter, glasses clinking—beckoned (she suddenly realized she had had nothing to eat except for two slices of pizza and a soda almost eight hours ago), but she marched resolutely across the lot to the far corner, where a sagging gate in the chain-link fence let her out onto Champion Street. Even in July, the lot was gritty with remnants of the sand strewn during the city's harsh winter, a tactile reminder of days past and to come.

This block of Champion featured a mix of commercial and residential buildings, mostly of a familiar and distinctive local yellowish brick; in some buildings both functions were combined: lower floor a shop, upper floors apartments. The Temple of Human Potential occupied one of these latter hybrids.

Kris advanced on the place, nodding to the half-familiar faces of the oft-seen but nameless neighbors sitting on their stoops.

Any vision through dirty plate glass windows on either side of an old wooden door with flaking green paint was stymied by water-stained beige curtains. The windows bore faded commercial decals for cigarettes, soap powder, and candy, indicative of the place's past life as a small grocery.

The door hosted at eye level a small brass plaque, newer than the decals, announcing the Temple's bare existence. The organization's precarious finances were reflected in its humble trappings.

Kris twisted the dented, tarnished copper handle and let herself in.

She generally arrived earlier than this and helped to set up the refreshments table, but a quick glance informed her that the coffee and lemonade, doughnuts, and bowl of snack-sized pretzels had already been arrayed. Her stomach rumbled at the thought of a doughnut, but she didn't want to disturb the offerings yet. So she quietly slipped into a folding chair in the back row and turned her attention to the front.

The single large room, all former partitions having been demolished sometime after its retail existence, featured a scuffed old wooden floor. Several fluted, cast-iron columns, painted industrial gray, marched abreast across the room to bear the load of the upper stories. The farthest wall, windowless, featured the nailed attachments for vanished shelving. Kris's rear row of five chairs abreast constituted the last of eight such rows, and more collapsed chairs rested in stacks, awaiting large crowds that never showed. Even the forty chairs were only half occupied.

The seats all regarded a small freestanding moveable stage just two short steps high, its complicated mechanical undercarriage showing, due to lack of curtaining at its edge. A tall portable screen of red cloth, held up by an armature of pipes, backended the stage.

Kris knew that behind this scrim, awaiting just the right dramatic moment to make his entrance, lurked Vardis Salthouse

As always each week, a handful of strangers, adults of many types and ages, had been attracted by the Temple's long-running advertisements in several of the region's free weekly papers. Chatting, some newcomers showed an irreverent desire to be entertained. They would probably never return after tonight. Others presented a more sober and earnest meditative air of being in search of the promised revelations, wisdom about becoming one's better self. These folks might come back, once or several times. A handful might even evolve into permanent adherents, like Kris herself.

Of these longtimers, Kris registered a fair number. Tucker Storch, a spry old man with long white hair and an enormous dirty-ivory beard. Storch wrote "cosmic ballads," long rambling epics employing tortured rhymes full of angels and other supernatural beings who eccentrically echoed the Temple's teachings. He was usually invited by Salthouse to read a few stanzas to conclude each Friday service. Kris saw the woman known only as Andorra, a skinny, manic-eyed blond with no ass or hips who had gifted herself as compensation with outsized breast implants. Tonight, she was dressed in stretchy black pants and a leopard-print top, with flat shoes decorated to match the animal theme. Impeccably attired in a good linen suit and fingering his tidy little ginger mustache, Roger Auldstane ran a rather chichi antiques store. Emilio Elorza, a lawyer specializing in immigration matters, always came straight from work in his uniform of a colorful guayabera shirt. Kris did not believe she had ever seen him repeat a color, and she pictured an enormous closet full of an infinite number of such shirts. Brown-haired and plain-looking, Lauren Long resembled a stay-at-home mother of three, actively involved in PTA work. Kris had done a double take when she learned the woman was the invaluable top aide to the state's most powerful senator, and rumored to be his mistress as well.

A few other long-haulers caught Kris's attention as well, nodding or smiling at her. Some of the regulars were among the missing. Kris wondered if that signaled a diminishment in Salthouse's allure, a waning of his powers.

Tonight's performance would be revelatory of any such sag.

The hour was approaching the eight p.m. starting time. A few latecomers drifted in, including another of the core acolytes: Bernie Vanson, a burly fellow who owned a small furniture-moving company. Disdaining office life for the frontlines, Vanson showed sweat-crescents under the arms of his denim shirt and thoroughly scuffed Herman Survivors work boots.

Those in the audience unfamiliar with the ritual presentation began to fidget as eight o'clock arrived and passed. The stirring of the red curtains a few moments later caused the intended anticipatory excitement, satisfied at last when, through an unnoticed slit in the backdrop, Vardis Salthouse finally burst.

Kris had always thought that Salthouse resembled nothing so much as a cartoon anarchist from the 1920s, a big brawny hulk with wild russet hair and aggressive beard to match, his eyes under thick tangled brows like two smoldering coals, his lips—insofar as they could be observed behind the hairy façade—perpetually quirked in a manner half-disdainful, half-rueful, half-leering (surely three halves could be allowed in such an exceptional figure). To complete his iconography, he should have been wearing the shapeless wool suit of some Balkan bomb thrower, with perhaps a cape and an outsized Borsalino hat. Instead, even in the midst of winter, as if he were not prey to such uncomfortable externalities as mere cold, he wore colorful tropical shirts—tonight's featured a tessellation of hibiscus flowers—and cargo shorts that showed off muscular hairy thighs and calves. Thick wool socks and chukka boots completed his ensemble.

Having made his dramatic entrance and cemented the attention of the crowd upon himself, Salthouse made no preamble but instead uttered a bold assertion and charge.

"My friends! You can all do better than you are doing. You can all become greater than you are. But you are too blind to see how!"

Kris settled back in her seat. No, there was no sign of fading power from Salthouse. She felt reassured—but also slightly let down.

If he had been less than himself, she might have permitted herself to quit all this.

But instead, she settled in for the night.

1

Ninety minutes had flown by on the wings of Salthouse's free-form, almost stream-of-consciousness oratory. The room's heat was ameliorated only slightly by a single oscillating elevated fan at the back of the space, but Kris failed to register any discomfort, although sweat soaked her shirt along her nape, as it did Salthouse's whole flowered garment. The bottled heat drove old grocery smells—coffee, camphor, pickle brine—out of the room's ancient floorboards.

A mélange of slogans and maxims, exhortations and accusations, appeals and implorings, all arrayed around the central theme—personal and societal uplift through a kind of magical thinking-cum-supernatural channeling effect—Salthouse's performance was delivered with gusto, fervor, and a seemingly infinite well of energy. The receptive audience, any scoffers at least temporarily disarmed by the speaker's power and sincerity, responded with a mix of rapt attention, moments of shock, and equal parts appreciative laughter and solemn hush. (Whether they would remain under his spell after leaving was the crux of repeat attendance.) When Salthouse let fly any particularly vivid or resonant motto or observation, interrogation or demand—"Every second is pregnant with infinite possibilities!" . . . "Your destiny runs in parallel with that of the entire universe!" . . . "No one ever failed to ascend who dropped the ballast from their soul!" . . . "Can you show me a vision of the future you? If you can't, then that beckoning person will never exist!" . . . "Believe in what you desire, or desire what you believe!"—the audience would almost lift off their chairs in excitement.

But the real showmanship and electric moments occurred during the one-on-one confrontations.

At certain points in his erratic, mystical, jargon-laden performance, Salthouse would single out and invite one of the listeners onstage for an "atmanic interrogation and counseling."

The first such client tonight was a middle-aged, slightly dumpy woman using a four-footed silver metal cane. Dressed older than her years, she wore a brave but wan smile, as if ready to confront yet another obstacle in an obstacle-strewn life with whatever remnants of good cheer remained in her armory. Negotiating the two small steps to the stage took her many long seconds that stretched to a trial for the watchers. But Salthouse exhibited no impatience, merely taking the time to push the damp tendrils of his mop of hair off his brow.

When the woman came face-to-face with the preacher, he immediately grabbed her wrists, and a kind of involuntary juddering went through her. Closing his eyes, he began his psychic reading.

"Your burdens are real, but they lie atop a stratum of organic strength, like a raft of floating seaweed atop a brilliant, colorful coral reef. Let a tsunami of resolution wash all the detritus away! I see in you a certain loneliness and despair. But these are only the unwelcome visitors you invited in yourself! Show them the door! Kick them out! Then you'll finally meet the angel who waits on the threshold."

Releasing the woman's wrists, Salthouse stepped back, opening his eyes and beaming through the foliage of his beard. Far from needing to slump after being forced uncomfortably to stand, perhaps past the limits of her normal endurance, the woman seemed to rise up straighter, and descend the steps more vibrantly than she had gone up them.

As the natural intuited climax of Salthouse's talk seemed to approach—he had cast a glance at Tucker Storch, as if to say, *Be ready with your poetry*—a sudden impulse surged through Kris, and she rose from her chair.

Seemingly not disconcerted at all by this unplanned audience interaction, Salthouse thoughtfully paused.

"Yes, Miss Troy, you have a query, or perhaps some insights to communicate?"

"Something really odd and unprecedented happened to me today. Could I have a reading, please?"

"Certainly! Come right up!"

With only inches separating her from Salthouse, Kris could register the rich male fragrances pumped out by his exertions and exhortations, pheromones that might have poured off Jesus expelling the money changers. His piercing eyes locked with hers, and she experienced once more some kind of certitude about his visionary abilities.

Quickly and decisively, since this time no cane interfered, he clasped not her wrists but both her hands.

And while Kris did feel some familiar unnatural and inexplicable spasming of her muscles and nerves, a kind of etheric current known from previous atmanic readings, in this surprising instance it was the preacher who experienced the greater jolt. His whole form stiffened as if some puppeteer had yanked all his wires taut. His words emerged as if from some deep well.

"You have met the ultimate reifier today. A power beyond

human ken. The lines of your two fates are inextricably tangled now. You must learn how to splice everything together."

Opening his eyes, Salthouse released her, and she involuntarily took a step back as he, too, staggered a bit, then regained his footing. Forcibly resuming his showman's domineering presentation, he said, "Thank you, Miss Troy, for sharing that very edifying glimpse of the vast potential we all can meet, during every minute of our lives. And now, if I can have Mr. Storch up here for some of his inimitable and inspirational versifying, we will conclude tonight's expedition into the wilderness of our common unexplored characterological domain."

Back in her seat, Kris could pay no attention to Storch's lame verses. She turned Salthouse's words over and over, examining them from every angle, seeking to tease out the real-world implications for her own life.

Eventually Storch ended his florid mystical declamations, and the audience rose to make for the refreshments like a horde of famished soldiers. Achingly hungry, Kris managed to snag a glazed cruller and a glass of lemonade; coffee at this late hour, almost ten p.m., would wreak havoc with her sleep. (Where was the Friday night party girl of yore? Shouldn't she be heading straight to the bar at Bryce's?) She had to practically fight for the doughnut with an unrepentant pimply teenage boy wearing a T-shirt touting "Van Halen III" and displaying a vivid retro image: in old-timey black and white, a ponderous male circus performer, shirtless, received the impact of a cannonball shot at close range.

Having been too late to set everything up, Kris stayed to break things down. Before she quite realized it, she was alone in the Temple with Salthouse.

The preacher took her by the elbow from behind. She pivoted and found this action put her almost within the half-circle of his arm. This time neither of them experienced any extra-natural frissons at the contact. But instead, Kris felt a decided twinge of sexual desire.

"Miss Troy—Kris—I want to thank you for everything you do at the Temple. You are one of our most loyal and responsible members. It's always a treat for me to look out over the crowd and spot your attentive and intelligent face. You've been with us for about six months now, I believe . . . ?"

This unexpected attention flattered Kris, but also made her uneasy. Could Salthouse's sudden extra interest in her stem solely from whatever he had sensed of her weird time at the Everett home today?

"Yes, that long . . ."

"Then you know that we all have to be ready at any moment to grasp the hand that Fate might extend to us. So I want you to tell me exactly what happened to you today. You experienced something very powerful."

Kris found she could not refuse his request. "Yes, I think I did."

Violating all client confidentiality, Kris recounted the bizarre doings involving Vangie, Mama Ginny, and the sibs. Upon recitation, it all sounded utterly unlikely. But Salthouse did not seem to find it so.

Salthouse absorbed all this information with a keen and swift mind. Nodding sagely, he said, "This child is obviously possessed of some kind of extraordinary powers. I want you to monitor her very closely, and report back everything, no matter how insignificant it might seem. She could be the conduit to the realization of all that we have believed in. An actual nexus for all our aspirations toward the enlargement and maximizing of our souls."

Kris hesitated. Salthouse leaned in closer. Despite hours of talking, with only a swig or two of water, his breath still smelled pleasant, like clover or a sliced green pepper.

"Kris, I ask this only because I feel extremely close to you.

And I believe you feel the same toward me. We are united in our shared desire to inhabit our best lives. Nothing we do together can go amiss. Am I wrong?"

"No . . . you're not wrong."

When he kissed her, his beard was much softer than she had expected it would be, not bristly at all, and his arm around her waist much stronger than imagined. She responded to his kiss passionately and placed her hands on his chest. He released her elbow finally, so he could cup her butt, first with one hand, then with both. He picked her up—perforce, she had to wrap her legs around his waist—and carried her to the edge of the stage. He set her down, and pressed her flat onto her back, her legs, bent at the knees, dangling off the short riser. The worn carpet atop the stage smelled musty.

Kris wondered if the last acolyte to leave had locked the door. But in the next minute she no longer wondered or cared.

8

The next three weeks for Kris revolved entirely around her job and the Temple. Not that this severely limited scope of her ambitions and intentions and preoccupations differed much from her past regimen. But at least before now she had carved out the occasional moment for the gym or a movie or a Saturday outing to the park, where she would enviously watch flocks of spandex-clad, awesomely muscled rollerbladers, inspired by the recent X Games, whipping down the curvy lanes. But none of these pastimes had prevailed against the demands of her job and her increased involvement at the Temple of Human Potential.

Her unwieldy caseload burgeoned even more as one of her coworkers quit and the man's assignments were divided up among Kris and her peers—"Just a temporary thing, until we can hire Alex's replacement. Don't worry, we'll make it up to you!"—and the various families under her care all seemed to enter crisis mode sequentially, as if they had arranged to pass the burning baton of chaos from one to the other, with Kris trailing behind trying to put out the flames. It began with Sally Burris, the moody and often despondent goth teen, attempting suicide. Kris got four hours' sleep that night, some of it in an emergency room chair. After that came a cascade of child and elder abuse, expulsions, evictions, shoplifting charges, and all the other ills that government-monitored families seemed to be heir to. The torture was almost enough to make Kris want to tear up her diploma. But what would she do for money if she did that? Her college-era stints as a waitress had taught her that lowly service industry jobs were hardly paradise.

Kris felt grateful that her altered role at the Temple offered her some pleasant contrast to the insanity of her job. Her new duties there were demanding, but at least she could feel that she was working toward a higher goal, not just spinning her wheels, as at work.

After their sex in the Temple that Friday night, and after Kris and Salthouse had reassembled themselves for the sake of public decency, the preacher had surprised her by asking for a ride home.

"I don't own a car, you see, and I generally walk. But I thought you might not mind helping me out. It's been a long day."

"Of course—Vardis. My car's right at Bryce's."

The barbecue joint was jumping, but Kris paid little attention to the clamorous scene, as she tried to figure out what had just happened and what it might entail.

In the car, Salthouse was quiet for several blocks. His masculine scents and the smell of their recent intercourse almost counterbalanced the car's busy bachelorette fug, and Kris's embarrassment modulated to a subliminal twinge.

Her attention only half on the dark, unbusy streets, heading toward the district Salthouse had named, Kris did not receive the impression that, having gotten what he wanted, her guru was acting cool or distant. He did not seem regretful or uncertain, neither contemptuous nor affectionate, not vain or self-satisfied.

Rather, it was as if he had integrated the new reality of their shifting relationship into some vast internal composition, a tapestry or painting, and was now contemplating the unfamiliar facets of the altered landscape for their potentials. Like a chess master looking six moves ahead. He chewed meditatively on a few coarse auburn hairs of his beard at the left corner of his mouth, staring straight into the night beyond the windshield.

Eventually they arrived at Salthouse's building, and Kris recognized it as an SRO where she had once met with a father separated from his family. The prospect of being invited up to a shabby lonely room—hot plate and shared toilet down the hall—made her wince. But Salthouse made no such offer. Instead, he turned to her and said, "There's much more to the Temple than our Friday night meetings. There's outreach to your fellow devotees. I think a more personal touch will boost loyalty and membership retention. And there's some networking with a couple of other organizations around the state as well. Not to mention recruitment at certain venues. Having your car to hand will help considerably there. Also, I've been doing some extensive research on various subjects at the downtown library and could really use your scholarly expertise. Can I count on you to help me with these lines of activity?"

"Yes. Of course."

"Wonderful. Meet me here on Wednesday after work then. Oh, we should exchange phone numbers, in case something comes up. Here's mine. It rings in the downstairs hall, and the super will come get me."

Salthouse left the car then, without so much as an offer of—or attempt at stealing—a goodnight kiss. On the sidewalk, he said, "Don't forget. Your primary mission is to keep tabs on that child. She could be the key to a quantum leap forward for us and the whole Temple."

Having issued that directive, he ascended the steps of his building without a backward glance.

Kris drove off, feeling a bit confused, but elated overall. That their quickly concluded sex, her first bout in months, had nonetheless been good and taken off some bottled-up bodily pressure didn't hurt.

The Temple duties Salthouse had outlined swelled to occupy most of her off-work hours. On no occasion of their time together did the subject or spontaneous possibility of more sex arise. Kris was somewhat pleased at not being taken for granted or used promiscuously. The lack of typical male neediness was welcome. But on the other hand, she would not have minded further intimate encounters, nor disdained the chance to advance their weird relationship to the next level. But such progress, apparently, was not to be—at least not in the immediate moment.

As for Vangie and the Everett household, the immense irony was that the Plank Street home and its inhabitants represented the only bastion of quiet and normality among all her clients. It seemed that having gotten their crisis out of the way before all the other clients, the Everetts could now enjoy a boring stretch of peace and ease.

Kris managed to squeeze in two visits a week, rather than the mandated single visit. The second, unofficial encounter each week, attained by sacrifice of any lunch hour that day, was not reported to the office. But she felt that she could not let Vangie go unwatched for too long a stretch. She salted each visit with a few small gifts for Mama Ginny and the children alike. Even just a package of ice cream sandwiches was met with appreciation.

Upon her first return, Kris found Mama Ginny restored more or less to her former personality after her bout of irrationality and her temporary post-unconsciousness calm. Irascible, self-centered, concerned only with short-term satisfaction, the woman continued grudgingly to provide the bare minimum of domestic safety and support for her fostered brood. But at the same time, Ginny Everett exhibited a subliminal underlay of uncertainty, anxiety, fear, and suspicion. She regarded Gavril, Toby, Drew, and Blaine with barely concealed ill will and disdain, as if they were *Village of the Damned* cuckoos she was being forced to harbor. But her attitude toward Vangie manifested even greater vehemence and abhorrence. She wouldn't voluntarily speak of the child or be in her presence. Queries about Vangie triggered a round of almost Tourette's-like swearing and, if pushed, physical flight from Kris's interrogations.

The first time this had happened, Kris instantly feared that such an emotional complex might bring Ginny to harm the insensate child. Out of Mama Ginny's hearing—the woman had retreated to her bedroom—Kris queried Gavril about the possibility.

"Miss Troy, I sincerely believe it won't happen. Save your worries. This is my discovery. When we don't mention Vangie to Mama Ginny, she does not even think of her, as if the girl does not even exist. I have seen her walk right past Vangie's room when the door was open, and she never even moved her eyes toward Vangie in her chair. It's only when the topic is forced on her that she freaks. And even then, I make the equation like so. Mama Ginny is more scared of Vangie than Vangie has cause to be scared of Mama Ginny."

"So Vangie is safe and getting good care?"

"Very true! I and the other kids do everything that must be done. Toby and the twins are truly good helpers. The strangeness of Vangie has grown on them. They really like her. You can trust me, Miss Troy, that little girl is doing fine. I mean, as fine as a dummy who does nothing can do."

Kris hesitated before asking the next question, but knew that

Salthouse, obsessed with finding "the ultimate reifier," would demand such information.

"Has Vangie performed any more, uh, tricks? I mean, has there been any other kinds of magic, like what you described to me? New sneakers and such?"

Gavril's face fell. "Alas, no! I will speak the truth. I wish we could get more magic from her, whatever its source. Wouldn't life be swell then! But she has turned off that faucet. In all actuality, the twins begged. They made her all kinds of compliments. Toby even left his favorite toy with her, his Furby. And I showed her how my old sneaks are practically falling apart. Nothing!" Gavril looked slightly bemused and baffled. "You know, I'm starting to wonder if maybe we didn't all just dream it up, as you said the night it happened, last Friday."

"You'll let me know if anything strange does occur again, won't you?"

"This is my pledge!"

"Maybe I'll go up and see Vangie for myself."

"Your compassion cannot go astray, Miss Troy."

Laid out in her patched recliner, wearing white leggings and a jumper dress embroidered with the faddish Teletubbies figures, Vangie struck Kris as some kind of Egyptian mummy or swaddled papoose—maybe an ice-wrapped Neanderthal baby, bundled up ceremoniously to greet eternity. The girl's dismal plain-Jane appearance, made more disturbing by her continual flickering eye tics, could be interpreted either as a stone wall leading nowhere or as a carpet laid atop a bottomless abyss.

Kris picked up the six-year-old child, sparking no reactions. Vangie's rubbery body complied with the new positioning with a kind of unintentional refolding of itself, the way a piece of rope would respond to being twitched at one end.

Kris looked down into Vangie's eyes and tried to establish

some kind of bond or connection but failed utterly. She murmured, "Who are you in there? What are you hiding? Are you frozen in place, or totally free? I need to know . . ."

No answers forthcoming, Kris set the girl down, then left the Everett home.

That night she recounted everything to Vardis Salthouse. He chewed a stray tuft of beard while he pondered the matter. Kris recalled his kisses, his hands on her ass. Wasn't that more important than the empty mystery of some freakish child? The Temple was all about becoming your best self. Couldn't she and Salthouse make a simple, unexceptional joint life together that maximized all their available happiness? Wasn't it foolish to yearn and strive for something supernormal and let all the lesser joys and rewards pass you by?

Finished thinking, Salthouse reached out and took Kris by the wrist. "That child is just biding her time, I'm convinced of it. But we could elicit from her the effects we seek. If only we had her under our control. We could enact a rigorous program of atmanic elucidation."

"And how would we come to control her?"

"I don't know . . . I don't know. But maybe Fate will lend a hand."

9

The ghosts had been tamed.

Somewhat.

To the degree, anyhow, that had delivered to the more mature Vangie a greater portion of self-assurance and confidence and self-knowledge, increasing her capabilities and visionary powers.

There was less fog, less confusion in her sphere of extended consciousness. An expansion of ease, motivation, and direction.

Her maturing brain, with its exfoliating powers, had topped a new plateau.

Looking back at her earliest memories, Vangie was amazed and somewhat embarrassed by her previous incompetence and helplessness.

Not that she chose to manifest any of this new self-knowledge to the world.

Everything that mattered happened only inside her, was visible only to her eyes.

At age six, Evangeline . . . Evangeline Everett . . . had learned better how to shunt and focus, trawl and cloak, probe and skim, choose and delete, minimize and maximize the visions that besieged her.

Still endlessly confronting a constant explosion of borderless windows, an infinitude of living, animated, noisy, almost tangible dioramas, all containing myriad Vangies in endless guises and roles, the child had acquired some powers of selectivity over the plethora of ghosts. She could grant as much of her attention to her choices of input as she wished, even freeing up a portion of her wide but limited channel of focus for the immediate surroundings of her real world, when any fleshly exigencies demanded. Not that she cared to grant more than a few shards of attention to the essentially boring mundanity of her own timeline. The vastly more entertaining, educational, and illuminating—albeit sometimes frightening—lives of her other selves were much more alluring than her own boring mortal conditions, limited in scope and possibility.

Studying the endless iterations of herself, all shapes and ages, types and characters, under all imaginable conditions, was her sustenance and pleasure. (Although there were indeed moments of terror and oppression, as she contemplated so many other selves, all ranked against her lone individuality. Sometimes she would lose all sense of her own uniqueness in the welter of Vangies, before clawing her way back to her own singular, somehow central identity.)

She saw much that was understandable, much that was incomprehensible. But every day brought fresh knowledge.

Continuing her endless survey of her selves, so long as her physical body was warm and fed and not abused, she relegated her exterior circumstances to mere background noise, the hum of a security whose interruption would require action on her part perhaps, but not otherwise.

But however fascinating her alternate lives were, she felt

no impulse to leave behind this timeline she had come to three years after escaping death, fleeing her native realm. Jumping elsewhere was not a desirable option.

That lone experience had been too scary, too draining of energy, too chancy, imprecise, and hazardous to risk again. Assimilating the memories and ego of the host Vangie, the toddler originally saved from the twister by that fortuitous grassy cradle, had taken her months of effort, and had been an awkward and itchy experience, like wriggling into a costume tailored for someone whose dimensions were just a little bit off from those of the wearer. To jump to one of the more radically divergent, exotic timelines, however appealing it might seem, would have required immense skill, desire, and inner strength, as well as reckoning with an uncomfortable aftermath of ego hybridization. Only the threat of imminent death had propelled Vangie on that leap three years ago. And why seek to inhabit another self, another world, when nearly all the benefits and pleasures of any such existence could be had vicariously, just by watching and listening to the ghosts?

Not that she hadn't succumbed several times over the last three years to the temptation to improve herself, or escape annoyances. But these forced exercises of her power had been the tiniest exertions she could conceive, mere lateral twitches across almost imperceptible and negligible barriers.

The first family to foster the miracle survivor, the Ralstons, had provided a suitable environment—until the day when the childless husband and wife brought home a dog. Seemingly cognizant of Vangie's peculiarities, her status as a freak, the beast had never stopped bothering her, getting past all pet gates, slipping all leashes, to bark and even lunge at her crib, her high chair, her playpen. And the visiting social worker never seemed to be present to witness any of this dangerous canine behavior.

Frightened, Vangie began to scroll through her surrogate selves. All the nearby timelines that involved the death or disappearance of the dog required bigger leaps than the easy hop she eventually settled on: to the universe where Mr. Ralston got a new career position with an out-of-state firm. Rolling over and into the ego of that barely divergent Vangie had been as easy as a snake slipping out of its old skin. Goodbye to the old and inconvenient timeline!

A similar event occurred with the foster family next in sequence, the Brents. Vangie's preferred hour-by-hour condition—extradimensional studious lassitude—had been threatened by the insistence of the Brents on subjecting her to a crackpot school of operant conditioning designed to lift her out of her "autism." The daily routine involved being wrapped in wet bandages and other indignities. And so, a foster-child-cancelling pregnancy was engineered for Mrs. Brent.

The Bannerjees, next in line, had earned Vangie's ire by boasting too imposing a family life. It seemed as if they had a hundred noisy and affectionate relatives, all of whom expected to see the poor little disabled foster girl attend one party or ceremony or outing after another, disturbing and diminishing her interior pursuits. Taking a lesson from her stay with the Ralstons, Vangie had simply hopped to a timeline where the elderly family chihuahua, already a resident, had suffered a momentary psychosomatic glitch, a spasm of nerves, irritable bowels, and a bad tooth, and attacked Vangie—just when the horrified visiting social worker was present.

Finally came the Hopps: a decent retired couple save for their insistence on travel. Possessors of wanderlust and an RV, the Hopps liked nothing better than to embark on long trips with frequent stops for tourist activities. The endless hours in motion in the RV were acceptable, still allowing Vangie the undisturbed time she desired to cast wide her nets of perception. But the forced climbing of towers and mountains, the duck-boat rides and museum lectures, the beach excursions and zoo rambles were too disruptive! How easy it had been to flee to that very nearby strand of the multiverse that featured Mr. Hopp's debilitating and transformative stroke that freed her again.

Finally, though, with the Everetts, Vangie had found a place that suited her. Having just one adult in the household—and a negligent one at that—decreased the likelihood that Vangie would be disturbed by any demands for affection, improvement, or performance. And having four other children around served as buffers for any adult demands. And these particular four—Blaine, Gavril, Toby, Drew—proved to be decent types, not bullies or aggressors or pests. In fact, Vangie had come to rely on their presence, to moderately enjoy their nearness, insofar as she could relate to any other human in her limited sphere. Never having received or been open to receiving love, she was clumsy with any kind of reciprocal gestures or emotions.

But there came a day when the self-indulgent demands on her powers of multiversal observation were slightly lessened (all the other nearby Vangies seemed to be experiencing a lull and quietude), and so she turned her attention to the twin girls who were dutifully giving her a massage and complaining about their lack of nice toys.

Whimsically, Vangie peered across a few nearby timelines and easily found one where the girls owned some desirable dolls. This life-thread was otherwise so identical to the one that Vangie and the twins currently inhabited, down to a subatomic level dimly sensed, that passage to it and accommodation to her new avatar would be trivial and painless. Altruism, however, was the smallest, almost nonexistent, part of Vangie's motivation. Lately she had been feeling that she wanted to test herself, to expand on her latent powers. And this would be a good test, since Vangie would not only have to port herself over, but also the consciousnesses of her two foster sibs. For without experiencing the jump, even at an unconscious level, they would gain no sense of change. If she traveled alone to the new thread, Vangie would merely encounter avatars of Drew and Blaine who had always possessed the nice toys. And where was the surprise in that?

To cause her magic to register on the girls, she had to yoke their mentalities, their essences, to hers, transport them, and insert their naïve minds into the new reality.

In this instance, Vangie was extending to the girls the ride she had denied to her foster parents, Steve and Becky, as they lay dying in the wreckage of the trailer.

And so she primed herself, leaped with her riders, and it was done!

Vangie enjoyed the new experience, a testament to her increased skills. It had proved safe and rewarding.

And so she did it again, several more times, culminating with the moments when she had gifted Gavril with new sneakers and Toby with sunglasses.

But then, the wild scene with Mama Ginny! The affront, the noise, the guilt, the accusations, the fear, the bodily assault—!

Vangie panicked.

Instinctively, she jumped—carrying five passengers—to a branch of reality with no new toys, but featuring, from whatever bodily cause, an unconscious Mama Ginny. Carrying so many put a slight strain on her abilities, but she handled it.

Then came the interval with social worker, Kris, and her threats to break up the household if Mama Ginny remained asleep.

Vangie didn't want that! So she brought the whole entourage—six people now!—to a parallel nexus where Mama Ginny came awake.

Experiencing this spontaneous flexing of her mental muscles, Vangie sensed herself growing stronger. But the whole affair proved too unnerving. Having to integrate so many of her own avatars in such a short time, despite their minuscule variations, gave her a small temporary headache. So many things could have gone wrong. And for what? Meeting the trivial demands of others, not fulfilling her own goals.

And so in the subsequent days she had idled her powers, gone into watching mode only, and refused to perform for her foster siblings when they asked. Best to let the situation remain safe and undisturbed.

But Vangie's actions had precipitated something she had not counted on.

Attention from the ghosts.

Not all of them. Just a subset.

The group Vangie would come to call the Council of Ghosts.

Nine Vangies, in assorted flavors.

Vangie had always known that just as she observed her other selves, so did many—but not all—of her avatars observe her. Their attention, mostly as diffuse and benign and intermittent as her own, actually felt good in a way, feedback from those souls most intimate, an acknowledgment that she existed, a kind of camaraderie not shared with normal humans.

But never before had any of her other selves joined in a group to directly address her.

This unprecedented attention from her doppelgängers almost caused Vangie to attempt to flee across the strands of the multiverse. But something stopped her at the last minute. She froze in place and paid special attention.

The nine Vangies occupied each their own timeline, did not exist together in some shared nexus. But their windows now swam together in an approximation of shared space, as if they all occupied an imaginary round table with Vangie at the center.

Three of the Vangies were elderly, three were mature adults, and three were young women, ranging from adolescent to twenty-something. The limited vision that Vangie had of their timelines, the backdrops behind the women, seemed to hint at a wide variety of circumstances, from peace and comfort to desperate travail. The faces and forms of the Council members were marked with variations, a map of their unique histories.

One of the elderly, white-haired women spoke first. Although Vangie herself had never spoken, she had heard her other selves speaking in many alternities, and the timbre of the aged Vangie's voice seemed utterly familiar and authentic to her ears.

"Little one, you are stretching yourself."

"This is as it should be," said a younger Vangie.

"Yes, agreed," chimed in a third. "But there are no steps without danger."

"You need to practice stealthily and with minimal exertion and disturbance. There are tricks and methods, techniques and clever tactics."

"For instance, why seek out a faraway thread where your desideratum is already extant, pre-formed but hard to reach and adjust to, when you can seek out a closer place where the twitch of a butterfly's wing will lead to the desired end?"

The youngest Vangie said, "Sweet spots! That's what I call 'em."

The older Vangies smiled indulgently. One responded.

"Yes, as good a term as any. Seek out those continuums with the desired sweet spots. You'll learn how to recognize them by comparison among their cousin branches. It might seem slow going at first, but soon your evaluations will become lightning fast and highly accurate. Remember you can also check the futures for a range of results. The higher orders of infinity presume that there is always a timeline that is chrono-accelerated to pre-cisely the degree you need. A second, a minute, a year or more. But looking laterally, you get a view of many future scenarios."

An elder Vangie bearing a large livid scar across one cheek and down along her jaw said, "But beware of looking too far ahead! Everything becomes nebulous and dicey. False outcomes prevail, and they can be very seductive. You can believe some-thing is destined to occur when it's not!"

The teenage Vangie jumped in. "Tell her about the Massive! Go on! She needs to know. It's only fair!"

One of the white-haired Vangies, not the scarred one—but was this one missing an eye?—said, "We were going to wait a little longer, dear. But now you've let that cat out of the bag."

A middle-aged Vangie, dressed in some kind of blue, gold-braided military-style uniform, said, "We refer to a certain individual. His name is Durant Le Massif, dubbed the Mas-sive. He is an entity unique among all the timelines, for he has no variants. He is unchanging across all possibilities. And this gives him a kind of invulnerability to anything we can muster against him. There is no deturning him, no twisting his fate. Everywhere we might jump, he is there, implacable, unmovable. And although he cannot communicate sensibly across timelines among his selves as we do, nor leap from nexus to nexus, he has a kind of subliminal awareness of probabilities and the forces of change. Picture him as a wall stretching laterally across all time-lines. This allows him to stymie or counter our efforts, should he choose to do so."

Impulsively, a young adult Vangie said, "I'll show you ex-actly why Le Massif is so horrible. Here's a travelogue of one world he's come to dominate."

The pane holding this woman filled up entirely with a kind of documentary audiovisual presentation. A giant urban plaza hosted ten thousand standing individuals, all attired uniformly and wearing the same blank-eyed handsome male face. They were hailing their master, the original of their image, who stood gleefully on the balcony of a palace. Then, the invisible camera pulled back, swooped away, and revealed a homogenous cityscape filled with a million identical clones of Durant Le Massif.

Young adult Vangie returned to her window. "Luckily, however, he is still relatively young, and not quite aware of his strengths yet. But just imagine this monocultural conquest extended across all the strands of our existence."

Presented with this confusing, ominous forecast, Vangie felt a tornado of conflicting emotions: fear and envy, horror and admiration. The Massive was one of the few presences she had seen in her alternity visions that impressed her.

An elderly Vangie sought to offer reassurance. "But the Massive should not be any hinderance to you—not yet. You can still test yourself freely, with the provisions we outlined. But more importantly, you must formulate your desires."

"Yes, to have a direction, a goal, a fervent wish—that's the key."

All this barrage of information and advice sent Vangie reeling. And this last injunction most of all. A fervent wish? So far in her short life, all she had ever desired was to be left alone, a spectator of her own many lives. Suddenly, however, that passivity no longer seemed sufficient.

Vangie tried to use her hitherto untested powers of speech to ask for help. How could she formulate a goal? What should she desire? What were her options?

But there was no time left in the session. Without so much as a farewell, the clumped spacetime windows containing the Council of Ghosts flew apart down myriad vectors of reality, dwindling to take their places among the nigh-indistinguishable multitude.

Just as well, Vangie realized. She suspected she would have

gotten no help toward any formulation of a goal that must necessarily arise from within her own heart and soul.

Kris Troy stood at the front entrance to the Everett home, the listing screen door moving slightly with the breeze. The early days of September had finally cooled down the city. The long weeks of assisting Salthouse on various Temple errands had modulated into a kind of familiar routine that was no longer so burdensome. She no longer felt stressed or tired all the time. But the predictable routine had also brought with it some boredom. That ancient night when Salthouse had sensed big things ahead—that night of their lovemaking—seemed a dim shadow now.

And here came yet another tedious visit to her most frustrating yet undemanding client. She tried to imagine some new line of questioning to direct at Mama Ginny, to elicit any new insights into Vangie's nature. So far, monitoring Vangie's doings for further unnatural miracles had led nowhere; the girl's utter adherence to a kind of "normality"—normal at least for her disabled state—had lulled Kris into a kind of bored placidity. If this child was the "ultimate reifier," she certainly didn't show it. No manifestations of any sort.

And yet, today, with her finger poised to ring the bell, Kris experienced some kind of heightened sense of expectancy, a numinous tremor of dimly apprehended change, as if she lay on a floating surfboard just as a giant comber began to ripple the ocean waters at her rear and barrel toward her.

Kris pushed the doorbell, and as it sounded within, she staggered, for a sudden barrage of new/old memories jumped fleetly into her brain. The disorientation was short-lived, though, and she quickly felt normal again. Just some kind of weird déjà vu, or maybe its less-frequent cousin, *jamais vu*. She felt as if her life were a train suddenly shunted off to a sidetrack.

The door swung open, and a smiling Gavril appeared. The teenage boy's grin was contagious, and Kris smiled back.

"Mama Troy! Your kindly nature makes you right on time, as promised. Be reassured! I have gotten everyone all packed, and we are ready to go! Even Vangie is up and walking on her own. How great she is doing lately."

Kris felt pride and a sense of anticipation. This was all going to turn out so wonderful. Mama Ginny's death just last week from mixing booze and pills seemed not to have burdened anyone with overmuch grief. The foster siblings, remaining in their Plank Street home under the supervision of a DCF operative (Kris had pulled some strings), had kept their sense of family intact.

The door opened wider, and the other kids stood revealed, duffel bags and knapsacks arrayed. Geeky Toby, corona-haired Blaine and Drew, all beaming.

Standing a bit to the rear of the others, Vangie, naturally, showed no animation. She retained her insensate, doughy countenance, but did clutch the hand of one of the twins.

Kris clapped her hands with genuine excitement. "All right, kids, off we go to your new home. I fixed up all your bedrooms so nice. The six of us are one big happy family now!"

PART TWO

PART TWO

I

The television, an expensive thirty-inch LCD Sharp flatscreen on a tall integrated silver base, played softly in the living room of the Troy and Salthouse family. The noontime news for Tuesday, September 11, 2001, unspooled, a dull, predictable catalog of local, national, and international commonplaces: elections and assassinations, upcoming autumn festivals and trade agreements, sports and weather.

Kris entered the nicely furnished parlor, done up all in subdued earth tones, leaving behind a conversation-filled kitchen. Children's voices followed her.

"Toby, my dear friend. Harry Potter is not my role model, as he is yours. This I will forever assert."

"Well, all right. But just don't rag on him then. I love those books. And now there's a movie!"

Gavril sighed. "Such a waste of dollars, when so much science goes unfunded."

"You're so boring!"

"And you are so foolish."

"Eat my shorts!"

"Oh, indeed, you can fuck right off!"

The girls chimed in. "If Mama Kris hears you swearing like that, Gavril!"

"What will happen? Mama Kris is extremely cool. And besides, do you imagine she could spank me? I'm bigger than her now!"

Smiling, Kris shook her head. A certain amount of friendly sibling banter was fine in private. But she would have to reinforce the lesson that in public no such behavior was permitted.

The family had an image to maintain, a united front to project.

The sunlight of a beautiful late-summer day poured past the tasteful drapes of the living room. Educational books, puzzles, toys, quiz papers, and art projects cluttered every flat surface, shelf, and couch back, as well as large swaths of the carpeted floor. The children were taking their daily lunch break from their homeschooling under Kris's tutelage. Tuna sandwiches as requested by the twins, hamburgers for the boys—and the usual Gerber's for Vangie. Today, sweet potato, green beans, chicken, and banana for dessert, all puréed.

At age nine, the child's practical motor skills had hardly progressed from those on record in her files all the way back to her adoption. She expressed no food preferences, and so the most nutritionally balanced and easiest diet was the toddler-style bottled stuff. Handling a spoon was well within Vangie's manual toolkit, and the regimen seemed to agree with her and to keep her healthy, according to her frequent checkups.

And a healthy star was essential to the family business, no matter her diet. The public did not come, after all, to see her eat.

The children had been withdrawn from public school after only the first semester they experienced following Mama Ginny's death three years ago. Even by then, the demands on the First Family of the Temple of Human Potential had become too great. The weekly Friday ceremony alone would not have interfered overmuch with their schooling. But there were many midweek appearances locally—within a day's drive, say—and also extended performances all around the country. (No international travel yet, but Kris sensed that such jaunts were imminent. Vardis did not tell her every last detail of the Temple's plans, but that was okay by her. So long as she could feel that her management of the kids—Vangie especially—made her an essential part of the Temple's functioning, then she was happy.)

These public occasions obviously dictated frequent absences from any formal state-run classroom, too many to be sanctioned by the vigilant authorities. And so Kris had stepped up and taken over the kids' education. These new duties meant, of course, that her career at the DCF had to end. But that was more of a blessing than a tragedy. Looking back at those demanding, tiring, pointless, rat-race days, tooling all around town in her smelly car, she could hardly believe that she had put up with such unfulfilling dissatisfaction and tedium for so long. The transition to her current truly blessed state was nothing short of a luxurious miracle.

And all because she had impulsively stepped in to foster the Everett kids when Mama Ginny overdosed. A most unanticipated outcome, seemingly arising from no particular circumstances . . . Funny how that adoptive urge had come unbidden to her, out of the blue. But such things seemed to happen around Vangie. And whatever the impetus, they were her children now, not Everetts, but Troy-Salthouses; no longer just fosters, but fully adopted.

She hadn't planned such a move when the news about her special client first reached her. But then Vardis's words from a short time before—"If only we had her under our control. We could enact a rigorous program of atmanic elucidation"—popped right back into her head, and she knew just what she had to do.

And her subsequent marriage to Vardis Salthouse—well, if it had launched originally as merely a cynical maneuver to impress the adoption officials with the stability and fitness of a two-parent household—and to give Vardis a legal hold on his "ultimate reifier"—it had developed, Kris felt safe in saying, into a real relationship, full of excitement and love, partners yoked in a common cause.

How funny that Vardis had speculated in that same remembered conversation that Fate might take a hand in their affairs.

Fate in the form of a mute autistic girl, Kris suspected.

For had Vangie not demonstrated often by now that she and Fate were one and the same?

Crossing the living room, careful not to step on hapless Bionicles or Polly Pocket dolls, Kris tracked down what she had come for: her current reading, an advance reviewer's copy of King and Straub's *Black House*, due out soon. She had loved its predecessor, *The Talisman*, about young Jack, a boy with strange powers, and when she heard of the long-delayed sequel she had been eager to get a copy. Luckily, Vardis had been able to snag her one through one of his many well-placed friends. Once the kids were done eating, she'd clean up the table, then sit down with her own lunch and the book while they enjoyed a little more free time. This daily interlude of pleasure reading was one of her favorite times.

As she headed back toward the kitchen, she turned her attention to the newscaster's speech.

"And today saw the arraignment of the nineteen Middle Eastern terrorists arrested late last month in their plot to hijack several commercial airliners and use them in acts of suicidal destruction. Speaking at the press conference after the arraignment, flanked by President Bush and Secretary of Defense Donald Rumsfeld, the United States Attorney General John Ashcroft revealed for the first time the intended targets of the conspirators, which included the World Trade Center in Manhattan . . ."

Kris paused, and a shiver coursed up and down her spine. How awful it would have been had these mad bastards succeeded. So much mass death and destruction. And there was the possibility the terrorist plan might have meant a personal tragedy for her and the kids. Vardis was in New York City this very moment, had been there for a week, meeting with patrons of the Temple, and the group had often dined at Windows on the World, the restaurant atop the WTC. What if—?

A sudden vivid image, almost like a real memory, of the Twin Towers exploding, burning, falling, bodies plummeting—

Kris shook her head to rid herself of the ghastly, gruesome scene, and then returned to the kids and her book.

Nothing King and Straub could imagine would ever equal that forestalled horror!

When Vardis returned home, in the early evening of September 13, he did not bring with him any presents or souvenirs from his New York City trip, for either Kris or the kids. But by now, after three years as a family, no one expected any. The potential recipients all knew that Vardis Salthouse was not that kind of father. While he never exhibited any ill will or hostility, meanness or disdain, or even impatience, he remained pretty much aloof from his brood—except when onstage. His manner derived not so much from any feeling of superiority or disinclination for intimacy. Rather, his mind was too preoccupied with plans and visions, schemes and strategies, tactics and what-ifs and theorizing. Kris had witnessed his otherworldly nature from the earliest days at the Temple and had not expected him to change. The children, however, had gone through a period of adjustment concerning the reality of having a father who was often "elsewhere." They had to discard any expectation of back-yard play with Dad, or paternal interest in their schoolwork or dreams, hurts or impasses. But their long histories as foster kids had helped to inure them to this distant, neutral attitude. They had all experienced much worse. And Kris's outgoing, bountiful nature more than compensated.

And so the return of their father to the family home was more in the nature of soldiers welcoming a visiting general to the base. Kris, having heard from Vardis when his plane touched down (he employed a top-of-the-line Nokia 8250 phone to stay in regular contact with the growing Temple empire), had the kids all fed and washed up in time for his arrival. As a benefit of their homeschooling, they enjoyed more relaxed bedtimes than their peers, who had to catch early busses and respond to hourly bells. But still, it was approaching ten p.m., the most generous bedtime for everyone but Gavril, when Vardis Salthouse finally walked through the door, suitcase in hand.

Kris admired her husband's looks even at this less-than-perfect moment when he was rough and bedraggled from travel and extensive meetings.

Long gone were the gaudy frat-boy shirts and cargo shorts and casual footwear. Realizing the need to impress newcomers to the Temple and aspiring to meet on even ground a host of rich and powerful and influential people, Vardis had swiftly educated himself about men's fashions. Kris had watched in amazement as he digested catalogs and magazines in an accelerated feeding frenzy. He emerged from his intensive self-education with a savvy grasp of couture. Nowadays, on a regular rotation Vardis Salthouse favored suits by Brioni, Dolce & Gabbana, and Erme-negildo Zegna. Tonight, he wore a Brioni plaid wool in charcoal. His shoes were from Allen Edmonds.

Unchanged, however, from their earliest days together were

Vardis's bulky frame, his unruly flame-tinged hair, and his fervency of expression. Although Vardis managed mostly to carry off an air of elegant style and affluency and dispassionate logic, to Kris, who knew him intimately, he still often looked as if someone had stuffed Rasputin into a costume acceptable to any top boardroom meeting.

The four children on the couch arose when their foster father entered the room.

Gavril, a handsome burgeoning teenager.

Toby, edging towards plump, and indeed resembling a bespectacled apprentice mage, his hero, Harry Potter.

The twins, dressed in cute matching pajamas that failed to conceal a certain maenad wildness.

They issued their welcomes—formal but sincere—and accepted a squeezed shoulder (the boys) or a peck on the crown of their heads (the girls) by way of return greeting. And then Kris quickly hustled them to their bedrooms, foregoing for the moment her own embrace with her husband, in deference to maternal duties.

When she reentered the room, Vardis was going diligently and scientifically through the mail stacked on the desk for his return. Kris came up and embraced him from behind. The memory of a similar encounter in the old Temple, that night they had first had sex, rose to convey a fleet of emotions: nostalgia, regret for a lost simpler time, but also happiness at what they now had, something much greater than those inchoate hopes and dreams.

A privileged state of affairs that was all down to the unique child resting upstairs in her lonely room.

Vardis set down the envelopes and turned around to enter into a full-bodied squeeze with his wife. They kissed with abandonment and eagerness, and Kris realized that she had been feeling a kind of subliminal emptiness and anticipation during Vardis's absence that only now dissipated.

"I wish you could have been with me in New York."

"Oh, really? Because the nights were so empty?"

"There was that. Although I hardly had time for such pursuits. Once I hit the pillow each night, I was out. But I could have used your insights into what several of our new sponsors and donors really believe they will be receiving from us. I tried not to overpromise. After all, we can't grant endless miracles. But I suspect they all will be showing up with the usual banal dreams and demands."

"We can handle them. We always have so far."

"Well, they are basically unimportant—small fry. But we are going to have a more consequential visitor at tomorrow night's meeting. Senator Calgary."

"Lauren did it at last!"

Lauren Long had been a member of the Temple of Human Potential from the earliest days. And as chief aide-de-camp to Senator Brad Calgary, she had gone also on a voyage that took her man from the statehouse to, just last year, Washington, DC. And now her boss was already being talked about in terms of a White House Cabinet appointment in 2004—should the Republicans win another term. Lauren had been trying to interest Calgary in the Temple for ages, but he had always begged off visiting. But some combination of his new status, plus the growing reputation and reach of the Temple, must have finally convinced him to check it out personally.

"If we could do a favor for Calgary, it could mean moving up to a whole new level, Kris. And I suspect that Vangie is fully capable of pulling off much bigger things than she's already shown us. Given what's she done so far, I project immense feats for her. Feats that will buy us the loyalty and gratitude of important people. Would you ever consent to using her that way? It wouldn't be any strain on her, I promise, and it would help the Temple infinitely. What do you say?"

The prospect of having Vangie perform larger-than-average miracles was new and startling at first. But the more Kris contemplated the prospect, the more she came to endorse it. After all, if something beneficial was within a person's powers, easily accomplished without harm, then shouldn't it be done?

"I'd have to hear the exact nature of the request, but I can't really conceive of any theoretical objections."

"Good! I needed to hear you agree. If we can earn Calgary's overt support and endorsement, the Temple would be able to reach so many more souls, helping them all to achieve their best selves. I feel it's a pivotal moment, Kris. It's really our goal and destiny."

Kris grew a shade worried about one practical aspect. "If only we could communicate in a more straightforward manner with Vangie. We think she understands us and what we ask. But there have been some awkward moments. You recall that woman, Deana Peavy—"

Vardis winced. "Don't remind me. A dramatic snafu. But we'll count on no such misunderstanding this time. We will drive home the desirable parameters of the necessary changes one way or another. How is she doing?"

"Oh, fine, no new developments."

"Let's go see her now. I feel I must commune with her atmanic self."

A night-light in Vangie's bedroom revealed a pleasantly decorated space, full of untouched toys and a rack of unappreciated books: *The Phantom Tollbooth, A Wrinkle in Time, If I Ran the Zoo, Harriet the Spy* . . .

Vangie no longer used or fit a traditional crib, but her new bed featured hospital-style bars to prevent rolling off by accident. Not that the child was a restless sleeper. In fact, most mornings found her pretty much in the same position she had been set into at lights-out.

Her blubbery visage slack and unprepossessing, Vangie rested now on her back, her eyes open and flicking from point to point. Kris no longer found the bizarre mannerism off-putting but regarded it as she regarded her husband's chewing on the corner of his mustache: an essential part of a loved one's inherent nature.

And Kris did love Vangie—perhaps more even than she loved the other four kids. The girl was so helpless and undemanding. And yet so compliant—almost always—to the demands of her parents.

Vardis laid a hand on the child's abdomen, as if taking some ethereal pulse or reading entrails without a gutting. With a penetrative stare from beneath dark brows, the guru regarded the child in silence for a long minute or two before speaking.

"Wherever your atman is roaming, child, hear me. There is great and glorious work ahead for you. And you must perform well. We won't settle for less."

2

Vangie was content—mostly—with the external life she had engineered for herself, starting with her decision to be rid of Mama Ginny. This family situation—sharing the house with her agreeable foster siblings, with Kris and Vardis at the helm—offered the most stability she had yet experienced in her nine years on Earth. With her material well-being assured, she was freed to focus on her continuing knowledge quest across all her ghostly lifetimes. Her education in the mutability of her manifold selves, in all the potential sorrows and joys of existence.

In her nine years, Vangie had witnessed a hundred hundred thousand iterations of her own life, from birth to death (thanks to universes downstream or upstream from her own across the objective clocktick of cosmic hyper-time).

She had witnessed herself feted and raped, crippled and cosseted, desperate and placid, sated and starving, broken and triumphant. A million Vangies had risen, striven, fallen, gotten up, and fallen again. Around herself, that prime nexus of observation, empires and cultures and governments of every stripe, from benign to despotic, came into being and toppled. Her alternate selves acquired friends, lovers, enemies, and victims. She saw herself perform acts of utmost nobility and utmost degradation, of sacrifice and selfishness, of cunning and stupidity. Ultimately, no aspect of her own nature, or of human nature, was left unexplored or foreign to her. And still, with all she had witnessed, she knew she had seen and heard only a tiny fraction of her possible lives. And she realized also that no path was privileged or destined to be the one that this particular Vangie mentality would necessarily experience.

She saw some worlds whose Vangies had no ability to work with or visualize the multiverse. These dead-end Vangies had no life-options outside their own singular paths. (And to hurl herself accidentally into their worlds would be to doom herself forever to the sterility of a single timeline.) But she and the other dimension-jumping Vangies had a plentitude of real choices—and hence no clear-cut or set-in-stone destiny.

At times, Vangie had felt intrusive efforts by her avatars to perform upon her the same act of possession she had imposed on so many of her own doppelgängers. But some unique aspect of her constitution acted as a shield to ward off such takeovers. Perhaps that feature of her brain *did* imply some special destiny for her.

The emotions that all these spectral visions had engendered in the little girl were titanic and disparate, roiling her heart and mind. Hatred, fear, envy, pity, compassion, pride—all these and scores of other feelings surged through her, as her ability to channel-skip across the multiverse matured. In her younger years, she had been buffeted by a random selection of ghosts, whipsawed from one sensation to another. But with her deepening powers and experience came a sense of control, of being a willing audience who viewed these ghosts with a purpose.

Before she was eight, the tumult of Vangie's vicarious lives had engendered in her a certain boundless yet somewhat naïve wisdom, and her bubbling pot of emotions had boiled down to a residue of calm, even bemused, acceptance. All the lives, even those where she was killed, had only made her stronger.

And so, with a more fixed sense of self in place, she set about honing her skills: crafting a self-directed practicum of multiversal exploration and exploitation.

That included, of course, some occasional, not-too-heavy-lifting exercises, rendered upon demand from the Temple. Mostly foolish, vain, trivial requests that involved very little effort on Vangie's part, and which she could fulfill quite easily, after these three years of further practice and study. (She smiled inside nowadays, to think how her first forays into this proactive realm—conjuring up Barbie dolls for the twins—had stressed and taxed her.) The mental errands she undertook at the behest of Vardis Salthouse, exercising whatever complex, rare, and strange organs provided her powers, were in fact additional testing and educational stints, and so she did not begrudge them, even though they sometimes involved more complicated rituals.

Vangie had had to learn a very important technique to accomplish what was asked of her when a change in the fortunes or status or destiny or appearance of a person was requested. The new technique amounted to a twofold ability. First, she had to be able to discern the identities of all the necessary observers quantumly linked to the primary subject, those people who also had to jump timelines for the desired effect to be perceived. Secondly, Vangie had to learn how to concatenate them all, like beads on a string or nodes in a web, and hold them firmly in her mind's grip during the jump.

It had taken her a long time to recognize the importance of this "primacy of observers" principle and to become proficient in the necessary technique, and even longer to fully understand why she had deployed it instinctively back at the start of the extension of her powers to others. But eventually it had all become intellectually clear to her.

Consider the hypothetical case when Vangie jumped alone to some new strand, out of all her infinite choices. Pretend it was a world where Vangie, and Vangie alone, sported shiny green skin. (She had indeed seen such a far-off continuum once.) In this instance of solo transport, upon alighting in her new home she alone would recognize that anything had changed, since she carried the memories of her prior pink-skinned existence with her. No one else in the green-skin universe would blink at the notion of a green-skinned Vangie, for they were the natural residents of such a place and had experienced no alteration in their lives when Vangie inserted herself into their timestream. She had always been green skinned from their point of view.

If Vangie wanted anyone else to marvel at or even just apprehend such a transition—going from pink to green—she would have to bring their conscious essences along with hers, from pink-skin origin to green-skin destination. Then, as they were ported crosstime and unwittingly alighted into their new selves, their memories of a pink-skinned Vangie would overlay the green-skin memories of their new hosts, producing the desired effect of an instant magical transformation. There might be some residual confusion as two sets of memories battled, but generally the intruder gestalt took precedence, as if through some codicil of transit, or perhaps the brute shock of insertion, or an infusion of extradimensional energy.

And so when Vardis Salthouse asked her, say, to heal a congregant of some illness or condition—a lame leg, a cancer, blindness—then Vangie, after trawling the timelines for a suitable destination that would fulfill the request, had to quickly suss out all the interrelated souls who would have to come along to validate the miracle. At a minimum, that list included everyone present at the Temple ceremony. But then the roster would exfoliate outward from the individual, to include everyone— or at least those most intimate with the subject—who knew of the subject's current condition and could be amazed by the transformation.

In the destination universe, any tangential percipient not subjected to an overlay would host contradictory beliefs to those of the new arrivals. Any vital individual left behind would represent, in the new universe, an unbeliever, a hole in the tapestry of change, sporting memories devoid of any earlier paradoxical existence. "What do you mean, you're cured? You were never sick to begin with!"

These nodes—the necessary fellow travelers—revealed themselves to Vangie's extradimensional vision by ethereal, metaphysical lines of influence and connectivity, luminous tethers of affiliation. In her landscape of ghosts, they stood out as constellations of affiliations. Once she learned to focus on these numinous lines and bring them to the forefront of her mind, she realized she had been half-seeing them for some time without knowing what they were or represented.

And so a typical show at the Temple for Human Potential would proceed in this manner for Vangie. Onstage, Vardis would make his request.

"Oh, beneficent Ultimate Reifier, she who cuts and reweaves the tapestry of our destiny, please free this supplicant of the affliction besetting her."

Vangie would instantly begin scanning adjacent timelines for the one where 99.999 percent of reality was identical to her current strand, but whose one exception was the desired element of change: the cure, the fix, the alteration. Then she would pluck all the connectivity cables radiating out from the subject—or nearly all of them; there was no point in dragging in peripheral figures like first-grade teachers or policemen who had once written the subject a ticket—and grasp them firmly. Of course, everyone at the Temple, her family and other congregants, was automatically swept up in Vangie's ethereal embrace. Then came the effort of jumping to the new continuum, dragging everyone behind her like fish in a net. That did take some internal resources, in proportion to the number of souls along for the ride and the existential distance between universes.

But Vangie always recalled the lesson given to her by the Council of Ghosts: she need not jump directly to the universe where the request was a fait accompli, but only to a more easily accessible one that boasted a sweet spot of inflection, a circumstance that could lead by natural causes to the desired result.

These factors explained why Vangie was occasionally unable to fulfill a request: either too many souls to be hauled across too wide a gap, or no sweet spot to be found.

And of course, there were her occasional mistakes and omissions, screwups and disasters. She was, after all, only nine years old, and still learning.

The worst instance had involved a Temple congregant named Deana Peavy.

Peavy's request had been an uncomplicated one. The woman's face had been horribly disfigured in an industrial accident involving chemicals, leaving her with a monstrous visage, irreparable by surgery, that frightened children and made adults blanch. She simply desired the return of her old face. Easy enough. Vangie hauled herself, Peavy, the Temple congregation, and all of Peavy's affiliates to the requisite timeline.

But the miracle did not sit well with Peavy's ex-husband, one of the transported affiliate souls. Years ago, he had abandoned Deana Peavy after her troubles. Now, seeing her suddenly and inexplicably restored, he experienced a reality break fueled largely by guilt. The man's madness had led to a murder-suicide, himself and Deana. In the subsequent news coverage, no actual guilt for the crime could be laid at the door of the Temple of Human Potential. Nonetheless, just being associated with the tragedy was unpleasant and bad for Vardis Salthouse's reputation.

Life in the Troy-Salthouse home had not been happy for many months after that.

And so now, Vangie always took the time to scan adjacent chrono-shifted timelines for possible fallout of her actions. In milliseconds, she could skip her attention across weeks and months and years, making bigger survey jumps after some close-scale ones, to assess the possible effects of her changes. No more Deana Peavy–type incidents would be allowed.

Oh, yes indeed, Vangie had become an expert at her game, if not yet a full master.

Certainly she would have progressed further and faster if she had received additional help from the Council of Ghosts, those nine alternate Vangies who had come to her years ago to enlighten her about the nature of reality and her place therein.

But the Council of Ghosts had hidden themselves away in the bowels of infinity.

Vangie sought her advisory avatars everywhere but couldn't find them, although of course she encountered many similar doppelgängers who were unable to communicate back to her, as the Council had done. For whatever reasons, her mentors had chosen to sever contact with her. Vangie puzzled over the whys. To allow her to develop and learn at her own pace, instead of just receiving predigested wisdom? Because she was proving to be disappointing and unexceptional, not living up to her promise? Maybe the Council of Ghosts had been wiped out! There had been mention of some potential adversary . . . What was his name? Yes, Durant Le Massif.

The Massive.

Remembering that disturbing display of the Massive's monocultural world, intrigued and also frightened by the thought of some lurker who might intend harm to her and her ghosts, Vangie cast about for some timeline where his course might intersect hers. If she wanted to meet the Massive, she had to metaphorically bring him to her, rather than she going to him. This was the only option open to her.

Vangie's powers of perception did not amount to some kind of panopticon. She was not capable of being some disembodied eye that could float at will across the surface of the planet or into the depths of space, seeing everything omnisciently. Her living visions were limited to representations of herself, the spacetime-bounded lives of her doppelgängers. Of course, when anyone intersected her path through the coiled dimensions of reality, she could then follow them also, at least until their destinies diverged from hers. Thus, when Deana Peavy had shown up at the Temple with her plea, Vangie had gained access to Peavy's ghosts, since they were entangled with hers.

The Council had told Vangie that the Massive was unique in that he was invariant across all timelines. So out of an infinity of possible lives, his should cross hers infinitely often. But scrolling through millions of existences that did not feature the Massive's life-thread joining hers was enervating and frustrating.

But at last she brought forward a vision of a world where Durant Le Massif announced himself.

In this iteration of her life, Vangie was a permanent juvenile resident of a squalid sanitarium in a country of ruins and poverty, where every day seemed overcast and stormy, a realm of grief and poverty. This Vangie was a dead-ender, lacking all the

Vangie powers. Vangie Prime could not visit this avatar safely in person but could still observe.

One day a man applied to adopt her, announcing himself to the caretakers as Durant Le Massif.

He was a compact fellow, perhaps in his early twenties, with aquiline features and eyes more jeering than serious, although he did not smile. His cockscomb of golden-brown hair gave him a boyish look. In this drab, impoverished world, he dressed very well and did not appear undernourished, like most of his fellow citizens.

He pulled a cord that rang the sanitarium's wall-mounted bell. A caretaker appeared at the door and beckoned Durant Le Massif inside.

Able to shift about her perceptions at will—within the intimate sphere of activity defined by her doppelgänger—Vangie had been watching this action as if from outside the sanitarium. But now, as she prepared to follow Durant Le Massif inside, she came to a silently screeching halt.

The Massive had turned around as if to face his invisible observer. His sprightly eyes had locked onto the metaphysical overlook occupied by Vangie.

And then he winked.

Absolutely terrified, Vangie instantly pulled out of that particular frame, fleeing for the safety of her home.

And no longer did she seek to learn more of Durant Le Massif.

3

After moving four times to progressively larger and larger rented quarters over the last three years, charting a steady upward trend in popularity and prominence, the Temple of Human Potential now occupied its own building. A midsized auditorium with attached offices, a basement kitchen, and a dining hall, the place had been deaccessioned by a local Catholic church when the impoverished parish closed for lack of congregants. The Temple had purchased the building with cash. Their finances were solid, and new income streams were being developed almost daily.

Vardis Salthouse appreciated the symbolism of the transfer. "Just as the old paths of spirituality fade and give way to our new disciplines, so too do the earthly accoutrements of our success change hands. Every day we are moving one step closer to our destined future."

This fuzzy sentiment of self-affirmation brought a rousing cheer from the congregation that had assembled for the jubilant first services in the new building. From the stage, standing by her husband and with her children, Kris Troy had felt an upwelling of pride and satisfaction. They had come such a long way from those humble nights in the dingy former storefront, all thanks to the drive and insights and inspiration of Vardis Salthouse—supported by his loving wife, of course.

And also thanks to one special child who could work literal miracles: Vangie Troy-Salthouse.

Along for the exciting ride had come almost all of those early faithful adherents, given new and prestigious positions in the organization.

That brassy cougar Andorra had been put in charge of catering and decorations, arranging each session's refreshments, and taking responsibility for the hiring and setup of remote venues. The former dealer in vintage tchotchkes, Roger Auldstane, now handled all travel arrangements—including the securing of lodgings for the traveling Temple officials and entourage—while interfacing with local authorities for permits and cosponsorships. Emilio Elorza now deployed his lawyerly skills in lobbying, community outreach, publicity, and publications. Burly Bernie Vanson, streetwise, had been delegated with all their security concerns.

And then of course there was Lauren Long, aide to Senator Brad Calgary. Absent from the mother church and busy in Washington, she performed no local functions but rather served as a conduit to the influential people who could funnel special benefits, donations, and interested parties toward the Temple.

And without a doubt, tonight Lauren had achieved a coup by finally getting her pet senator to attend a service.

The only old-timer missing from the current retinue was Tucker Storch, the elderly hermetic poet given to declaiming his cosmic screeds at service's end. Deeming his long-winded poetry incongruent with the new style and presentation and personality of the Temple, Vardis had officially discontinued those performances. He had tried giving Storch the job of driving the elegant tour bus that ferried the family around on their shorter excursions—the man already held the proper licenses from past employment—but Storch had balked at what he legitimately regarded as a demotion, an insult to his religious artistry. Kris had witnessed the severing of the connection.

Storch seemed to have shrunken in the past several months, looking dispirited and wan. "No thanks, Mr. Salthouse. If I can't share my visionary verses with the congregation, then I won't be sent down to the servant's quarters. In fact, I suspect I won't be attending Temple nights at all anymore."

Reluctant to lose even such a minor follower, offended by the dismissal of what he deemed a generous employment offer, and perhaps even a little nostalgic for Storch's presence, as a token of the old days, Vardis replied, "But why not just stay on in the audience, Tucker? Surely you can benefit from the preaching. That's what brought you here in the first place, isn't it? And we haven't even submitted your desires to Vangie yet. There must be something you want that we could coax from her. I'm sorry that favor hasn't come sooner. But we dread overtaxing her, and there were others with greater needs ahead of you."

Storch regarded Vardis intently from rheumy eyes. "Mr. Salthouse, when I first came to you, your preaching was all about how we could bring out the inner potential in our lives, how we could make the most of what we were born with and overcome the forces that were holding us back. But now it's all about what your magic little girl can give to us, not what we can accomplish on our own. I don't like that. Maybe she can do all you claim. Maybe it's all just people deluding themselves about stuff that was gonna happen anyhow, seeing her hand in changes that they really made for themselves. But whatever's going on, I think you are relying too much on something you can't really control. And it's gonna come back and bite you in the ass."

Feeling too exalted by all his successes, Vardis Salthouse took no offense at Storch's rebuke. He smiled broadly and clapped a hand on the old man's denimed shoulder.

"I'm very sorry you feel that way, Tucker, and I appreciate your concern for me and my family and the Temple. But given your fears and disapproval, I suspect it's best if you don't attend services anymore. Kris, can you make a note for all the ushers about Tucker's severance from the Temple? Thanks."

Storch left his interview with slumped shoulders, but no further words.

As she busied herself with the hundred-and-one last-minute preparations for tonight's service, memories of the old man's expulsion drifted back to Kris. A sad occasion, certainly, but, like the Peavy affair, just a small bump on the road to success and the fulfillment of their grand vision: a world where every individual could hyper-potentiate their destiny.

As always, the services were slated to begin at seven p.m. The family-friendly hour allowed for attendance by children—always conducive to a festive atmosphere—and also facilitated a commensurately early hour of dismissal so that the working-class attendees could call it an early night and get ready for the next day's demands.

Around five p.m., Kris was in the auditorium's greenroom, checking on a bouquet and snacks intended for Senator Calgary. (Andorra had arranged an actual wreath with a banner that read WELCOME SENATOR CALGARY!) Lauren had gotten off their train at a planned brief stop. She needed to phone from the platform and inform Kris that she and the senator were on schedule and should arrive by the start of the service.

Loudspeakers in the room were active now. During the service, they would relay what was happening onstage to whoever awaited in the greenroom. But right now they were tuned to a National Public Radio station, which was offering the news.

"The captured terrorists who planned to hijack four planes and destroy various United States targets have been subject to intense interrogation sessions at the US Naval Base in Guantanamo, Cuba, and have begun to reveal, it is rumored, the foreign state actors who were behind their plot . . ."

Fussing over the arrangements, Kris was excited. She ran through all that remained to be done, knowing that a host of competent Temple personnel should have matters well in hand. Still, she resolved to double-check them all. She knew that tonight would be a pivotal moment in the Temple's onward march to greater influence and success. Vardis had something big planned to impress the senator, some large invocation of Vangie's powers. Exactly what, he had not told her.

But about Vangie, she worried little. The child seemed rested and content—insofar as her emotional state could be ascertained—and she had never failed them yet. No one really knew the extent of the girl's strange powers, but Kris suspected they were vaster than anyone conceived. What they asked of her probably barely scratched the surface of her abilities, and she was hardly overworked.

On a practical level, the wonder girl needed little supervision. Her semi-autism meant she was not able to stray or get into any dangerous situations. And as for receiving love and affection—well, that was what her foster siblings provided. Under the command of the newly adult Gavril, Troy, Blaine, and Drew waited in attendance on Vangie, petting her, putting her through her muscle-toning routines, reading aloud to her (for whatever good it did), and generally providing companionship. The five of them would make their entrance and take their place onstage tonight together, a tableau signifying familial unity and the yoking of simple human strengths with the supernatural talents of the chosen one, the Ultimate Reifier.

Leaving the greenroom, Kris was surprised to encounter Emilio Elorza in the backstage corridor. (An old, faded church poster, permanently pasted to the wall, proclaimed IN MY FATHER'S HOUSE ARE MANY MANSIONS.) She was doubly surprised to find him accompanied by a stranger.

Elorza gave out with his best press agent's bonhomie.

"Ah, Kris, I'm glad I found you! I'd like to introduce you to a respected scholar who's taken an interest in our little mission, and who has a special request to make."

Kris focused on the stranger. His betel-nut-brown complexion, perhaps slightly jaundiced, overlaid a set of features which, in toto, Kris associated vaguely with the Indian subcontinent: cleanly and classically composed, non-Anglo, somewhat prominent nose and mouth. Far from young, as evidenced by his floppy white hair and elegantly trimmed white mustache, the slim man still possessed a kind of youthful bearing. He was dressed in a style that could only be called "shabby professorial," his suit having been modestly stylish a decade or two in the past. Thick lenses in his eyeglasses contributed to an owlish look. A subtle cologne like cloves and other unidentified spices emanated from him.

The man tendered his hand and Kris took it. His grip was competent. He spoke without accent.

"Ms. Troy, I am very honored to meet you. My name is Professor Vivek Kocchar. Please allow me to offer my card."

Kris took the card, recognizing the seal of the state university in one corner. "Professor of Consciousness Studies? What exactly is that?"

The professor preened his mustache, a gesture that Kris intuited must precede his classroom lectures as well. "It is a relatively new discipline which seeks to plumb the depths of the mind, to learn the cellular or existential basis of thought and selfhood and rationality and awareness, to assign scientific underpinnings to the habits of mind which we all take for granted. A noble, albeit perhaps impossible quest. But one which I have chosen to pursue wholeheartedly."

"I think I understand. But what brings you to the Temple?"

"What else but the accounts of your wonder-working child, Evangeline. From what I have read about her feats, I have a suspicion that she possesses unique talents that could illuminate my own researches."

"How so?"

"It all comes down to qualia. These are the hypothetical components of consciousness. The atoms of self-referentiality, if you wish. It is my theory that some people possess stronger qualia than others, and that their mentalities might be forceful enough to influence the minds of others, or perhaps even bend reality to some small degree. Now, as David Chalmers has shown—"

Kris signaled a pause in the lecture. "That's all very intriguing, Professor Kocchar, but somewhat beyond me. I'm more concerned with the practicalities of your observations, and whether they might interfere with the services."

"I only need to be close by Evangeline when she is performing, to take readings with a small unit, my electrophotonic gauge. Totally inconspicuous, I assure you."

Kris considered. If this fellow could learn more about how Vangie's powers worked, surely that would be of use to the Temple . . .

"Let me consult with Mr. Elorza a moment."

Stepping a few yards away, Kris and Elorza conversed in low tones.

"Emilio, I assume you brought this guy here because you thought it was a good idea."

"Yeah, of course. We haven't had any interest from the academic crowd yet. This guy could generate some good headlines for us." Elorza made air quotes. "'University prof says miracle girl is next stage of human evolution.' That kinda stuff. Scientific cred could draw in a whole new crowd, really expand our allure to a whole different set of people."

"Have you cleared this with Vardis yet?"

"No, I figured I'd run it by you first, and you could take it from there, if you approved."

Kris looked back to Professor Kocchar. Obviously overcome by a sudden brainstorm, the savant had taken out an old-school reporter's notebook and was scribbling away, possibly even solving equations, judging by the non-alphabetic flicks of his pencil.

Kris said, "Okay, Emilio, I think you might be on to something."

She returned to the visitor. "Professor Kocchar, the final word on allowing you access to our daughter rests with my husband. But I will plead your case, and you might be taking the stage with us in a couple of hours. Do you have this meter gadget of yours handy?"

Smiling broadly, Kocchar dipped a hand into one capacious pocket of his baggy suit coat and removed something that resembled a pistol-grip label maker or retailer's pricing gun, but festooned with wires and dials and some twinkling varicolored LEDs.

"Ms. Troy, the pursuit of knowledge is an around-the-clock activity. I am never to be found without my essential probe!"

4

The Temple's band, a jazzy young sextet neatly attired in uniforms designed by Andorra, had been playing show tunes for nearly an hour as the excited audience filtered into the auditorium. Vardis saw no need for solemnity nor piety nor sanctified silence before a show. The accomplishments of the Temple were entirely consonant with mundane needs and desires and pleasures. Any spiritual enlargement was derived secondarily, from the satisfaction of achieving one's practical goals. This sprightly familiar music engendered a lively ambiance in the crowd that would encourage attainments.

Standing in the wings, stage right, unseen by the audience, her anticipation building, Kris focused her attention on the uncurtained platform, as-yet unpeopled, where the magic would happen. Even after all these years and miracles, she still got butterflies before going on. Her duties were limited to overseeing Vangie and the other kids, not preaching or testifying, but she still found it exhilarating and nerve-wracking to be at the center of so much massed expectant and worshipful attention.

Behind her stood a calm and obedient Professor Kocchar.

If the thought of appearing onstage in front of several hundred people unnerved him at all, he did not show it other than by fussing with his detection gadget as if to ensure its crucial working. His certification to attend had been given swiftly and unbegrudgingly by Vardis Salthouse, once both Kris and Elorza had made their cases in private. Instructed in the protocols of the evening, Kocchar had promised to remain unobtrusive and silent, taking his readings covertly, behind the shield of Kris's body as she stood next to Vangie.

The furniture on the stage was simple. A tall bar stool hosted a cordless microphone on its cushion. Here was where Vardis could rest from time to time, like a weary comedian, when he tired from his exhortations that had him stalking furiously up and down the stage. Kris had always deemed her husband a bundle of inexhaustible energy, but of late he had begun to tire more easily, and Kris worried that he was pushing himself too hard. But he wanted so badly to boost the Temple up to new heights as fast as possible. She hoped that, coming off this New York trip, he was not starting the performance from a low ebb.

Dominating the middle of the stage was an expensive customized lounging chair, burgundy leather with gold piping, permanently reclined at a slight angle that would still allow the audience to keep the face of the seated person in view. The resemblance to a throne was intentional. Flanking this seat, two on each side, were a total of four modest upright chairs. In this suite of seats, the five children would take their places, Vangie in the center, of course. Behind the reclining chair was a small riser that allowed Kris to hover, standing over her adopted daughter like a beneficent guardian angel.

Three top-of-the-line Panasonic camcorders on tripods were spaced in an innocuous semicircle, so as not to attract attention from the audience. No technicians would operate them during the service—Vardis did not want to share the stage with any extraneous personnel—and so they had been activated before the first congregant entered. Their 120-minute tape cassettes would be replenished during the service's planned intermission.

Suddenly the band was playing Steve Winwood's "Higher Love," the song that would usher Vardis Salthouse onstage. The congregants erupted in applause and celebratory shouts. Allowing the tension to reach a perfect apex, Vardis delayed his entrance till the final second. He bounded out from stage left, tracked by a golden spotlight. Grabbing the mic, Vardis reached the very edge of the stage and stood smiling, letting the band bring the tune to a climax. Kris saw no signs of fatigue. He seemed perfect to her eyes, commanding and assured. When the shouts and clapping had subsided, he finally spoke.

"Who wants to be their best self!"

"We do!"

"Then listen to my words!"

"We'll listen!"

That ritual ended, Vardis began his free-style, almost stream-of-consciousness riff about tapping into the ur-currents of the plenum, channeling them through one's karma and atmanic core. Although it varied from service to service, the rap had enough repeated elements to form a kind of scripture, which the Temple had self-published in a small book, sales of which constituted a very respectable revenue stream.

The sweaty, high-energy performance went on for a full hour, marked by a few quieter interludes upon the stool, where a water bottle and towel also saw use. Kris marveled afresh at her husband's physical capacities and visionary's tongue.

At last his dramatic peroration came, followed by extensive applause. When quiet resumed, Salthouse said, "I know that you are all anticipating the arrival of my daughter, Evangeline, the Ultimate Reifier. We pray that tonight she will be able to instantiate one of her life-changing miracles for us, to edify and enlighten us as to how we too can grasp the live wires of reality and guide the potent charge through our intentions and dreams. But first, as always, let me bring out the Temple members who help to keep our mission flowing so smoothly."

Responding to their boss's wave, Andorra, Roger Auldstane, Emilio Elorza, and Bernie Vanson trotted out to receive their accolades. They shifted then to stand behind Vardis.

"And of course, you all know who's yet to appear. My lovely and irreplaceable wife, Kris, the woman responsible for finding and fostering our daughter Evangeline. The woman who first recognized the Ultimate Reifier's talents. Without her, we would all still be stumbling in the dark. Here she is, folks. Kris Troy-Salthouse!"

Kris signaled to Professor Kocchar that he should continue to wait backstage until after the scheduled break. She, however, responded to her cue by swiftly crossing the platform to her husband's side. He gave her a hug and a peck on the cheek. Grinning, all her senses amped high, swept up in the sea of noise from the congregants, Kris was overcome by a sensation that the Temple stood at a decisive turning point. Was it something conveyed by Vardis's stance and elation? She couldn't say.

"We have to leave you for a half hour now, to make sure our little Vangie is ready for her challenge. Please enjoy the refreshments in the lobby and consider purchasing a book or tape!"

Kris exited stage right, while the others retreated stage left. She found Professor Kocchar looking ponderously pensive.

"My electrophotonic gauge detected no surge in meta-qualia during your husband's presentation. So we can rule him out as a source of any transreal waveforms. Any such manifestations must come from your daughter Evangeline. That is, unless any of your other children are equally talented?"

"No, I'm afraid not. They're just normal, good-hearted kids who love their special sister."

Kris excused herself and raced off to the greenroom. (The children had a special room—the "Nursery"—devoted to their comfort. Kris did not feel obligated to check on them, since Gavril showed such care and competence in his mentorship of the brood. And besides, Vardis would probably poke his head in anyway.)

In the waiting room, Kris encountered Lauren Long looking dapper, efficient, and businesslike in a tailored outfit that bespoke subtle Washington finesse. With her, of course, was Senator Brad Calgary.

Lauren rendered the introductions.

Knowing men's fashions from Vardis's interest, Kris speculated that Calgary's suit must have cost at least three thousand dollars. Classically handsome, blond, smelling of a subtle, elegant cologne, Calgary displayed a mix of boyish, Kennedy insouciance with a substratum of hard-bitten mastiff meanness. Kris knew that his tenure as a local Republican politician had been marked by cutthroat bargains, some shady deals, and an overweening ambition. His transition to the larger sphere of national politics had been long assumed, and after just a short time in the capitol he was standing out in the eyes of the Bush administration.

"Senator Calgary, we are so thrilled you could make it tonight. I think my husband has something special planned for you."

Calgary's sonorous tones seemed tailored for broadcast and the pages of history books, even when no cameras or crowd of observers were present.

"You know that I've been very impressed by the seeming miracles your Temple has recorded, the good you've done for so many suffering souls. Lauren has assured me that everything is on the up-and-up, which is the only inducement that could bring me here. I rely on her acumen tremendously."

Kris thought Lauren's face might outshine a hundred-watt bulb.

The senator continued. "I'm counting on ascertaining the reality of these phenomena tonight with my own eyes. You realize, naturally, that I cannot afford to endorse anything that smacks of chicanery or scam. However, if I emerge tonight with proof of the tangibility of little Vangie's talents, then it might be that the Temple and I can come to a certain understanding that will prove mutually profitable. And not just in terms of money. But rather in the currency of power."

Allusions to some kind of important and consequential deal convinced Kris that Vardis was indeed planning something stunning for tonight. Had he already been in negotiations with Calgary? Regarding what? And would Vangie come through?

"You can have complete and total confidence in the honesty and integrity of our practices and beliefs, Senator. My husband is a sincere philosopher and a very wise and compassionate man. As for Vangie—she is utterly innocent, and a conduit to the real higher forces that drive our universe. There's no trickery within her."

"That's extremely reassuring, Kris. Because I'm trusting that my public presence here will in no way compromise my reputation. For if it did, the fallout would be severe.

"And I would ensure that nine-tenths of the damages fell on the Temple."

5

Back in the wings, amidst the bustle of techies and the smells of old stage curtains, cobwebbed rafters, and the ghosts of church incense, reunited with the superhumanly patient Professor Kocchar, Kris experienced a bout of déjà vu, as if she had always stood here, or stood here serially for uncounted iterations. Working hard to shrug off the odd sensations, she focused instead on the savant. He seemed quite calm, having evidently gotten his gadget into satisfactory working order. All to the good.

The rows of seats were rapidly filling up with the returning congregants. Another packed house tonight. Soon they would have to consider moving to even larger quarters. Kris could envision a stadium filled with roaring adherents as Vardis delivered his upbeat maxims from centerfield, a giant TV screen shadowing his every gesture. Anything looked possible tonight, especially with the mysterious hints of support from Senator Calgary. Kris felt confident that his full expectations would be met, and his blustering threats would never come into play.

The houselights went down, the spot came on, and Vardis crossed to the forefront of the stage.

"Welcome back, seekers! Tonight, we have not one but two special guests. I'd like to introduce our first visitor."

That was Kris's cue. She motioned for the professor to follow her into the spotlight.

Once the frowsy academic was beside Vardis, presenting a vivid contrast of types, the preacher draped an arm over Professor Kocchar's shoulder, as if they had been longtime pals. "I want to introduce Professor Vivek Kocchar, an expert in brain science from our fine state university. He's here tonight to observe whatever miracles our Evangeline chooses to manifest, with an eye toward placing her marvelous abilities onto the spectrum of all creation that runs from the lowliest single-celled creature to the gods we are all capable of becoming!"

Instructed to remain silent, Kocchar gave a small regal bow. Kris noted with gratitude that the professor was exhibiting no stage fright or bumbling, but rather showed some calm and innate dignity. She supposed that standing in front of a classroom for years had somewhat inured him to this parallel spectacle.

"Our second new participant tonight hardly needs my introduction. You will all instantly recognize our outstanding junior senator, Brad Calgary. Truly one of those rare open-minded politicians, he is here to learn about the wonders that the Temple encompasses. Please make him feel at home!"

Calgary emerged with a jaunty gait and a broad smile, as if officiating at some mall ribbon-cutting ceremony. He shook hands all around and said a few innocuous words into the borrowed mic. Resuming command of the mic, Vardis issued a command.

"And now, let the miracle children step forth!"

A second spotlight tracked the arrival of the quintet. Solemnly flanked by the neatly dressed boys on her left and the

charmingly frocked twin girls on her right, Vangie moved with
a kind of awkward hip-rolling ambulation that bordered on
a continuous falling forward. She wore a kind of utilitarian
ivory front-zippered coverall and flat slippers, dancing shoes
almost, like the garb that might be worn by an acolyte of the
most unimaginative cult possible. Vardis had always insisted
that her presentation should be deliberately drab to counterpoint her startling powers. At age nine, Vangie retained a kind
of still-gestating face and physique, lumpish and uncontoured,
homely as a dishrag.

The crowd that had applauded raucously at Vardis's exhortations offered no clapping or cheers. They had seen this small
creature perform too many miracles to countenance frivolity.
Despite Vangie's unassuming appearance, she radiated much
power and mystery.

The foster siblings raised Vangie up to her throne and got
her settled down before taking their own chairs. They offered
the semblance of the staff at mission control, there only to help
launch the real explorer into the unknown.

Vardis broke the silence of the ritual. "Friends, you know
that generally at this point we select a deserving member from
our audience for Vangie's intercession. One of our own kindred seekers in need of our daughter's aid. But tonight, we
have chosen a different candidate for Vangie's numinous touch.
During my visits to our city's various charity wards, I was deeply
touched by the plight of two small girls—orphans, actually, just
like our Vangie once was. Eight-year-old sisters named Tippi and
Risa Perkins. And so I've arranged for them to be here tonight,
in the hopes that we can work a miracle for them."

Onto the stage came Tippi and Risa Perkins, accompanied
by a fellow whose white lab coat and stethoscope plainly sig-
nified his official medical stature. The girls—plain-faced but

innocently charming, with long tresses and modest matching plaid dresses—seemed averse to being separated, so closely did they hug each other as they marked a kind of crablike progress across the boards. It was only as they reached the front of the stage that Kris—and the audience—discerned their true nature.

The girls were conjoined twins. The bridge of flesh that joined them must have begun about collarbone-high and continued down to waist level, leaving them slightly canted toward each other, but with four more or less functional legs. Their innermost arms had to perforce hug their partner's shoulder when not in awkward use, although their outer arms hung normally.

Vardis first congratulated the girls for being here, eliciting some shy smiles. Then he turned to their guardian.

"Dr. Troutman, you've been attending the Perkins twins for some time now. Would you care to say a little about their condition?"

"Certainly. Although basically healthy now, the girls have had to undergo many surgeries during their brief lives. They share several unduplicated organs, and of course their nervous systems and circulatory systems are a maze of entanglements. They have adapted from infancy quite well to a conjoined existence, although of course their lives can hardly be called normal, and their sad condition constrains them from enjoying many of the simple things that all of us take for granted. And of course while they are deeply bonded emotionally at this point in their lives, I foresee a day—should they be lucky enough to reach adulthood, which is not a given—when matters of privacy and individuality and the impossibility of separation become matters of distress."

"So you're telling us that medical science has no way of surgically altering these girls—no way to grant them the individual personhood that should be their birthright?"

"That is correct, Mr. Salthouse."

Vardis paused, as if hesitant to utter his next statement.

"Dr. Troutman—if the girls consented, might we all see the fleshly barrier that's frustrating the surgeons?"

The doctor squatted to put his face on a level with those of the girls. "Tippi, Risa—do you mind sharing your condition in a modest way with the good people here? They're all friends, and you've certainly been examined by large groups before. And perhaps your bravery here tonight might actually lead to a solution somehow."

The twins regarded the doctor and then each other gravely, before nodding their assent.

Feelings of unease and even a small bit of shame had begun to creep into Kris's sense of excitement. Was this right, to parade these children before a mass of strangers? And yet, Vardis must know what he was doing. He had never failed the Temple before. And besides, it was all for the good of the poor sufferers.

The doctor caused the girls to turn around, so that their clothed backs were presented. From Kris's proximity, she could see that the custom-designed double-sized wraparound dress featured a line of snaps down the middle.

Dr. Troutman popped the snaps, not all the way, but nearly. Then, like a surgeon parting an incision, he pulled back the wings of plaid fabric.

The florid naked ligature of flesh that bound the twins together was not smooth, but ridged and welted and crisscrossed with scars. It seemed to Kris more like some fungal parasite yoking the pair than common flesh.

Troutman refastened the girls and they faced again the audience, apparently unflustered at this familiar routine.

Vardis said, "Thank you, girls, doctor. Indeed, this is a horrible affliction. Doctor—can you put aside your scientific rationality for a moment and endorse our principles of faith, when I tell you it is quite possible that our Ultimate Reifier can grant these girls their freedom?"

"Science and faith are not incompatible in my book, Mr. Salthouse."

"Good! Very good! Because I truly believe that we are about to witness a miracle. Our Evangeline is not always able to attain the impossible for us. Sometimes the universe conspires against her. And also, sometimes her miracles are infinitely subtle. The fulfillment of her willpower might mean that six months from now, a surgeon from across the globe might step forward and reveal he can cure the Perkins girls with some new technique. Would that be a coincidence, just the progress of pure science? Or would it be the fruition of a cosmic seed that Evangeline plants here tonight? Although I could never prove that our daughter was responsible in the latter case, I would firmly believe so, having seen her earlier workings come true. But let's not anticipate failure, my friends! Let's trust in the mechanism of the plenum, a mechanism whose tiller is guided by the Ultimate Reifier. Friends, as always, I am going to ask you to concentrate your own atmanic power-selves and direct them toward the fulfillment of our goal. Lend your beliefs and strengths to Evangeline, and they will rebound to your favor. As you strengthen your own psychic muscles in the cause of these two little girls, so too will your path to unleashing your own potential become more straight and smooth!"

Vardis now guided the twins, Dr. Troutman, Senator Calgary, Kris, and Professor Kocchar to stand in front of Vangie's throne. The four serious-faced fosters rose to their feet in deference to the gravity of the moment. The half-recumbent girl took no notice of any of the activity.

"Evangeline Troy-Salthouse, Ultimate Reifier, we beseech

you with the purest of intentions. Please give these innocent misshapen children standing here before you the gift of normality, the benison of separation, the blessing of being untethered each from each. If you can perform this task, if you deem it worthy of your unfathomable talents, then let thy will be done!"

At these moments of invocation, Kris always felt her perceptions escalate into some kind of hyper-awareness. She could see the beads of sweat on Vardis's brow like giant spheres of liquid. She watched an expression of mixed avidity, doubt, and longing infiltrate the senator's face, creeping though every incipient wrinkle and fold of his physiognomy. The doctor radiated to her a kind of tug-of-war splitting of his very being, science versus faith. She plumbed the hearts of her four foster children, sensing their play of emotions: pride, anticipation, even a shade of boredom and defiance. She felt from Professor Kocchar an intense buzz of curiosity, as he covertly played his gadget upon Vangie's form. From the audience came a wave of almost bestial excitement, spectators in the Colosseum.

The only participant she could not delve into was Vangie.

Past miracles had always produced a kind of subliminal quiver in the very fabric of reality, and Kris felt that familiar subdimensional warping now. But no other miracle had ever produced such a dramatic incident as this one: for the twin girls suddenly fell insensate to the floor as if struck down by lightning, sending a wordless rush of bewilderment, awe, and concern from the audience gusting through the auditorium.

Dr. Troutman was instantly kneeling by his charges, deploying his stethoscope. From offstage, Bernie Vanson, as security head, was frantically dialing a wall-phone, probably summoning an ambulance.

But when Kris looked back to the spectacle before her, she saw there would be no need for an ambulance.

Now the girls were standing, wild-eyed, and they were instinctively straining their dress to its limits, striving to move as far apart as it might allow. And then the dress's snaps gave way, and the girls shucked off the cumbersome, unnatural garment to pool at their feet.

Their immature chests were bare, for no separate camisoles could have been configured for them. But they wore individual skivvies down below, and so modesty was preserved.

Preserved for two completely normal-looking girls unbound by that former natal bridge of skin and blood vessels. Two girls who stood six feet apart for the first time in their existence, before they hurled themselves into each other's arms, weeping.

The crowd went mad, as did everyone onstage and behind the scenes.

Everyone but Vangie.

6

It could not be said of Vardis Salthouse's largish office in the Temple HQ that it was ostentatious, pompous, baroque, elegant, or even luxe. Not for the leader of this church any of the expensive trappings that other TV ministers arrogated to themselves. The room and its furnishings were strictly functional, so banal and austere as even to preclude false modesty: a Steelcase desk suitable for the workstation of a shipping clerk, an assortment of office chairs and side tables, a watercooler, some laminate bookshelves sparsely populated, various lamps, and, finally, a couch so uncomfortable-looking that any thoughts of worktime naps or seductions seemed utterly impossible. As an inner room, the space did not even feature any windows.

The desk's surface held an assortment of office tools (stapler, letter opener, Rolodex) and the only incongruous item: an iMac G3 in pastel blue, a personal computer that resembled some missing plastic divot stolen from a child's toybox.

Kris always felt proud of Vardis's renunciation of—actually, more like an active disinterest in—the status symbols that could have—and, some might have said, should have—accompanied his stature as the founder and head of this growing and influential organization. Aside from his expensive suits—a taste cultivated tactically, only for its abilities to impress those whom he needed to and wished to impress—he remained the same rough-timbered, otherworldly, unassuming man she had fallen in love with several years ago. Basically he hadn't changed, despite a new and broader sphere of action. Except, she often whispered to herself, in one regard: his drive and ambition. Those qualities had intensified by orders of magnitude, to a level that sometimes scared Kris. But so deftly did Vardis Salthouse conceal his desires for greater and greater stores of worldly and eternal powers, even from his wife, that Kris could for the most part convince herself of his unshifting altruism and his elevation of wisdom above all.

But now, pacing agitatedly in his office after Vangie's historic and stunning miracle, the preacher seemed overtaken by a kind of hyperbolic ecstasy. Kris hoped this manic moment was just a manifestation of a natural flood of endorphins, a burst of brain chemicals and hormones. She knew that if Vardis allowed her to intercede, she could bring him down to earth, deliver unto him a more practical reaction to Vangie's latest blessing.

However, the office hosted not just husband and wife—a situation that would have permitted Kris greater intimacy and leeway—but several other people as well.

Senator Calgary seemed almost as beet-faced and high as the preacher. Rather than express his agitation by pacing, though, he had perched his butt on the edge of the desk, while continuing to mutter, over and over, variations on a theme: "If I hadn't seen it myself. But I did see it, I know I did. How could it be? Did I see it? Yes, yes, I know I did!" Every few moments he would go to the watercooler, decant a paper cup's worth, then swallow it in a gulp, as if attempting to quench some inner blaze.

Another attendee at this highly unusual post-service confab

(usually Vardis and Kris relaxed alone together, after any last-minute issues had been dealt with) was Professor Kocchar. A somber but intellectually ruminant expression on his face, the fussy university man kept fiddling with his detector gadget, explaining to no one in particular: "Those readings were off the charts. It was a qualia storm! Unprecedented. I never thought to see such numbers."

The high-pitched emotional and mental fallout of the public spectacle just ended, shared by all four of them—Kris, Kocchar, Calgary, and Salthouse—was not mirrored in the fifth adult in the room. Hefty and solid Bernie Vanson, ex-furniture-moving man and now head of Temple security, showed a stolid face and cool demeanor as he sat behind the desk in Vardis's chair. Occasionally the man tapped out a sequence on the computer keyboard, presumably doing something on the "worldwide web," a domain Kris knew little about.

And of course the final occupant of the room showed even more unruffled aplomb in her semi-catatonic way than hard-nosed Vanson ever could: sterile, frozen, perhaps even removed from the adults' consensus reality.

Still wearing her prisoner-style garb, Vangie had been placed on the couch, sitting upright, by Gavril, who had carried her offstage. Her limbs like jelly, the girl had exhibited a sudden loss of her will or ability to walk under her own power. Kris suspected that the monumental effort of separating the Perkins twins had taken more out of the child than Vangie herself had anticipated. Although no one knew how Vangie's powers worked, one universal rule must still hold: no physical result was obtained without an input of energy. And what tremendous energies Vangie tapped and drained could only be imagined.

After setting Vangie down, Gavril had spoken softly to Kris. "Mama Kris, why do I not bring Vangie home with us as usual?"

Kris touched the teenager reassuringly on the elbow. "I'm not sure, dear. It's your father's wishes that she stay here for a while."

"Well, okay, I guess Papa Salthouse has fine reasons. But I usually try to feed frozen-face sister something nourishing after the service. Helps build her back up."

"I've got a couple of granola bars in my purse. That should be enough until we get home. I can't imagine we'll be very late. I appreciate your love and concern, Gavril. But everything's all right."

Still looking dubious, the boy nodded his reluctant assent. He moved to kiss Vangie on her brow, then departed, saying, "I'll take good care of the others."

Kris had offered the protein bar to Vangie after Gavril's departure, but the wonder child had shown no interest in eating it. Kris managed to get her to swallow a cup of cold spring water, but that had been the extent of her replenishment. Kris tried not to worry, telling herself that the girl had eaten a good supper prior to the show, and was in no obvious distress. She wished that the nice Dr. Troutman were still here, but he had left with the exultant Tippi and Risa. Restrained and demure in front of the audience while still conjoined, those two, freed from their lifetime bondage, had been transformed into joyously chattering, jumping magpies, almost unable to make their way to the car that would take them back to the incredulous staff and residents of the orphanage. Surely tomorrow's newspapers and other media would be bursting with reportage on this miracle. Vardis would need to summon up all his savvy and the aid of all his staffers to respond to the miracle and to fully exploit the event for the greater glory of the Temple. And there would be doubters and naysayers galore, of course, to contend with. Kris could envision that the days ahead would be a madhouse and circus. Had her husband this time truly anticipated all the repercussions of his actions? Had he taken the wisest course? Was it all just to impress Senator Calgary? What exactly could the politician bring to the table that would justify the hullaballoo?

Kris noticed that Professor Kocchar had taken a seat on the couch next to Vangie and was continuing to monitor her with his device. That seemed so harmless that Kris said nothing.

Vardis was the first among them to reassert control of himself. He took a cup of water from the cooler and splashed it on his own face. Then, without warning, he did the same to Senator Calgary!

Spluttering but not indignant, the senator bladed the water off his face with the edge of his palm. A look of calculation and strategy filled his eyes.

"All right, Salthouse, you did what you said you'd do. I never actually believed you could, but you did. Or your little monster baby did, when you asked her. So that means that we can go ahead with our deal."

Kris was bewildered, and not a little peeved, at the term "monster."

"Deal? What deal?"

Vardis came to her and attempted to soothe her doubts with some affectionate husbandly stroking and dulcet tones. "The senator wants us to employ Vangie's talents to aid him in a very noble quest. He now believes that although his goals are larger perhaps than any Vangie has attempted before, they are well within her powers. Seeing what she did tonight convinced him. And if she can fulfill his wishes, then it will also wonderfully benefit the Temple and our whole family. Just listen to his pitch with an open mind, dear. Keep an objective attitude, and I think you'll see that this is the only possible path for us to take, if we're ever to maximize our own futures."

Vardis leaned in closer, to whisper in Kris's ear: "And remember what you promised me just a short while ago, that you'd trust me and consent to something big, once you had heard it through."

Vardis stepped back, and Kris awaited the senator's pitch. She herself was still so over-the-moon at what Vangie had achieved that she felt inclined to go along almost without hearing the details.

Finished composing himself, Calgary, despite his water-spotted finery, fell instinctively into his smoothest and most sincere addressing-the-United-Nations manner.

"Kris, it's like this. I am extremely concerned with America's place and status in the world. Our security and the nation's flourishing. You know that since the fall of the Soviet Union ten or so years ago, we remain the globe's only superpower. Our hegemony—our ability to do what's right and what's best for the whole planet, to promulgate our unique American ideals—remains unchallenged. Or at least it saw no real opposition until this latest incident of terrorism."

"You mean those Middle Easterners who tried to hijack the aircraft?"

"Yes, precisely. The incredible arrogance and temerity and hatred shown by those plotters, backed by the militant theocracy of Saudi Arabia, among other nations, indicates that the US still has many enemies who are intent on bringing our glorious country down. Separately, they stand no chance. But together, even if uncoordinated, they could inflict massive damage on the nation. I want to prevent that from ever happening. I want to ensure the continuing strength and prominence of our country."

"Well, I'm sure that President Bush feels the same way."

Calgary gripped Kris's forearm painfully. "That's where you're wrong, Kris. Oh, his instincts might point him there, but he's surrounded himself with officials who exhibit much less guts and gumption, starting with that airheaded vice president of his, Liz Dole. Keyes, Hatch, Forbes, Nader, and a bunch of others in his Cabinet—they're all counseling him to make nice with the Saudis, to try these terrorists in court as if they were mere criminals. And he's going to do it! Instead of regarding this incident as a declaration of war, he's going to pretend that these insane ragheads were a bunch of pickpockets or litterbugs! My sources have confirmed this for a fact. And when he goes ahead with such a strategy, then America's image goes down the toilet. We will look like a weak sister, and we'll be inviting a world full of predators to start circling for the kill."

Kris tried to fathom all this sudden influx of geopolitical information. "But what do you need us for? Surely you can round up a coalition of other senators who think like you and change Bush's plans . . ."

"Nope, I'm afraid not. He's got everyone bamboozled. And even if I could organize the opposition, it'll all happen too late. Those trials start soon, and then there's no turning back. We need to prosecute these terrorists like the war criminals they are and go after their backers. No, Kris, I've thought this through thoroughly. The only way to save the country from extinction is with the help of your little girl, Vangie.

"I want her to make me president."

"But—but that's impossible!"

Calgary laughed with brutal force. "Impossible! After what she just did on stage tonight? I think not!"

"And what would the Temple gain from this huge change?"

"Once I'm president, the Temple of Human Potential becomes the officially endorsed state religion—or faith, if you prefer—of the United States of America, with all the perks and powers thereof."

"I—no, that's just wrong . . ."

Vardis stepped in. "Kris, you know that I've never sought

to use Vangie's reifying abilities to leapfrog our organization into a position it has not earned. Instead, I encouraged her to perform miracles that helped others, knowing, yes, that the reflected glory would ultimately elevate our reputation in a gradual, well-deserved manner. To employ Vangie to instantly install the Temple over and above all other belief systems with a mere snap of her fingers would result in an unnatural world, out of harmony with the cosmic principles. But if we install the senator as president, and he then anoints us by his legitimate powers of office—calling a Constitutional Convention or declaring a national state of emergency or some such executive action, to establish our primacy, first among equals—then we've achieved our goal in accordance with the laws of the nation and of the universe. Not to mention of course that President Calgary's tough-minded policies will have preserved the country from utter ruin and extinction. Can't you see that it's the only logical and wise course for us to follow?"

Having little faith or interest in any politician, Kris wondered if Vardis weren't right. What difference could it make who sat in the Oval Office? And if Vardis finally reached the top rung on the ladder of his own ambition, maybe he could relax, lighten up, and they could all just be a family together. And then again, there was her former vow to go ahead amiably with his plans . . .

"All right, I give my consent."

"Wonderful! We knew that, as Vangie's mom, you had to be fully on board with this. I believe she has a unique bond with you that we could not contravene, even if she can't express it. After all, you were the first to discover her and her abilities. Thank you, dear. You won't regret it."

"But I also reserve the right to have her change everything back if it looks like this was a dumb decision."

"Of course, of course, that's just a smart failsafe measure. I wouldn't have it any other way."

"When would we attempt this?"

"Why not right now, this very minute?" Calgary urged.

"Don't we need time to consider—?"

The senator's tone changed from wheedling to demanding. "All the deep and thoughtful consideration has already happened. There's no time to lose."

"Okay, I guess . . ."

Vardis, Kris, and Calgary now stepped to the couch, while Bernie Vanson remained behind the desk. Professor Kocchar, having paid little attention to their talk, looked up with mild puzzlement about their intentions.

"Professor Kocchar," said Salthouse, "your meter registered the psychic efforts of our daughter when she separated the twins?"

"Yes, indubitably. All quite accurate and, I am happy to say, in line with my theories. But I realize now I must install some kind of recording mechanism in my electrophotonic gauge, to archive the telemetry."

Vardis brushed off the professor's future plans with a wave of his hand. "Very good. That's why I wanted you here now. Please continue to employ your device and let us know if Vangie is exerting herself in a similar fashion as we attempt to get her to use her powers again."

"I suppose there's no reason for me to object to a simple scientific measurement . . ."

"Fine, fine. Kris, why don't you sit and hold Vangie? That should bolster her comfort levels."

Kris did as she was asked, taking the small supple and unresisting child into her embrace. The girl smelled as she always did, of baby powder and jarred mushy fruit and veggies.

Vardis kneeled before the mother and child, a quiveringly
alert Calgary standing close beside.

"Vangie, my little girl, hub of all sanctified atmanic power.
Listen closely to me. I want you to make this man standing by
my side, Senator Brad Calgary, into the duly elected president
of the United States!"

1

It had been a Friday night like any other, a night where she would be taken from her reveries at home, her fascinating incessant surfing among alternities, and forced to perform for a crowd. Vangie never resented such small demands since they formed a tiny part of her observerly student existence. If this was the price she had to pay for the protection of a stable home life, it was not outrageously high. And oftentimes the requests that her "father" made of her were interesting tactical and scholarly problems in their own right. Interpreting the full parameters of the request. Surveying all her jump options and destinations. Correlating all the linked participants that would have to be entrained in the jump. Scanning the various possible futures subsequent to her nascent interference for harmful outcomes— these activities all helped to perfect her skills. Life was good. Tonight would be no different.

When the conjoined twins had first been paraded onstage, they also marched across a million ghostly alternative timestreams, and Vangie regarded these spectral duplicates with mild curiosity. The various entities that swam, second by second,

into and out of her ken, all those individuals whose lifestreams
intersected hers, held some interest for the girl, since they represented tokens on her gameboard. The constant figures in her
life—her sibs, Kris, Vardis—had even come to occupy mildly
affectionate niches in her museum of other entities.

So almost effortlessly, Vangie sized up the Perkins girls,
noting that for an almost infinite number of adjacent timelines,
radiating out in all vectors, they remained a conjoined pair.

When she had been asked to separate them, she knew
she would have to cast her senses far abroad, across a
wider-than-average span of the multiverse, in order to find
a viable ghost universe where such a miracle could naturally
obtain, without altering any other parameters in great degree.

Although to the tensely expectant outsiders that night the
searching seemed to take only an eyeblink, to Vangie's hyperextended
consciousness the quest took an incredibly long time, wearying in
its magnitude. Finding a universe where unconjoined Perkins girls
had a rationale to be present on the Temple stage took extensive
reconnoitering. Then, dealing with the twins' ancillary coterie—
all the many, many people who knew of them as conjoined—as
well as sweeping up everyone present in the Temple—that all required immense draining effort. Finally, making the actual snap
to the new continuum, bearing her load of other souls, was a vast
and purgative expenditure of strength. The feat left Vangie voided
for the first time of all her physical and mental energies.

She felt extremely grateful when Gavril sensed this and carried her off.

Sitting on the couch in Vardis's office, striving to recoup
her losses, to regain her strength, she could only accept a drink
of water before retreating into her inner sanctum.

And now, what was this? Her mother had picked her up, her
father was ordering her to perform again. So soon? Too soon!

Nonetheless, Vangie, willing and obedient, not wishing to destabilize any of the roles and relationships that provided her with peace and safety, moved to obey. Too proud of her talents to admit defeat or beg for leniency, she would accept the challenge. She parsed the request—make this man president—and began the requisite correlations.

Finding the suitable timestream where President Calgary ruled was fairly easy. Many of the probabilities already existent in a stochastic cloud about him conduced toward such an endpoint—although not necessarily at the short timescale desired. That required some finessing. But ultimately the desired continuum was pegged.

However, when Vangie exercised her painfully learned diligence (the Peavy tragedy was always looming in her mind as a warning) and examined the myriad futures radiating outward from Calgary's installation in the White House, she was brought up short.

The thick bundle of adjacent future-forward timelines all showed the most ghastly results of this intervention—most of them, in fact, included all-out nuclear war. Calgary's treatment of the terrorists, using them as a stick against Saudi Arabia and other countries, eventually brought in the Russians, Chinese, Israelis . . .

The ICBM missiles with their poison payloads started flying in every feasible alternative, and soon the entire planet was a radioactive hell. Cities in ruins, citizens crisped, civilization shattered.

Vangie certainly had no desire or willingness to deposit herself and her family into such a timestream. But searching out some far-distant continuum where President Calgary could still rule and yet things went better was beyond her stressed abilities at the moment. Her focus and attention were drifting.

And while a certain saturation of ghostly visions over the

years had left her relatively unperturbed by disasters and trag-
edies (yes, some particular timeline might see the death of a
certain cute little puppy, but he also survived quite well in a
million other planes, so where was the actual harm?), Vangie
still possessed a certain sense of artistic elegance and economy
and balance. No outcome where Calgary became president was
more esthetically or righteously appealing than this timeline,
where he stayed just as he was.

And so for the first time, Vangie refused silently to carry
out her instructions. She did nothing, and simply resumed her
recuperative somnolence.

The tension in Salthouse's office was stretched thick and painful as the ligaments that had yoked the Perkins twins, as all
the adults waited for the instant displacement and transmog-
rification that would accompany Vangie's fulfillment of the
command. How would it manifest? Perhaps a Secret Service
agent would knock on the office door and, entering, say, "President Calgary, Marine One is waiting to fly you back to DC now
to deal with the Saudi ambassador." Or would the alteration
be even more magically disruptive, with all of them suddenly
blinking and finding themselves in the Lincoln Bedroom? How
would Vangie handle the transition?

But after a few minutes of expectancy, it began to dawn on
the party that nothing had changed at all.

Vardis addressed the professor. "Kocchar, what did your
gadget show?"

"Some small fluctuations similar to those that I detected
onstage just before the huge output. I would speculate that
they indicate preparatory groundwork before launching the big
change. But that latter superstorm of qualia never happened."

Kris spoke up. "Vardis, she's obviously tired now. She's just not up to doing this. She needs her rest. Let's try again tomorrow, or the next day even. Surely such a small delay can't matter."

Calgary said, "That's an obvious false reading of what just happened, Kris. The doctor here showed that she made some initial efforts, then abandoned the attempt. Why?"

Beginning to sweat, Vardis said, "Some time ago, we had one miracle that didn't come off so well. Bad repercussions. But ever since then, never a glitch. So we suspected that Vangie was vetting our requests. Refusing to honor any that led down bad avenues. That was our explanation for the occasional dud event."

"Are you saying that my presidency would be one such 'bad avenue'? Does that mean that elevating the Temple to new heights is a bad thing too? You can't believe that, Salthouse, not about me or yourself. You know that our requests are absolutely righteous and essential. Put it to her again."

Before Kris could object further, Vardis laid hands on Vangie—a useless but resonant gesture—and repeated his demands.

"Mighty Reifier, make this man standing by my side, Senator Brad Calgary, into the duly elected president of the United States!"

Again, nothing changed.

Kocchar spoke up. "This time there was not even any lower-level preliminary activity."

Stocky and imposing Bernie Vanson had left his seat and come to join the tableau. Now Kris noticed that from Vanson's belt depended some kind of collar threaded onto a small box. He also had something concealed in one hand.

Vardis said nothing, but merely nodded with some slight reluctance to the security chief.

Before Kris could shield Vangie, Vanson acted.

He forced open Vangie's mouth and with a glass and rubber-bulb eyedropper squeezed a jet of liquid down the back of her throat. He held her jaw shut until she chokingly swallowed whatever the dose was. Then he quickly clamped with a decisive click the collar around her neck.

Kris whipped Vangie away from the man, but her move was much too late. She looked in deep angry consternation to Vardis and saw that he held some sort of rudimentary control box.

"Vardis! What are you doing!"

"It's harmless, dear, really. We've just administered a small dose of quick-acting scopolamine to make her pliant and less willful—more amenable to suggestions. It will wear off in a few hours, leaving her just fine."

Kris inserted a finger under the collar, but it was locked in place. "And what's this?"

"Only a shock device, such as certain institutions use on mentally ill patients. Our daughter really is mentally abnormal, you realize, despite her talents, and we probably should have resorted to this tactic long ago, rather than rely on her capricious goodwill."

Kris imagined she had gone crazy herself. None of this could be happening! Could it?

Professor Kocchar had gotten to his feet. "I really must protest. This is highly unethical, especially when performed on a juvenile, and certainly not the proper way to conduct any kind of experiment. That drug will skew the qualia formation. Any results will be chaotic—"

Bernie Vanson planted a paw on the professor's chest and shoved him back down onto the couch. Vanson's voice brooked no resistance: "Your objections have been registered, Doc. When President Calgary conducts any hearings, you'll be in the clear. Now just get that meter of yours ready so we can see what happens next."

Distorted by his emotions, the senator's handsome face wore a look of avarice and a partially sated appetite for dominance. "I warned you, Salthouse, that it would come to this. We should have just taken this course from the start. Get busy now, while the drug is at its peak."

Vardis turned his gaze from Calgary back to Kris, and she saw nothing familiar in his eyes, no trace of the man she thought she knew, no husband, no leader, no visionary. Just a man bent on getting what he wanted at all costs.

"I'd put Vangie down on the couch now and stand up, Kris. Otherwise you might get some of the leakage from the collar. It's not a pleasant jolt, I've sampled it. Plus, she's bound to spasm a little."

Reluctantly, Kris complied.

Vardis pressed a button on his remote and turned a dial.

Vangie was far away from the office and from her current baseline reality when the assault came. She was actually conducting one of her intermittent perennial searches for the Council of Ghosts, the nine avatars of herself that had once surfaced to advise and counsel her. She felt somehow that their wisdom could be useful at this moment.

The wrenching at her jaw, the harsh infusion of liquid down her throat, all at first seemed like a bad dream. But strange and unpleasant and unexpected as it was, the sensations did not appear to constitute any large immediate threat, any lethal harsh condition—like a tornado hurling one through the skies—from which she would have to instantly retreat across the multiverse in order to save her life. Such jumps into the unknown were not to be taken lightly or in haste or without planning and forethought, if they could be avoided.

Even the securing of the collar around her throat did not radically alarm her. She was used to being fed and handled, dressed and bathed, almost without her intervention.

And by the time she realized the enormity of her plight, it was too late.

All the focus and sensitivity of perceptions that she had cultivated for six years evaporated in a flash. Thanks to the drug, her mind was an undisciplined whirlpool. Suddenly she was back to those earliest years of infantile semiconsciousness, where the ghosts were invaders, an out-of-control assault force smashing into her awareness from every angle, leering, taunting, showing unrecognizable things to her. Every defense and leash she had installed, every fortification and subjugation she had established fell to pieces, and she was helpless against the onslaught of spooks.

Now she realized she *had* to jump, flee to any halfway decent timeline that might swim into view. Any alternity that did not feature these physical tormentors, the people she had formerly trusted and relied on. She flailed about internally, her mind like a fish flopping on dry land. Was that an exit? Maybe. She reached out—

And then came the first horrible electrical shock, disrupting her escape.

Vangie did what she had never done before.

She screamed.

When her daughter screamed, Kris yelled, "No!" She shot to her feet, clutching the girl. She took a step toward the office door.

Calgary snatched Vangie out of her grip, while Vanson pinioned Kris brutally by the wrists and forced her back on the couch, coming to loom over her.

Clutching the girl around her midriff, Calgary shook Vangie two-handed like a sack of flour. "Salthouse, get this little monster to obey!"

Vardis gave the dial another twitch upward, eliciting another wail from the girl. "Vangie! Listen to me! Just do what we ask, and you'll be free! Make Calgary president! Now!"

Kris had a sudden revelation. Vangie could never go free after this, because when she was in command of herself again, she would instantly undo everything, or perhaps even take a swift and potent revenge. Maybe she would be maintained alive, on a constant drip of drugs. Or maybe this would have to be her last miracle, with death to follow.

Vardis dialed down the electricity, and Vangie subsided into pained grunts.

Calgary yelled, "You're not being hard enough! Take this brat and give me the box. I'll do it."

The men swapped, and Calgary spun the dial to near maximum. "Make me the president, goddamn you! Do it!"

Vangie now only spasmed silently. Kris began to weep.

Staid, forgotten, harmless, Professor Kocchar was suddenly part of the dynamic. No one had been watching him. He came armed with a letter opener taken from the desk. He feinted at Calgary, at Vardis.

But then, he made his true move, driving the point of the opener into the plastic case holding the shock mechanism. The impact drove the box forcefully against Vangie's throat, but also succeeded in shorting out the electronics.

Freed from the painful current, Vangie ceased her vocalizing. Everyone else remained silent too. Time seemed to stretch like taffy.

Kris felt that wavery wavefront of a Vangie-born miracle approaching, ripples across reality.

And then the wave was upon them.

PART THREE

PART THREE

I

Retirement agreed with Professor Vivek Kocchar. Not that he hadn't enjoyed his several decades of teaching—inspiring young minds, doing his own research into the quantum nature of consciousness (he was a firm adherent of the Penrose-Hameroff school). But as with all passions, his blisses had naturally cooled over the years, rendering his daily duties and disciplines often more drudgery than delight. And then there was the matter of his health, as he entered his seventy-fifth year. His prostate cancer was not the most aggressive in nature, but surgery and treatments had sapped his baseline energy level. His doctors assured him that he had a good number of years left, but Kocchar was realist enough (a man could not always keep his head in the lofty realms of theoretical neurochemistry) that he knew there were no guarantees.

All in all, Kocchar was glad to have stepped down from his faculty position when he had. He knew he must conserve his energies. Retirement left him mostly content, as he puttered around the house, keeping up his garden and even working occasionally on what would no doubt be his final paper for the

Journal of Consciousness Studies: "An Inquiry Into Microtubule Timebinding and Dislocative Transposition." About the only thing that worried him these days was the fate of his daughter when he eventually died. She was a very special person, and not at all capable of being on her own in this harsh world.

Kocchar's wife, Adya, deceased herself for some three years now from congestive heart failure, had extracted from her husband—without much arm-twisting, to be sure—his fervent promise that he would place the welfare of their child above all else.

Kocchar patted his wife's hand and tried not to notice her stertorous breathing. "Yes, yes, of course, *chellam*, you need give no worry to that. I shall see that no harm comes to her, and that she flourishes to the best of her abilities."

Adya gripped her husband's wrist. "I always knew you would, *jaanu*, but I just needed to hear you say so."

The memory brought a rivulet of tears to Kocchar's cheeks. Despite attaining their fiftieth wedding anniversary before Adya's sad passing, he could still wish for additional years together, could he not?

The Kocchars had had a son by birth, Havnesh Kocchar. But they had lost him at age twenty-four. All three Kocchars possessed dual citizenship with the USA and India, and Havnesh, motivated by a youthful burst of idealism and patriotism, had enlisted in the Indian Army during those turbulent years when the collapse of the People's Republic of Formosa had brought much chaos to the border regions of India. During the campaign to liberate Tibet, Havnesh had fallen to a sniper's bullet.

Upon Havnesh's cruel death, Vivek and Adya, already in their fifties, had been unable to bring into this world a new child of their own, and they had resigned themselves to an empty nest. Then, some ten years ago, when they were both in their sixties, had come an unlikely chance to adopt, long after they had firmly abandoned the idea. The child was a girl of six, and a problem case. Apparently somewhere on the autism spectrum, nonverbal and generally unresponsive, the girl had seemed doomed to an institutionalized life. Vivek had been introduced to her plight by a colleague at the university, a woman from the school of social work named Kris Troy.

It took only a few visits to the orphanage for the Kocchars to come enthusiastically around to becoming parents again. They needed this child, and she needed them.

And so little Evangeline had come home.

The seven years when the three of them had constituted a family had been wonderful. No longer out in the workplace by this time, Adya had devoted herself to Vangie. Her endless patience and creativity and love—along with some skilled professional help—had brought the girl much further along the path to a "normal" existence—a benefit that orphanage life surely would not have conferred. Showing herself capable of emotional bonding and some speech, as well as sporadic interest in a few simple pastimes and crafts, Vangie had come out of her shell and won over all those she encountered outside the family setting.

Admittedly, the past three years as a single parent had been harder on Vivek, contributing to his desire for retirement. But a reduced teaching schedule, along with the help of a very fine specialized school (not inexpensive) had allowed both him and Vangie to maintain their equilibrium in the wake of Adya's passing. For some six months, Vangie had been disconsolate. But one day she seemed to cast aside her grief, without discarding memories of her mother, whom she still invoked regularly with the phrase, "Amma gone, Vangie cry."

And so Vivek Kocchar continued to honor his promise to Adya, making sure that Vangie received all his love and all the professional care he could afford. As for her life beyond her father's death, Vivek had secured a fervently binding promise from a young nephew back in India that Vangie could live there with family. The transition would be hard on the uncomprehending girl, and not ideal, but it was the best that Vivek could arrange.

Everything, then, seemed to promise that life would proceed without storm or turbulence, at least until Vivek himself had to meet his Maker.

So indeed it did go, until the morning that Vangie's school called to alert Vivek Kocchar that his daughter was having some kind of unrestrainable fit—and speaking in voluminous full sentences that made no sense at all.

The staff at the Applied Behavior Academy were of a type all too familiar to Vangie: solicitous yet domineering do-gooders. As they reacted with consternation and constraints to her excited exclamations of relief at having escaped her previous timeline, she realized she must tone down her instinctive outbursts and assume the mindset of her new host. But it was hard at first to shuck the horrors that had precipitated this jump. Her mind replayed it all . . .

The pain in her throat, the chemicals in her brain, the disorientation in her mind, the swarming of ghosts. Vangie fastened onto her one steady foothold, an unexpected savior, the man who had broken the leash around her neck. With an almost kinesthetic cellular memory of how to select an alternative, she raced through myriad alternate lives, and selected one.

With this intelligent man, perhaps, for the first time she could be somewhat more free and open, could be understood—

Could express herself in carefully observed and mentally re-hearsed but never uttered words, not just magical deeds.

All now shunted to a dead stub. But it still felt so real . . .

The head of the Applied Behavior Academy was a sincere and ingratiating fellow in his forties named Brian Knickle, always sharply dressed and affable. Vivek had generally found him a warm and efficient figure in his daughter's life, full of wisdom and empathy. But today, sitting in Knickle's office, with its deliberately soothing decorations, Vivek just wanted to strangle the man because he was keeping Vivek apart from his daughter in distress.

"Just be patient a moment longer, please, Mr. Kocchar. We feel that bringing your daughter into your presence before we have a chance to apply some standard de-escalation techniques would prove problematical and counterproductive. That's our expert opinion, and you have indeed hired us for our expertise, right?"

Kocchar finally had to calm down and admit that perhaps Knickle was doing the correct and professional thing. Nevertheless, the interval of waiting until two teachers finally escorted Vangie between them into the office seemed an eternity.

Kocchar took in his daughter's appearance and attitude with a father's perceptive eye, cultivated from ten years of familial care and affection.

At age sixteen, Vangie exhibited an average height. But in most other respects she deviated far from a normal adolescent. She was noticeably overweight, and all the official playtime and physical therapy the school could provide had not firmed up her physique into any kind of well-toned muscularity. Her unfashionable and blunt pixie-cut hair showed the lackluster shade of dry grass, and nearly as coarse. Her facial features seemed stamped into waxy ivory Play-Doh with an imperfectly carved template. Normally her gaze was always half-abstracted, turned inward, and only reluctantly confronting her exterior environment when cajoled or prompted by necessity. But at this moment her eyes kept darting intelligently around the room, as if to measure every contingency, to catalog every escape route and opportunity for self-preservation.

When Vangie saw Kocchar, she attempted to lurch toward him. But the woman and the man shepherding her restrained her with minimal force, and she reluctantly complied. But she could not resist calling out.

"Professor, you saved my life!"

This hyperbolic assertion, uttered in a fully formed and mature fashion totally unheard-of from the girl, set Kocchar aback more than all the prior news of her unwonted rebellion and distress.

Knickle lifted an eyebrow in a manner that signaled, *You see? What did I tell you?* "She's been fixated on something imaginary which you apparently did on her behalf, Mr. Kocchar. Stopping some assault or violation. It's all she could talk about. She tried to escape the building, to find you. We have no idea what instilled this misbehavior, or what she can be referring to—and all while displaying such an atypical instance of high-functioning verbal proficiency. Has she manifested any such changes in her speech abilities at home this week?"

Kocchar was as baffled as the director. "No, not at all. You know her vocabulary is just a few hundred words. And she always calls me 'Baba.' Never 'Professor'! Why suddenly this mental upgrade? Is it some experimental new therapy you've been employing, perhaps, without my consent?"

Knickle showed a horrified face, plainly anticipating lawsuits and scandal. "No, not at all! Vangie has been receiving only the mandated treatment you and your wife approved from the start."

The object of the discussion had visibly been following the conversation, and suddenly her whole manner changed, as if she had donned a disguise or reverted to some discarded and outmoded shell or carapace or cocoon. She spoke with familiar slurred intonations.

"Baba take Vangie home now? Vangie tired. Vangie sad. Go home with Baba please?"

Upon hearing these accustomed pleas, delivered in their accustomed way, the two teacher-guards smiled and relaxed. Director Knickle also brightened.

"Vangie, your father will be happy to take you home now. Why don't you return to the classroom and get your sweater and backpack first?"

Vangie nodded enthusiastically, with a simpering dullard's grin, and her custodians left the office with her.

"Mr. Kocchar, this incident, while very strange, is not totally unprecedented in the annals of the condition your daughter shares with many others suffering from her same abnormalities. Children classified with her behaviors and intelligence have been known to experience quantum leaps in their abilities—sometimes permanent, sometimes temporary. The delusory aspects of her behavior are more troubling, but even those can be explained and dealt with. I would suggest this course of action. Bring her home to her comfort zone and safe space. Monitor her behavior over the next several hours until bedtime. Of course, if she displays any dangerous or distressing behaviors during that time—although I doubt she will—immediately call nine-one-one first, and then the Academy. If in the morning she is doing fine, please bring her back to the Academy as usual. I will have our staff physicians and therapists on hand to administer a few essential but rudimentary tests. If they deem it necessary, we will bring her into the lab with our affiliated experts for a larger battery of diagnostics, including a complete physical workup, just to rule out things like infections, brain trauma, et cetera. Does this sound like a safe and valid and logical course of action to you?"

Kocchar considered. Although Vangie's behavior and speech had been anomalously disconcerting, nothing about her seemed unsafe or critical. He was certain that she was still the little girl he and Adya had adopted a decade ago.

"Yes, I consent to this approach."

"I'm very glad to hear that. I will mention now that our conversation has been recorded—just to provide accountability on the part of all parties. Well, Mr. Kocchar, I'll see you in the morning, and I'm sure that Vangie will be just fine."

Vivek waited outside, as he always did when picking up his little girl in the late afternoon. The early position of the sun was the only indication that the day was unlike all the others.

Vangie emerged. She smiled at the lone teacher, the woman, who had escorted her out.

"Bye-bye," she said, with a clumsy wave.

Kocchar strapped his daughter into the shotgun seat of his old 2015 Rambler Typhoon, stretching the belt across her belly. He must do something about her weight. But food was such a pleasure and solace . . .

The drive from the Academy to the Kocchar house—a lovely old Victorian on the edge of the university campus, in a leafy and friendly neighborhood—took a half hour. Kocchar did not attempt to make conversation about her day, as he usually did, feeling that a quiet ride would be best, and Vangie did not choose to speak until they pulled into their driveway.

"Professor Kocchar, I have so much to tell you. But first, you must promise never to send me back to that place. We need all our time together to help me become myself."

2

Since the anomalous incident at the ABA facilities, two years of homeschooling had ostensibly resulted in a few increased proficiencies in the resume of Vangie Kocchar, age eighteen, carefully forged results suitable for public consumption.

The relevant and sincerely concerned educational and child welfare authorities were quite pleased to perceive that the young woman could now do some simple math, read a kindergarten primer, and cook such easy items as toast, a soft-boiled egg, and hot dogs and beans. Mac and cheese from the box was a landmark accomplishment. And Vangie even held a job. For four hours one day a week, every Saturday, she filled orders at a boutique cookie shop, the Happy Harbor, that specialized in hiring the handicapped. Of course, she was not able to actually operate the cash register, but all the customers loved her cheerful manner and foolish small talk.

And now that the girl had turned eighteen, she was positioned nicely to handle—one day soon, when circumstances demanded—as much semi-independent living as she could, whether with her distant non-blood relatives in India, as arranged by her father, or more locally, in some group home.

Vivek Kocchar, doting father, also regarded Vangie's accomplishments as satisfactory. Her convincing, albeit tedious, subterfuge of dim-wittedness had allowed both of them all the freedom and time they needed to catalog, explore, scientifically rationalize, and refine her extraordinary powers of skipping across the multiverse. These past two years had been the flowering and culmination of all of Vivek's professional aspirations. Being able to firmly document the connection between at least one exceptional human brain and the workings of the cosmos—to map the interface between soul and substance, mind and timespace machinery—had been thrilling, and gave him hope that their findings could one day be extended to the neurological underpinnings of all humanity, even those who showed no ability to escape their natal timeline. If only he had been able to publish his findings, perhaps the field would already be far advanced. But of course, all the work that Vivek and Vangie did together had to remain secret, at least for the present, for very good reasons.

And that present moment-to-moment-to-moment life was all Vivek Kocchar really had. For his prostate cancer, once deemed subdued and nearly tamped out, had roared back into a conflagration, and the best that his superlative medical establishment could offer was nothing but palliative care. Not in much pain yet, or experiencing much diminishment of his physical and mental faculties, Kocchar enjoyed the daily attentions from regularly scheduled visiting hospice personnel. They were all so caring and competent. And of course he relished the ministrations and tenderness of his loving daughter, a girl who embodied both the child whom he and Adya had raised for ten years, and also a perfect stranger, cognate with his Vangie but so different. They both inhabited the same body, in a fusion of minds.

My God, if only he could have another lifetime to study

these phenomena! Surely that path would have led him to a Nobel Prize and revolutionized several branches of science.

But such was not to be.

Oh, he had been offered the chance to continue his work beyond his allotted fate. But he had felt compelled to turn it down.

Enough on that subject, he thought, until the day came when such a decision would be irrevocable.

That first night of the arrival of the hybrid Vangie, neither child nor adult had slept a wink. There had been too much to tell, too many seemingly impossible realities to recount.

Inside his house that fateful evening, everything seemed strange to Vivek Kocchar, from the vintage poster depicting Sophia Loren in *The Seven Year Itch* (Adya had been the cinema fan) to the pile on the coffee table of unread issues of *Jack Kennedy's Mystery Monthly*. (Kocchar loved a good mystery tale whenever he needed to take his mind off work, but of late had let his reading lapse.) He wondered if his life would ever regain its wonted feel and dimensions.

Vangie had begun the evening, once her shocked father had followed her inside and they had settled down on the couch with cold soda and newly delivered pizza, by saying, "Professor Kocchar, father, Baba—I am your daughter, but I am not. There are two of us now in this brain. Actually, more than two, given all those I carried within me already, upon my entry into your daughter. But not to worry—shortly there will be just one again, compounded and integrated. I, me, the visitor—I have come as a disembodied consciousness from a different timeline, a continuum you have no access to."

For one wild moment, Kocchar recalled the superstitious tales of his youth about the *bhuta*, ghosts who could possess people. Had that happened to his daughter, invasion from the spirit world? But then all his scientific beliefs and training reasserted themselves. Literally shaking the notion out of his head, he regarded the girl severely. "Child, if some bad prenatal wiring in your brain has spontaneously repaired itself and you now choose to mock me and my fascination with the mind—!"

Vangie looked alarmed. "No, no, this is all the truth, I swear!"

And then she proceeded to share with Kocchar, the only other being ever so trusted, the story of her life, from her earliest memories to the present eruption into his existence.

Kocchar listened to this miraculous biography with near-gapemouthed astonishment. Their pizza grew cold and their drinks grew warm. At points he interpolated a few questions and restatements of what he thought he understood, just for clarification. But mainly he just listened to his new-old daughter talk.

Her speech was both mature and juvenile. She handled large concepts deftly, and then muffed simple quotidian conventions and idioms. She mispronounced certain words as if she had never actually heard them spoken before. She did not know how to maintain eye contact with her interlocutor, as if she had never had a reason or chance to do so until now. She talked faster than the conversational norm. She let awkward pauses build while she inwardly meditated over things. But despite all these unconventionalities, she managed to deliver a quite vivid picture of her life.

And then, as dawn percolated through the windows, she came, by her reckoning, to the events of the year 2001, which had just occurred in the past few hours.

"So just a few minutes before they called you from the school, I was being tortured by my father, Vardis Salthouse."

"One moment, please. That year, 2001, was some twenty-five years ago. You are not even that old. How can this be?"

"It's all down to the differential between our two streams.

There's a higher order hyper-time or super-time in which all the strands of the multiverse are embedded. At least that's the way I've come to think of it. So the big bang for your universe occurred twenty-five hyper-time years before the big bang for my universe of origination, and so you're that much advanced from me."

Hearing this theoretical jargon from the mouth of his nearly nonverbal daughter, as if she were a speaker at one of his professional seminars, caused Kocchar's head to swim. The whole world seemed unreal. Kocchar tried to integrate the concepts, and finally gave them a tentative pass. "You have obviously spent a lot of time considering these matters."

Vangie laughed, replicating precisely the well-known snort that old Vangie always produced on such occasions. "Professor, it's really all I've done with my whole life!"

"Please continue then."

"As I described, I had been betrayed by those closest to me, leaving me staggered and confused. Then I was drugged and made helpless, put under the lash of a pain collar, unable to employ my powers to save myself or defeat my antagonists—the very people I had come to love and trust. What a shocking horror and lesson that was! There's no telling what would have happened to me if they had continued with their torture. But then you heroically intervened."

"You say I was present during this encounter, armed with some kind of detector—and wearing a mustache?" Kocchar fingered his bare upper lip, which had never been graced with any such fuzz.

"Yes, you had come to take scientific readings on me, having heard about my performances. I hardly paid any attention to you at first. But then, at the crucial moment, you saved my life! You drove some sharp object into the pain-making mechanism and shorted it out. So even though I was still disoriented from the drugs, I was able to focus well enough to make the jump that eventually brought me here."

"You did not jump here directly?"

"No, I had other plans besides my personal escape. I wanted to punish those who had hurt me. So I first brought my mother and my father and Senator Calgary, and even their hireling, Bernie Vanson, along with me to the very world they had desired."

"You left me behind, though?"

"Yes, I felt that you'd be safe, once I removed the bad actors from that continuum."

Kocchar pondered a subtle theoretical point contingent on this removal of a unique consciousness from its original continuum, a factor his own studies had tentatively postulated. But he refrained from raising the issue right away, eager to hear the finale of Vangie's long tale.

"Go on. You made the decision to give your attackers what they wanted, to get them to stop their abuse. And somehow to punish them as well?"

"Yes, because their destination was not exactly what they wanted or expected. My concentration and thinking were too scattered by the drugs and torture to pick out a fresh timestream that might make a fitting punishment for them. But that night, under their orders in the back office, I had been cataloging and studying the various timestreams where Calgary was president. So I transported all of us to one of those preselected future-shifted continuums, just as the atomic bombs began to drop out of the stratosphere, aimed at Washington, summoned by President Calgary's long incompetent administration. Calgary and my mother and father and Vanson experienced extreme mental disorientation from the jump, and at first that inhibited the actions of their host bodies. But once they realized what was happening, as their new local memories started to flood in and aides clamored around them, they made a rush for the presidential bunker, but I don't think they got there in time."

"And you were resident in that doomed continuum as well, having journeyed with them as their guide and engine of travel."

"Yes. The Vangie avatar I landed in, kept always by their side for immediate use, was more or less brain-dead. Years of abuse had rendered her into an automaton. But her powers remained intact, and when I infused her, I had access to them. I only needed a few moments. Free of the drug and the pain, I cast about for a new destination for myself. Maybe I was still thinking a little woozily, but I fastened on the image of you— how you had saved me, at no small risk to yourself. And so when my questing vision settled on a timeline where you were my father, I jumped right here. I hope my choice was the right one?"

Vangie looked imploringly at Kocchar, and he could only answer, "Yes, my dear, this is your home. You chose correctly."

She brightened at this acceptance and confirmation. But she could sense that Kocchar still puzzled a bit over the newly displayed verbal aptitude of his "little girl."

"You realize, Baba"—she deliberately employed the term of affection to further endear herself—"that although I was preverbal in all my other existences, I had plentifully conversed with my avatars and also 'read over their shoulders,' so to speak, as they perfected their own language skills. So coherent speech was always innate in my being."

Kocchar nodded with understanding. "A skill you practiced in secret, but never used."

"Exactly. And it manifested once I arrived in the body of your Vangie, when all my physiological parameters were reset to normal, and I encountered the simplistic mind of your Vangie, and began to integrate her into my dominant being. I thought I had it all together, but I guess I was really still unsettled by everything that had happened so quickly. So instead of acting 'normal,' I began babbling to my teachers. I wasn't even used to talking, you know. I never did it till now! And that account brings us right to us sitting in our home this minute!"

Kocchar had to get to his feet at the climax of this tale. One leg was prickling with pins and needles, and he felt a dull pain in his lower back—a pain that would become much too familiar over the next two years as his cancer worsened. He walked off the awkward sensations, back and forth across the parlor.

Vangie did not press her father for any conclusion or judgment or reaction to her long tale. Instead, she just said, "I have to use the bathroom, Baba," and left the room, walking with her typical and familiar misarticulated gait.

Kocchar's mind was spinning, as he tried to assimilate everything he had been told. But in a moment, just as he expected his tired brain to explode or shut down, the opposite happened. All these new concepts settled down or jelled into a coherent matrix, and he experienced a kind of intellectual and emotional acceptance of this new revelation about the structure and workings of the multiverse. It had a kind of elegance and authenticity in his eyes.

Over the next two years, especially with further proof of Vangie's powers, this initial acceptance, intuitive and unsupported at first, would only grow more solid.

But one thing still puzzled him—an aspect of her story that even the girl herself seemed not to question or acknowledge. And, being the dogged scientist that he was, unable to let a thread of investigation go unfollowed, when Vangie returned to the room that very first fraught evening-gone-sunrise, Kocchar brought up the thing that baffled him, not wanting even to wait until they had had a good sleep.

"Vangie—have you ever gone backwards in your transitions?"

Seated once more, toying with her drink, as if the simple act of using a straw in a soda can was miraculous, Vangie replied, "What do you mean?"

"Have you ever tried to return to the exact identical time-stream you once inhabited? Not a parallel continuum, however closely related, but the precise point of your origin. I assume you could distinguish among such alternatives, pinning down a timestream uniquely out of untold trillions?"

Vangie's puffy dull mask of a face showed a distinct anxiety and unease. "Yes, I certainly could. All the continuums present a unique aspect to my vision, even before I examine them closely. I can't put the distinctions into words, but each strand out of infinity has a distinct signature. But why would I want to go backwards?"

"Let's forget about the why for a moment. Could you just try something for me? Try to sense such a past stream. Try for the timeline where I saved you. That's recent and close, in some meta-physical sense. Can you bring that strand into your perceptions?"

"I'll give it a go . . ."

Vangie's attention went away from her environment, roaming among multiversal ghosts.

Kocchar went to the kitchen and drank several glasses of cold tap water. He wetted a cloth and laid it across his brow for a few minutes. Ah, that helped a little . . .

When he returned, Vangie was still wandering.

An hour later, she resurfaced from the deep ocean of space-time and hyper-time. Her voice was trembly.

"I can't find that timeline, Baba! I can't find any of the universes I once inhabited. They don't exist anymore!"

"That confirms something I suspected, based on my own theories. I believe that if you devoted any thought at all to the subject, you imagined that when you jumped, you left behind an empty mindless shell of a Vangie, a vacant soulless doll that collapsed, and the same for any riders you took with you. After all, you weren't cloning a copy of your unique consciousness, you were ripping up the original by the roots and flying away. But however we phrase it, you imagined that the abandoned timestream continued to function, albeit with the fresh enigma of your unsouled body.

"Yet I suspected from the outset, based on your descriptions, that such could not be the case.

"My prior theoretical calculations and theories caused me to believe that something else must happen when you jumped. When you removed your consciousness from any given timestream—and the consciousnesses of any of your riders—you caused the collapse of that particular starting-point continuum into nothingness. In a moment of Heisenbergian state-change, the universe just winked out, once you departed, like pulling a prop out from a pile of sticks. It's a corollary of the quantum theory of false-vacuum decay. Everything dissipated into nothingness in an instant."

"Do you mean that I've—I mean, every time I've jumped, even for something trivial, I killed an entire universe . . . ? Billions and billions of lives, of worlds, just wiped out . . . ?"

Kocchar sat down beside his daughter. "I'm afraid so, my child. At least that's what your lack of results just now would seem to indicate. But we can certainly refine our investigations once we get some rest—"

Kocchar suddenly could not breathe, so tightly was Vangie squeezing him, before she burst out into a gale of tears and sobs, which did not stop until she was utterly exhausted, and he put her into her familiar, unknown bed.

But as he was bending low to pull up the covers and kiss her brow, she said in a voice gone cold and certain, "When you subtract one from infinity, the sum is still infinity, isn't it, Baba? One universe here or there gone missing can't matter. Not when an infinite number remain. Not when my survival was at stake. I had to survive, at any cost. Those billions of deaths were the price. But I do have one regret."

Slightly horrified, Kocchar said, "And what is that, my child?"

"I regret that when I jumped out of the atomic war timestream, my parents winked out, easily and painlessly, and did not suffer through the bombs."

3

When Vangie turned nineteen, five weeks after the hospice workers had started coming to the house, her father wanted to celebrate with a special dinner and a cake. But, wan and pinch-faced, Vivek Kocchar seldom left his bed these days, fortressed between stacks of books he was now unable to peruse and study, and he was in no condition to cook, a practice he had once enjoyed, along with his gardening, and which he had refined after his wife's death. Vivek asked Vangie if she wanted him to arrange for a takeout meal to be delivered, anything she fancied. But as someone raised on baby food mush, she had never developed an appreciation for traditional hearty food. And if Kocchar could not share the meal—he was mostly subsisting on liquids these days, protein shakes and such—she did not see the point. As for a cake, she had never been the recipient of such a ceremonial treat before, not even when living with her foster families, neither with the Everetts nor the Troy-Salthouse ménage. Such extravagances for an unresponsive and uncommunicative child were surely a waste. And so that celebratory, candle-festooned dessert was nothing she would miss.

And there was no one else to invite to any hypothetical party anyhow. Vivek's old faculty peers? Vangie's coworkers at Happy Harbor? Hardly. Vivek and Vangie were a family of two only, a household strictly delimited and isolated due to Vangie's unique and secret nature.

In the half-light occasioned by drawn curtains and a small lamp, although it was still an early sunny afternoon outside, standing by the side of Vivek's bed, the noticeable but not distasteful odor of a sickroom, sweat and salves and antiseptic wipes, pungent in her nostrils, Vangie felt some small undeniable sadness for the current terminal state of her father. Overlaid memories and feelings residual from this timestream's Vangie whose body she had invaded stirred her to a mild grief. The sentiment was compounded by some genuine gratitude accrued during the past three years, since Vangie had popped into this universe, the period during which Kocchar had come to embrace her talents enthusiastically and help her to sharpen and cultivate them, providing her with the refuge of peace and freedom, acceptance and stability that she had always sought.

But the tender feelings were compromised by irritation and anger at Kocchar's stubbornness, his refusal to accept the gift she could bestow. She raised the touchy subject with the bedbound invalid once again.

"Father, you know you don't have to suffer like this. Your life doesn't have to be over. Just say the word, and I'll transport the two of us to a continuum where you'll have full health and many years ahead."

Vivek regarded his daughter with a keen eye and not a little actual aversion and rebuke. He recalled that long night of confession when she had first arrived, and how her sorrow at the serial apocalypses left in the wake of her travels had quickly turned to denial and self-centered affirmation of the necessary rightness of her actions. During the subsequent years, her attitude had not changed, but only hardened into a utilitarian certitude.

When Vivek replied, it was with a lifelong clarity and acuity unimpaired by drugs. In this year of 2029, mind-dulling opioids were no longer prescribed in situations like his. Kocchar had been fitted with a smart pain-blocker from NeuroMetrix, and he was able to maintain his usual sharpness of intellect. In a way, though, he had decided it was almost a crueler fate than going out on a dark tide of druggy somnolence. Unshielded by dreams and hallucinations, one was forced to apprehend every new tiny step toward total system failure. Eventually, of course, his physiology would degrade too far to support his mind. But that span would comprise only his final few hours.

"Daughter, I have made my ethical stance clear to you many times now, I hope. I will not let any selfish move on my part bring about the extinction of the entire cosmos. To save my one life at the cost of billions of others? Not a bargain my soul could endure."

Vangie made a sound of exasperation. "You know that once you die, I'm going to jump out of this timestream anyway, and so it's doomed already."

"I realize as much. To your credit, you have not kept your plans a secret from me. But that action will be accounted against your karma, not against mine."

"But your objections are ridiculous! Every timeline has uncountable parallel mirrorverses that differ from it by only the position of a single atom! In other words, essentially identical iterations beyond enumerating. Right this very second, across the spectrum of hyper-time, you and I are having this conversation over and over and over, preserving everything in the histories of those billions of continuums. Nothing is ever lost when I jump, even though one whole strand vanishes! It's simply the pruning of an infinite tree by an immeasurable iota, with no consequences. Not even as damaging as plucking one hair from your head."

Vivek reached his right hand out from under the blankets and rapped his knuckles weakly but defiantly on the bedside table. "You cannot convince me that this strand of creation is negligible, or just some ghost world whose disappearance matters to no one. All the duplications or backup copies in the universe do not negate the existential worth of any given timeline. The beings on this strand experience their lives just as keenly as those on another. When they vanish, something irreplaceable will be lost, no matter how many other almost identical iterations continue. I will not be responsible for such a diminishment of creation."

Vangie readied a sharp retort but stifled it at the last minute. What good would it do to argue with someone so adamant? Everything had been said, many times. She would have liked to preserve and extend the life of Vivek Kocchar—after all, his insights and aid had helped her, and he might continue to serve her as a foil and assistant and hedge against the curious public— but she would not move against his explicit wishes.

"Baba, your choices are your own." She bent to kiss his brow. "Is there anything you need before I go to my room?"

His arm still extended, Vivek wispily stroked Vangie's cheek. "I am all set. Oh, maybe you could shift that photo of your mother from the dresser to my nightstand, where I can see it better . . . Thank you, dear."

In her own bedroom, Vangie lay down atop her coverlets to conduct her regular daily practices meant both to hone her skills and to provide some solid security. Nearly three years of constant drills had helped her powers to evolve into a dynamic and sophisticated toolkit, much more useful and extensive even than the repertoire she had developed when carrying out the challenging assignments from Vardis Salthouse. How simplistic those seemed now!

Vangie briefly recalled the face and actions of her foster mother, Kris Troy. Had she been wrong to make the woman share the same fate as her savage and cruel and power-mad husband, Vardis Salthouse? Kris had shown her some affection and care. And in that Temple office, when the torture began, the woman had made an attempt, however ineffective or half-hearted, to stop the assault. But on the other hand, she had played along with Salthouse's program for years, blithely conducting Vangie down a path that led only to that ultimate degradation, the horrifying lack of control over her own destiny. No, Kris Troy deserved those moments of shock and fear, as the nuclear warheads dropped toward the White House. And she deserved also the ultimate negation that she had received minutes later, when Vangie ported out of that timeline, and in so doing wiped it out as if it had never existed.

But of course, in a very real sense, Kris Troy and her reprehensible crimes against the majesty of Vangie continued to flourish. In billions of timelines where Vangie had not managed to save herself, where Vivek Kocchar had not intervened with a dagger thrust, or where he had not even been present to begin with, or where he had been killed before his intercession could succeed, Kris and Vardis had triumphed, and lived to flourish. And also, on an equally uncountable number of strands, Kris and Vardis had refrained from their villainy, and Vangie had continued in her role as miracle-worker for the Temple of Human Potential, with ultimate results ranging from fame to infamy, from wealth and power to poverty and oblivion.

But she was no policeman, tasked with choosing between "good" and "bad" timelines and pruning them. She was only concerned with her own escape and future.

Vangie had psychically witnessed all those outcomes and more since her escape to this timeline. But of course, barring an actual jump, she could not get inside the minds of any of her avatars to experience what they were undergoing intimately. She could only observe their lives—her alternate lives—from the outside, charting the various decisions and aftermaths, possibilities and pitfalls, in a manner calculated to provide herself with the most advantageous outcomes.

This inability to fully experience the gut realities of her doppelgängers—they remained in the truest sense just ghosts to her—had led Vangie to the tentative conclusion that she was unique in all the multiverse, that only she, Vangie Prime, had assumed control of her destiny, and had full agency. All the other Vangies she observed—or rather, the large majority of them—apparently shared the ability to jump streams, and to observe the ghostly multiverse. Some of them even chanced to be looking back at her at the exact moment when she was looking at them. But none of them, so far as she could tell, had taken the same kind of proactive measures that she had taken. They all seemed content to endure whatever their original universe chose to hand out.

Naturally, Vangie realized that if any of her avatars had also jumped, they would have destroyed their original timestream, leaving her nothing to observe and perhaps skewing her conclusions. But surely in all her probing she should have encountered some scenario in hyper-time where a jump was imminent or likely. And she really had not seen any such scenario, lending strength to her deductions about her own specialness.

There remained, of course, the enigma of the Council of Ghosts, those nine avatars, elderly, middle-aged, and young, who had contacted her just that once. Vangie felt that they somehow shared her special status and could educate her. But despite her best searches, they remained secreted away, in some hidey-hole beyond her ken.

Oh, well, she could continue to burnish her abilities and hope to reach them someday.

Just now, lying in a near-hypnagogic state of concentration, Vangie moved to build up her sheaf of fallback universes.

That moment of torture, when she had longed to leap to safety but had no immediate recourse, had strengthened in her the resolution to maintain a good mental catalog of safety universes. Through diligent searching and categorization of ghost branches, Vangie had accumulated a dozen timelines whose numinous jump-coordinates were always uppermost in her thoughts—or at least floating on the top of her subconscious, available in an instant. These universes were ones where Vangie avatars enjoyed full autonomy under peaceful conditions, universes where no threats harassed her. To jump into any of them would require just the briefest of triggering events.

She could have gone into any one of them already. But she had not, for two reasons.

One was that while they were nice places, none were optimal. And part of the problem was that she had no real definition of what was optimal for her. Her ultimate desires and course of action were still nebulous, unsettled. Why make a jump to some intermediate place—an action requiring no small expenditure of energy and post-jump recalibration—when one could just as easily make a jump to some perfect destination?

A destination Vangie could not yet fully envision, that world of her heart's desire.

And the second reason was that she had made a vow to herself not to jump until Vivek Kocchar either died or could be convinced to accompany her. Sentimental, yes, not necessarily survival minded. But she felt she owed it to the man who had once upon a time, elsewhen and otherspace, saved her life.

And so as her anchor to this reality lay slowly dying just a room or two away, Vangie spent some hours enjoying the sights and sounds of those safe-haven worlds where she lived like the princess she had never yet been.

4

In the end, the Council of Ghosts came to Vangie, rather than her ferreting them out.

It was a week after her nineteenth birthday. Was that a coincidence? Did the calendar mark some new stage of maturity, for either her powers or her personality? No matter, she felt ready to confront and quiz the Council, to obtain any information she might need to ensure her continued survival and ascension through the multiverse.

But toward what ultimate goal or epiphany, she still could not say.

Vangie had just left her father's room. The hospice nurse had been by this morning and assured Vangie, in baby-talk sentences, that her father was comfortable and not in pain. A social worker had also been by to monitor Vangie and prep her for the forthcoming transition in her living arrangements: group home, or off to India.

Vangie did not choose to enlighten the woman about how large and majestic a transition would actually occur when her father died.

Kocchar mostly slept now, and drank hardly any nourishment, plainly loosening his grip upon the mortal world. When he was awake, he seemed with-it but dreamy, preferring to talk nostalgically about events long past: his happy times with his wife, his early academic career, Vangie's youth.

"You were such a helpless thing. But cute! We loved you so much. We hoped we could be as good for you as you were for us. How we missed Havnesh! He was such a fine son."

"Baba, have you changed your mind about jumping to a new strand, where you'd have a nice strong body again?"

His face—still clean-shaven thanks to aides, but semi-collapsed like an eroded hillside—displayed a look of puzzlement and irritation. "Do not speak of impossible things, my child."

Had he forgotten who she was, and the nature of her powers? Or was he referring to his own ethical stance? Either way, she was balked again.

Not for much longer, of course. If Kocchar had more than a day or three left, it would be a miracle.

And at that point, she would have to decide where she was going, all alone for the first time in her life. No guardian, however vile. No foster siblings either.

Vangie thought for a moment of Gavril, Toby, Drew, and Blaine. Their sympathy and camaraderie and dutiful attendance on her needs had constituted a small pleasure.

Back in her own room, Vangie slipped into what she sometimes thought of as "scrying mode," intending to reaffirm for the nth time her list of safe worlds and perhaps seek inspiration for her own destiny.

Almost immediately upon lowering her eyelids, swimming up from out of dimensionless, directionless depths, angles, and hidden coigns, there came a constellation of nine oval windows, each one featuring a Vangie: three elderly, three of a certain maturity, three younger than she was now.

Before they could speak, their mere presence had an un-precedented impact on Vangie.

Vangie had never given much thought to her looks. Looks were for relating to others, for enticing and appealing, conform-ing or pleasing, and those actions were not things she did or cared about. What did the exterior shell matter anyhow, when all the important essence was invisible inside? She had astrally visited universes where the Vangie avatars looked different than she did—some more malformed, some even attractive. But such outward signifiers held no meaning for her.

Until this moment. Now, suddenly, she saw herself and these other Vangies as oddities, beyond the consensual pale of people whom others enjoyed seeing.

But before the revelation could result in any further con-clusions or actions, the Council chose to address her, the oldest Vangie speaking first.

"Child, your climacteric is upon you. You have survived everything that has been thrown at you, and you have whet-ted your tools to an acute edge. But the question we asked you on our first visit still remains paramount. What is your fervent desire or goal? Let us suggest that you have two alternatives."

A middle-aged Vangie now spoke. "You may set yourself up in a world engineered to provide long-term safety and stability, a universe where you can indulge both your idle curiosity and your physical needs without hinderance. A cocoon, a cradle, a lotos-eaters' island. But we believe, from personal experience, that such a choice would eventually leave you bored and deca-dent and unfulfilled."

A teen Vangie jumped in. "Or, you could help us kick the Massive's ass! He's out to make the whole friggin' multiversal kit and caboodle into his personal circle-jerk!"

The first Vangie resumed the talk. "We spoke to you once

about Durant Le Massif. His iterations are invariant from one continuum to the next. While he cannot travel across strands as you do, and while the level of communication among all his avatars is subliminal, he has just recently made a quantum jump in what he can accomplish. He has achieved parallel processing across the continuums. He is able to harness large networks of his infinite minds for problem-solving and ratiocination. In effect, he has bootstrapped himself by multiplicity to genius levels of thought."

Teen Vangie added, "Every continuum he comes to dominate becomes a white-bread, vanilla landscape. He's turning the multiverse into a giant soggy bowl of cornflakes, no bananas or raisins allowed!"

Frowning, a fourth Vangie said, more soberly, "You might suspect that any such network of minds would approach the Singularity and become godlike. Luckily for us, that is not quite so. A hundred billion idiots linked together would still be an idiot. A hundred billion men of average intelligence like Durant Le Massif, pooling their brains, will perform maybe an order of magnitude or three better than the individual components. Very formidable, but not like a demigod."

"And what does the Massive intend to do with his new talents?" asked a fifth Vangie. "He wants immense wealth and power and dominance, of course, on any single timeline. But beyond that, he wants to remake the multiverse in his own image. He wants to prune away all the branches where his own genetic line is not dominant. In effect, he wants a multiverse full of Durant Le Massif clones. And to accomplish that, he needs you.

"The Massive wants to enslave you and force you to cull the timelines he wants culled, until the whole multiverse is made in his image, a monoculture. It's an insane plan, one that would take an eternity to carry out, given the infinity of time-lines to be deleted. But he's not a sane person. Incredibly smart and cunning and canny, but not totally sane. And what does he care about eternity, when he imagines he can go on forever?"

Vangie listened to this incredible story with awe and surprise, but also with not much doubt. She recalled the time she had encountered the Massive's gaze, when she went looking for him. It had been full of a smug superiority and cruel ambition even then, and that had been years ago. Surely he had grown into his inheritance as much as she had grown into hers.

"What can I do to stop him?"

"First, obviously, you must stay free of his clutches. To accomplish that, you will probably have to accumulate as much influence and riches as he. But how to shut down his larger ambitions, when he is omnipresent across all strands? That solution we have not yet devised. But simply for you to stay free of his dominance is the essential prerequisite. Given time, we should all be able to devise a solution to the larger problem."

The Council of Ghosts did not beg or implore Vangie for her assent. And that wise, respectful move on their part was probably the factor that tipped the scales toward cooperation.

Of course, the Council, being composed entirely of herselves, had always known how best to enlist her.

The eldest Vangie smiled for the first time. "Daughter, we leave you now for a while, confident that you are well-equipped to craft your own tactics and strategies. But we shall be back when we can again be of help."

The Council of Ghosts swirled away like polychromatic water down an eleven-dimensional drain.

Vangie opened her eyes. She felt suffused with a newfound sense of destiny and power, and a desire to probe her enemy, pushing his boundaries to see where they might be weakest.

She got out of bed and walked out to the parlor, where she found her father's smartphone. As she used its apps to search online for the vital contact information she needed, she recalled the night three years ago, when she and Vivek had sat here with pizza and soda, while she disclosed her true origins and nature to him. It seemed ages, a lifetime, ago.

Almost without volition, as if fated, her pudgy fingers succeeded in their task.

Onto the phone's screen came the living, animated face of Durant Le Massif, the Massive. A knifelike smile and an arched eyebrow were the only marks of any mild disconcertment at Vangie's contact.

His chiseled, handsome yet coldly inhuman features were as she remembered them. Vangie thought to detect new lines of strain around his piercing eyes, as though the overseeing of his many minds required intense and painful focus.

The man's wry smile widened, and he spoke.

"At last, the contest begins. I will see you again soon."

The screen went blank.

Vangie set the phone down. Was her hand shaking? No, she would not let that be!

Eyes closed, an ashen line of dried saliva around his lips, Vivek Kocchar had not spoken for many hours now. Vangie had tried to rouse him, but ultimately desisted. His broken breathing exhibited all the conventional signs of an imminent passage to the beyond.

Two hospice workers awaited outside the closed bedroom door. Vangie had asked to be alone with her father, and they had consented.

Stroking Kocchar's papery hand, and for once thinking of nothing in particular, Vangie was startled to hear her father whisper. She put an ear closer to his lips.

"Daughter, you know what was . . . strangest thing . . . ever told me? The Vivek who saved your life . . . he had a mustache!"

Vivek gave a small chuckle, then died.

The nurse and the social worker, a woman and a man, standing outside the bedroom door heard a short burst of sobbing, and knew the moment of death had come and gone. Respecting the young woman's privacy, they refrained for a couple of minutes from entering. A small, almost liminal tremor of psychic disorientation was experienced by both, but they were too well acquainted with the oft-strange happenstances surrounding death to pay much attention to the ghostly sensation or give it much weight.

The bedroom door opened, and Vangie Kocchar emerged.

The woman who stepped through the door shared the elegant lines and classical curves of some apex-dwelling fashion model, alluringly contoured at bosom, waist, hip, and ankle. Long, polished, supple blond hair crested atop her powerful shoulders. Her heart-shaped, strong-jawed face was comprised of gleaming green eyes, pert nose, and the lips found on some classical statue of Athena or Hera. Dressed in a tailored suit of tulip-yellow and cocktail heels, she strode with a bold and swaying gait.

She shook the slack hands of the two aides, smiled, and said, "My father is dead, and I must be going. Goodbye, and thank you for all your help."

And before the hospice workers could find their tongues, she was gone.

BOOK TWO

BOOK TWO

PART ONE

PART ONE

I

Fresh out of Cascadia State University at Yreka, age twenty-three, Gavril Bainbridge was in search of a good job. His BSc degree in spintronics, with a concentration in neuromorphic engineering, promised to secure him a well-paying and intellectually rewarding position at any one of Cascadia's many high-tech firms: MacroGate, Howlett-Snekt, RiboMechanics. Since they were all multinationals, Gavril would probably be able to take his pick of where to relocate. After spending some harsh early years in the heat-blasted wastelands of Phoenix, Arizona, and then a relatively pampered middle-class youth in Ann Arbor, Michigan, followed by six years in the pleasant but still mainly rural college-town precincts of Yreka, Gavril was up for some travel to exotic, cosmopolitan venues, a general change of scenery. He felt he definitely needed to broaden his outlook and life experiences.

Not that he hadn't come a long way already.

The climate-change depopulation of Phoenix (average temperatures ranged from December's 85 degrees Fahrenheit to August's 125) had proceeded in a more or less orderly and controlled fashion. But the exodus, teardowns, and rewilding had not affected every resident equally. As always, there were massive inequalities. The rich and even the merely well-off had many options when leaving the city. The poor had fewer. Many of the underprivileged balked at abandoning their familiar environs for the preselected government destinations. Residence in the "temporary" FEMA camps often stretched to many years, under sustainable and humane but less-than-optimal conditions. Enrollment in the Citizens Contributory Corps involved military-style living and lots of heavy lifting, often in some desperate and even dangerous scenarios—admittedly with commensurate paychecks. But for those who lacked the ability to finance their own resettlement, options were limited.

And of course there were folks who could have plausibly moved, but who were just too stubborn or eccentric to heed the summons. After a time, the authorities ceased trying to convince them of Phoenix's uninhabitability.

Gavril's grandfather fell into that category. Gavril had come to live with his grandfather at age seven, when the boy's parents had died in a terrorist-fomented crash of the Chicago to Atlanta high-speed rail. Grandpa Iorghu, Mama's dad, was the only relative willing or able to take the boy in.

A crusty relic of the Great East European Displacement of 1999, Grandpa Iorghu lived in an inoperative RV parked at the Desert Sands RV Resort outside Phoenix. The sixty-three-year-old military veteran, combatant in such famous campaigns as Operation Formosa and Black Whirlwind, had purchased the vehicle, a high-end Mahindra & Mahindra Thar model, with his mustering-out pay. His military pension had sufficed for him to secure and maintain a slot at Desert Sands, along with purchasing daily necessities, with the option of picking up and traveling elsewhere someday if he wished.

But in the low-level chaos of the Phoenix exodus, Iorghu's

vehicle had been scavenged by looters one day while Iorghu was out visiting the local charity food and water distribution center. (The Desert Sands RV Resort enterprise was defunct by then, with no staff to guard the premises, and just a few scattered slots still inhabited.) The looters hadn't bothered with any of the pitiable possessions or fittings inside the RV. They had been concerned only with taking all the vehicle's tires, its engine, and its valuable catalytic converter. They thoughtfully substituted cinder blocks for the wheels.

Iorghu swore up a storm, but then, realizing he really didn't want to go anyplace else other than his current location, he resigned himself to the inevitable.

It was into this situation that the Chicago authorities had consigned the orphan in their care, seven-year-old Gavril. They had been reluctant at first to send a child to such a hellhole, but Iorghu, still a legal resident of the state of Arizona, had threatened to go to court to secure his legal rights of guardianship, and they had relented.

Gavril loved his grandpa and found the novel situation exhilarating. Of course, he missed his parents terribly (a loss which, however, abated daily with surprising rapidity). But Grandpa Iorghu—preoccupied most waking hours, when he wasn't securing their sustenance, with replaying his old campaigns on a VR rig—let his grandson do whatever he wanted. There was no school, of course, which suited Gavril just fine. He never saw another child during his stay in Phoenix—except once, at a long distance. Exploring the abandoned landscapes of the city in his fluky knock-off of a high-end MacroGate stilsuit allowed Gavril to indulge in all sorts of vibrant postapocalyptic fantasies. And he was able to hone his skateboarding skills in all the empty swimming pools, including the indoor one at Desert Sands. (Formerly indoors, really, since the roof of the building now sported gaping holes where scavengers had roughly removed the solar cell arrays.)

Gavril gave no thought to his long-term future and was very happy to be a free-range juvenile savage. There was no telling how long he might have continued in this lifestyle, nor where his life might have led, if another tragedy had not intervened.

One day, Gavril returned to the RV to find its door inexplicably ajar. Of course, this malfeasance was highly frowned upon by Grandpa Iorghu, and it was unlikely the savvy vet had forgotten such elementary precautions. The intensively retro-insulated trailer, sheltered under a tarp canopy painted with super-reflective ultra-white barium sulfate paint, relied on a balky heat-pump to maintain even the semblance of a livable temperature inside. The open door would stymie all those measures.

Calling out his grandfather's name with some growing alarm and venturing tentatively inside the RV, Gavril soon discovered the horrible reason for the open door.

His grandfather's corpse, half-dragged out of his patched recliner, with VR rig still attached, showed all the ravages of a wild animal attack. Partially eaten, Grandpa Iorghu had been left behind as a cache for further meals by whatever killed him.

Gavril learned much later that the probable predators had been a pack of pumas. These large, fearless cats, used to attacking fierce animals much bigger than themselves, had been further enhanced for the rewilding campaign by federal genetic engineering programs that increased their intelligence and instilled pack behaviors in the formerly solitary hunters—all thanks to the Viridian Party lobbying efforts. Much later, Gavril had seen a FreeClips video of pumas cooperating to flip the handle of a door and swing it open, and so the mystery of his grandfather's demise had lessened.

The Bainbridge family of Ann Arbor, as Anglo and as white

as the barium sulfate paint on the RV's tarp, had heartily welcomed Gavril, his skin burnt dark by the Arizona sun, into their bosom. They rehabilitated their new formerly feral child with speech lessons, professional counseling, and lots of love. Wiry, funny, enamored of camping, Dad Bainbridge, Chet, taught economics at the University of Michigan, while Mom Bainbridge, Tina—blond, elegant, a crack pickleball player—operated her own interior design business.

Right from the start, Gavril—product of a lower-class stratum inhabited by many transplanted eastern Europeans in the USA—had felt privileged and happy to be fostered by the Bainbridges, and his eventual adoption after a couple of years merely certified the reality of his reciprocally beloved status. He instantly acquired three siblings, a sometimes vexed privilege he had never before enjoyed. Nerdy Toby, a boy younger than himself, and twin sisters—enigmatic and self-contained, but frighteningly smart, observant, and loyal to family—named Blaine and Drew, even younger than Toby.

For many years, even right up to his departure for the university, Gavril had always harbored a subliminal sense that this arrangement was too good to last. Whenever his foster parents traveled, as they often did for business, Gavril envisioned some spectacular transit disaster. When the whole family went camping at their favorite place, the Sleeping Bear Dunes in the Upper Peninsula (scarily named!), Gavril kept a sharp eye out for pumas and the like. When his vigilant behavior became noticed and questioned, he confessed his fears. The initial soothing reassurances, with tears flowing from all parties, evolved after some time, after all the emotions had been defused, into a family joke, where the humor bore an edge of whistling through the graveyard. For instance, Toby was prone to hum the *Pink Panther* theme at appropriate or inappropriate moments, while the twins would bare their teeth, growl, and shape their hands into claws if Gavril did something to annoy them.

Frequent happy trips back to the Bainbridge home in Ann Arbor during his time of studies at Cascadia revealed to Gavril that any attachments he might have had to his barely remembered days in Chicago, or his more dreamlike years in Phoenix, had been amalgamated, burnished, and domesticated into his identity as a Bainbridge.

And now, as he cast about for his first real employment, Gavril had the dual objectives of not only satisfying his own desires and proclivities but also of doing his family proud. Those parallel demands were the main reason why he was so hesitant about which company he should apply to. He had been headhunted vigorously and knew that any application he might submit would probably result in an instant job offer. He was very concerned with getting off on the best foot. Not that he couldn't switch jobs after a year or two. But why jump into a position that you knew would be only temporary or not a good permanent fit?

It was already June, and the lease was running out on his off-campus apartment, when Gavril received an unexpected job offer. And this proved to be irresistible, perhaps his dream job, one he had never even bothered to consider, deeming himself inadequate for the assignment until he had accumulated more work experience.

The opening was for a junior engineer at what was undeniably one of the two richest, most innovative, cutting-edge companies of this era, a firm whose many ingenious, invaluable, and indispensable products and programs had come to underpin people's quotidian lives.

VKC.

The Variant Kinetics Consortium.

Rivaled only by DLM Industries.

2

Despite breezing through both his first and second interviews at VKC—surprisingly, his nerves had been as unruffled as a calm day on Lake Siskiyou, almost as if the interviews were a fait accompli—Gavril could hardly believe when the actual offer of employment came through. Not only would he receive an enormous salary and great bennies, but he would also be positioned at the elite corporate headquarters right here in Yreka and assigned to a research division seemingly aligned superbly with his discipline. (He'd know more about his duties, of course, when he started work.) For a few minutes, he regretted that he had not been granted some foreign posting. Reputedly, the VKC facilities in Greater Hong Kong, right outside Shanghai, and those on the Island of Havana were swinging spots. But then he felt happy to be remaining in this familiar college town, his home for the past six years, with its mountain-girt beauty and manageable population of some one hundred thousand (not counting the inhabitants of the FEMA refugee camps in the hills; but then they were only temporary residents, here until they could be relocated to other needful locales, such as Detroit, Appalachia, or the Isle of Bronx).

As soon as Gavril signed his contract with VKC—his start date was just a week off—he re-upped the lease on his apartment and booked an impulsive flight back to Ann Arbor. His three weeks of vacation privileges at his new job wouldn't kick in for six months, and he hadn't seen his family in too long, since Christmas. And this way, he could deliver his good news in person.

Gavril found his parents happy and equable as always, leading their charmed lives into early middle-age, hardly showing any signs of graying or slowing down. His mother, for one, had just landed the plum remake of a dozen interiors in a small restaurant chain, Wolvie's Waffles.

The folks greeted him with the usual hearty glee and were as excited and pleased as he was to learn of his good fortune. His dad added a surprising codicil to the news. Chet Bainbridge was starting a sabbatical to produce a book on, of all things, the competition between Gavril's new employer and DLM Industries. The working title was *Dance of the Disparate Duelists: How Two Rival Corporations Sought to Divide the World Between Them.* The focus, Chet said, would of course be on his own field, economics, but there would also be cultural and sociopolitical angles.

Pouring Gavril a Goebel beer as they sat outside in the backyard that evening, a fragrant barbecue underway, Chet said, only half-jokingly, "Maybe you can feed me lots of fresh insights and tidbits from your insider's niche, Gee."

"I don't know, Dad. That NDA I had to sign was about six pages long. I'd be afraid to tell you what I ate in the company cafeteria."

Tina Bainbridge, working the grill, said, "Oh, leave the poor boy alone, Chet. You want him to get fired on his first day there?"

"Just joshing, honey."

Gavril's brother, Toby, having just finished his junior year

in the computer science department at Elihu University, all
the way across the country in New Haven, Connecticut, was
home for the summer, having snagged an internship at a local
firm, Glowworm Graphics. They produced CGI for Hollywood
movies, with their major claim to fame so far being their work
on *Tiger, Tiger!* starring Heath Ledger as Gully Foyle.

Arriving later than the others, Toby entered the backyard
and immediately gave Gavril a big hug. "Hey, bro, good going
with the VKC gig. Did you know that Glowworm does all their
rendering on VKC machines?"

"No, but I'm not surprised." Gavril began to wonder if his
entire life was going to pivot around his new employer.

"On a more vital topic, any news in the romance department?"

For a time, Gavril had lived with a fellow student named Starla
Mosley, and everyone had foreseen theirs to be a long-term rela-
tionship. But Gavril and Starla broke up when Starla got religion
and joined some tiny, obscure cult called the Temple of Human
Potential. And this last year of studies had been so demanding that
Gavril hadn't had time for anything more than a few casual dates.

"Nothing on the radar, Toad. Just keeping my options open."

Slim and darkly pretty in their CyberGoth fashions, Drew
and Blaine, still in high school, sat side by side at the picnic
table, entwined as usual, heads together as they whispered. They
giggled now, apparently at the picture of their brother having
a girlfriend. Looking up, they chanted in unison, "Gavril and
VKC, sitting in a tree. There'll be K-I-S-S-I-N-G!"

Gavril had to chase them around the yard to make them stop.

Lying awake in his old childhood bed past midnight, sated
with food, drink, and talk, Gavril felt simultaneously comfortable and estranged, pivoting between the known past and the
unknown future. He pondered for a while how different his
life would have been with just a few twists and turns. If he had

accompanied his birth parents on their fatal train trip . . . If the Phoenix pumas had eaten or just mangled him too . . . If he had reacted to the white-bread, middle-class circumstances of his foster home in Ann Arbor with ungratefulness or suspicion, bitterness or prejudice . . . Just taking one unwonted step sideways could change your whole life.

Early Monday morning after he returned from Ann Arbor, Gavril stood at the front entrance to the gigantic postmodern building, sheathed in smart materials, that housed the Yreka branch of VKC—not in its entirety of course, for there were many satellite buildings on the 150-acre immaculately land-scaped campus. But this one, the biggest, nicknamed "the Bean" for its leguminous shape, contained office space for twenty-five hundred of the campus's three thousand people.

Including the idolized, mysterious, brilliant, capricious, wealthy, and enigmatic founder, dominant stockholder, and CEO of VKC, Evangeline Kocchar, a woman who, despite her long tenure at the root and helm of her organization, having kickstarted it into life nearly twenty years ago, still managed to look ageless, eternally young, and beautiful. Her fabled office, high up in the structure, just where the roof dipped to mimic a bean's curves, was the unapproachable, unassailable, glowing nerve center, the Aerie, of the whole enterprise that had come to infiltrate its myriad sleek and desirable products and services and even its philosophies into roughly half the globe's marketplace, the other 50 percent being dominated by DLM Industries—a firm that seemed to cater to more authoritarian and old-school regimes. (Not that they entirely lacked customers and partisans here in the USA.)

Gavril had of course seen numerous photos of the legendary office and its inhabitant, in one magazine puff piece or another, and so he retained a vivid image of that nexus of power, status, and innovation. But he knew that his chances of setting foot in that rarefied realm were as minuscule as the odds that a twister would lift him off to Oz.

Gavril was dressed in hip, casual engineer clothes, as per the famously relaxed atmosphere at the headquarters. And when he stepped into the main lobby with its soaring ceiling, statues, whirligig mobiles and fountains, benches, and automated information kiosks (the public could enter and savor this much of the Bean, but no more), he was pleased to see that the ambling or scurrying folks wearing employee badges on lanyards were dressed with equal informality.

A cheerful male receptionist at a broad desk that bore the VKC logo—a mythic tree with a multiplicity of branches that exfoliated fractally to an implied infinity—found Gavril's name on his screen and issued the somewhat stunned newcomer a temporary badge that allowed him to penetrate further, all the way to the human resources department, reached by following the badge's voiced directions. And there, in a whirlwind of activity, Gavril signed a plethora of digital documents (was his life really now insured for one hundred thousand dollars?); received a new VKC Qualia phone (a model not yet available to the public, and which hosted various specialized company apps); trained a new VKC BrainySlate to acknowledge both his fingerprints and facial scan as biometric security; and accepted a lanyard around his slightly bent neck. Studying the photo of his own just-digitized face, Gavril saw a slightly goofy, slightly querulous stranger. Oh well, he had lived with worse ID shots.

While Gavril tried to find an extra pocket to accommodate his new phone (his old phone, up till now quite acceptable and beloved, suddenly seemed mere trash), a woman emerged from an inner office of HR. A decade or so older than Gavril, confident, poised, well-assembled in a sporty outfit that made her look ready for a day of kayaking or cycling, she displayed a big sincere smile that made her somewhat plain features—dark bangs, blue eyes—more radiant and charming.

The woman offered her hand for shaking. Gavril complied. Her grip was strong.

"Hello, Gavril. My name is Kris Troy. I'm the director of human resources, and I just wanted to extend a warm welcome to you, on behalf of the whole company. We're very pleased to have you onboard."

"Thanks. Thanks so much." Something puzzled Gavril, and he voiced it at the risk of seeming impolite. "Do you come out to greet every new hire? You wouldn't have time for anything else."

Not offended, Kris Troy laughed. "No, I just try to keep my hand in by picking random newbies now and then. You just happened to grab the golden ticket. I'm going to give you a tour of the campus before I deposit you at your new workplace. I hope those shoes are good for walking. We might have to pause for lunch before we get to your ultimate stop."

"And where exactly is that?"

Troy's eyes widened. "Didn't they tell you that, the most important thing, in all this bureaucratic shuffle? I'm going to have to whip some butt. Just kidding! I'll bet the info is on your BrainySlate. Why not try to bring it up?"

Feeling as if he were a lab mouse being tasked with an intelligence test, Gavril poked around at the screen until he stumbled on the information. Not quite believing what he saw, he turned the screen to Kris Troy.

"Is this it?"

"Bingo! A really special assignment. Gavril, you're going right into the Ghost Factory."

3

Gavril's supervisor at the Ghost Factory—the unit was housed in a long, low structure that resembled a boathouse or a beer garden, shaded by a stand of black oaks—turned out to be an Asian-American woman even younger than himself named Kumiko Willcutt. Chipper, sparkling, and bright, she refracted off Gavril's more sober and tentative nature like sunlight off a stolid mica cliff face. After half an hour of introductory patter, her unstoppable enthusiasm had worn down Gavril's natural sense of reserve (heightened by the circumstances of being a newbie), and he loosened up enough to meet Kumiko's sallies and exclamations with some fervor of his own.

The tour of the campus with Kris Troy had been both mind-revving and wearisome. Gavril had been introduced to so many people and so many concepts and projects that his head was left spinning. Then he had made the mistake at lunch of drinking a beer. Hard to resist when the VKC refectory featured a row of kegs full of local craft offerings to accompany the gourmet menu, all for free. By the time Troy deposited him at the door of the Ghost Factory and said goodbye, all Gavril wanted was a nap.

But Kumiko had taken her new worker firmly in hand, no slacking allowed despite the collegial atmosphere, and commenced bringing Gavril up to speed with the layout and personnel and specs of the unit. A small freshet of novel faces and names went by without any retention, and Gavril tried to let go of any feelings of anxiety or guilt. All these people and things would surely come to seem as familiar as his own left hand after a few weeks.

Eventually Kumiko brought them to the heart of the Ghost Factory itself: a room full of high-end VKC processors: not off-the-shelf machines, but uniquely configured for the Ghost Factory's mission.

The young woman had grown somewhat serious, as if she had entered a temple. "We are, of course," Kumiko said, "concerned with creating the best neuromorphic hardware and software available in the world today. The VKC aspiration! But there's a special angle to our particular project."

Neuromorphic engineering, the interdisciplinary craft harnessing math, physics, biology, and more, to which Gavril had devoted six years of his academic life, concerned itself with emulating—in the media of silicon, spintronic memory chips, and quantum memristors—the architecture of the human brain. The miracle-producing organic workings of squelchy synapses replicated in a box.

"Our template is one particular brain. That's all we are trying to instantiate. We are not shooting for a general model, but a specific one. All our efforts are bent toward a perfect emulation of the candidate brain."

Gavril wondered at the eccentricity of the project. Didn't one always begin with generic models before trying to tailor them? "And who would that be?"

Kumiko regarded Gavril as if trying to ascertain that he had really signed all his nondisclosure agreements and would be a team player. Apparently deciding that he was wholeheartedly invested in VKC, she finally answered him.

"The brain of our founder, Evangeline Kocchar."

Attempting to build an analog silicon brain perfectly replicating the skull-housed original (presumably still functioning in that woman ensconced in the Bean's Aerie) involved a fairly gruesome everyday task. And that was studying slices of the original gray matter.

Gavril knew quite well, from her numerous documented appearances—on campus, at galas, with visiting politicians—that Evangeline Kocchar was very much a dynamic, living, breathing resident on this globe. So how these slices had been obtained was just one of the many mysteries inherent in Gavril's work at the Ghost Factory. The best solution to this enigma that he could conjure involved somewhat unethical "brain in a petri dish" cloning. But he quickly learned that full answers to many such questions were not forthcoming, and that he would have to put aside his curiosity and just employ his learning, intuition, and skill.

And so, every day, Gavril would pore over digitized images of brain slices, each one precisely five micrometers thick. (He could actually consult the organic originals if he ever needed to, each one preserved in its own separate jar filled with artificial cerebrospinal fluid, in the room dubbed the "Brain Library.") Mapping the neurons and their connections, he would work on translating that to computer architecture. He also got to do some coding, which was a nice break from the hardware protocols. It was fascinating and challenging work, and while at first Gavril felt somewhat out of his depth, he soon got up to speed. The day that one of his coworkers came to him for advice and insight, rather than Gavril going to them for help, was a milestone that ignited a warm sense of pride in him.

Their unit, under the direction of Kumiko Willcutt (she had finished *her* neuromorphic degree in only four years, while simultaneously earning a BA in the history of Japanese art), was called the Ghost Factory for one obvious reason: that old phrase "ghost in the machine," coined by philosopher Gilbert Ryle to illuminate mind-body dualism. Gavril and his peers were constructing the ghost and the machine in parallel. And while their unit's work was vaguely known to many employees on the VKC campus, and even to some outsiders (*Life* magazine had done a jokey little feature titled "Variant Kinetics is making a chip that could become your best friend!"), there was another aspect of the project that also earned the ghost nickname.

The replicant of Kocchar's brain was not being built in adult modules which, when joined all together, would suddenly self-assemble into the totality of her mature consciousness. Instead, progress was being chased just the way that embryonic and postnatal brain development happened. Starting with just a few digital synapses, then accumulating more and more in the proper interrelated patterns, growing the brain just like a fetus, and then, after "birth," mimicking the childhood and adolescent neural development and rewiring. This silicon Evangeline would mature just like a human child.

And the datasets that the brain was being trained on at each stage were variant timelines, ghostly counterfactual histories, encoded by another division of VKC entirely. These datasets were huge, modeling as they did entire planetary gestalts, albeit at a very reductionist, coarse-grained, and highly symbolic level. (Whatever their granularity or complexity, these useful models had been tinkered with and enhanced enough over the past several decades to perform very well for economists, climatologists, politicians, sociologists, and other experts.)

If one could imagine somehow capturing the current fleeting

state of the planet—climate, politics, history, geology, oceans, flora, fauna—in a detailed simulation (and this was hardly new territory), then these counterfactual models were ghost versions of reality.

Hence, the Ghost Factory.

It was as if the nascent baby silicon brain were being deliberately exposed to a welter of counterfactual realities at every stage of its growth, rather than just letting it focus its learning on a single consensus timeline, as with all previous attempts at machine-self-education.

Privately, Gavril thought this was a recipe for inducing insanity or catatonia in the artificial construct. That a mind could develop in a healthy fashion when faced with infinite flux, all confusion and no certainties, was a leap beyond his faith.

Why the Kocchar Brain should be receiving this kind of stimulus and education, no one knew. But the staff of the Ghost Factory had their directives, and they carried them out with all their well-paid talents and enthusiasm.

As the anniversary of Gavril's hiring approached, he discovered that for the first time in his episodic, eventful life, he really felt a new level of stability and confidence not present at any earlier stage. Memories of his earliest childhood in Chicago had been retroactively tinged with mortality by the death of his parents. His time with Grandpa Iorghu in Phoenix had of course been some kind of way-out-there *Empire of the Sun* interlude. (Gavril was a big fan of Harold Pinter's sci-fi novels, including *Empire of the Sun*, his mainstream account of his time in a Shanghai internment camp.) And even during all his peaceful middle-class years in the bosom of the Bainbridges, he had felt both the pressure to live up to the gift they had given him, and also some kind of sense of contingency, that his future was never certain.

Now, however, he felt he had found a niche, a purpose, and lots of satisfaction, both monetary and companionable.

The staff of the Ghost Factory was tiny for what they were attempting, just six of them. The smallness of the force served to bond them and drive them even harder, as if they were a platoon on some cyberbattlefield. More hands would have just dissipated their drive, added dissenting approaches, and generally encumbered the project with layers of bureaucracy and decision-making. Working alongside Kumiko and Gavril were:

Stan Dresser, a plump fellow who hailed from Massachusetts and MIT. Stan's family was old-line Bostonian, but he had disdained the family wealth and put himself through school by working for the Providence Grays MLB team as a statistician.

Mafalda "Maff" Cataldo had grown up in Argentina, her great-great-grandparents part of the nineteenth-century Italian diaspora that had followed the failure of the Risorgimento. She danced a mean tango.

Mateo Bilbao had spent his childhood in Macau, where his father had owned a high-class casino. Gavril had quickly learned not to play cards with Matt for money.

Sanura Darwish was the daughter of the British governor of the Egyptian protectorate and had grown up in Alexandria. She ofttimes still spoke fondly of her favorite "uncle," a wryly intelligent but dissipated civil servant named Lawrence Durrell.

Gavril spent not only his working hours with this crew, but also much of his recreational time. They went hiking and weekend camping, barhopping and clubbing, concertgoing and lecture-listening. (The Pinker-Dawkins Chautauqua was their favorite brain-stretching occasion.) Gavril eventually slept with both Maff and Sanura—serially, not alternating—and while the sex was good and did not harm their work relationships, it petered out in both cases and led to no long-term romance.

Attracted also to Kumiko, Gavril had held back because of

the supervisor-underling dynamic. When Kumiko introduced him one day to her girlfriend, the attraction became moot.

One day in May, Gavril was sitting in the refectory, drinking a very nice boutique IPA and trying to let his brain unknot from the day's exertions. Visions of circuits danced in his head. He was admiring the many beautiful women walking around the cafeteria, since he figured this activity was as far from mapping brain slices as he could get.

He was surprised then to see Kumiko hastening across the floor toward him. She wore a puzzled and earnest look.

"Gee, I just got a directive to loan you out for an indefinite stint to another department. Technically, you start your new assignment tomorrow, but you've got the weekend off."

"Man, that's a bummer. But I guess the higher-ups know what they're doing. Anyway, it will probably last only a week or two. Who do I report to?"

Kumiko consulted her BrainySlate again, as if to reassure herself of the information. Her eyes were wide when she said, "To Evangeline Kocchar, in the Aerie."

4

Never possessing much of a fashion sense, Gavril had had to place an Eye'n'Ear call to his mom as soon as he returned to his apartment after receiving the incredible news of his primo assignment. Tina Bainbridge's pretty, maternal face filled his phone's screen, smiling at the unexpected contact. (Gavril usually called home nowadays only about once every three weeks, generally on a Sunday morning.) After their hellos, Gavril related the startling work developments, concluding, "Mom, you've got to help me pick out what to wear. I don't want to go ridiculously formal. But I don't want to look like a slob either."

"Let's investigate your closet."

Conducting a tour by phone lens of his wardrobe, Gavril was subject to a steady stream of tsk-tsking, oh-mys, and really-nows.

"Do you actually wear a madras jacket with a pocket crest that says 'Yreka Dive Bar Inspection Team'?"

"C'mon, Ma, it's just a joke thing among my posse when we go cruising."

A final long sigh terminated the inspection. "I am going onto the Biggest River site right now and ordering you a perfect ensemble, with overnight delivery. When it arrives I want you to model it for me, to make sure maybe you don't put the shirt on backward or have a lollipop sticking out of your blazer pocket."

"Ma!"

"No backsass! Just do what I say."

When the package from Biggest River arrived, Gavril opened it with a mix of gratitude for the assistance and embarrassment that his mother was still clothing him at his age. He worried for a few seconds that she might have picked out something dorky. But he should have known better, given his mother's design sense and vast experience—albeit only with such nonhuman decorating tasks as selecting the perfect tablecloths and napkins for the Ella Fitzgerald Lounge franchises.

The box contained a pair of light gray linen trousers; an unconstructed microwool jacket in a darker shade of gray; several collarless, buttonless silk shirts in different soft pastels; and a pair of classic loafers. There were even socks to match the shirts! An enclosed card said, *Knock 'em dead, kiddo!*

As he had promised, Gavril showed Tina Bainbridge that he could dress himself adequately. Expressions of love, affirmations of success, and virtual kisses concluded the fashion demo.

With this hurdle out of the way, Gavril had nothing left to do over the weekend except ponder, angst, and rehash practically every professional decision he had made in his year's employment, hoping that he would commit no flubs when he met Evangeline Kocchar. He even rehearsed saying his name out loud. By the hundredth practice iteration, he was unsure of even the pronunciation of "Bainbridge."

His crew from the Ghost Factory called him for their usual weekend carousing, but Gavril politely declined. He didn't want to rack up a Monday morning hangover, nor did he want to deal with an endless stream of questions and speculations from his friends—who, to be quite honest, might be harboring a little jealousy, subliminal or otherwise. Not having to face their naked emotion could preserve their friendships intact when he returned to the Ghost Factory. His buds would have to be content at that future date with any anecdotes of the stratospheric upper echelons he might generously choose to relate.

Then he started fantasizing that maybe Kocchar wanted him only for some kind of public relations program. Maybe Kris Troy at human resources, or some statistical AI data tranche, had singled him out as a useful icon for the Consortium's PR purposes. VKC was always mounting one new informational campaign after another, touting their products and visionary attitudes over those of archrival DLM Industries, in what sometimes amounted to a propaganda war. And after all, Gavril's refugee identity had earned him points all his Bainbridge-era life—deserved or not, Gavril couldn't say. He felt he had always succeeded on his own merits, without extra credit for an accident of birth. But, subjectivity aside, his life story was indeed fairly exceptional, an example of triumph over adversity. How many VKC employees had had their grandpa eaten by a puma? Could it be that Gavril Bainbridge was being groomed as some kind of poster boy for VKC, after putting in a year's worth of credible effort, just long enough to establish his utility and allegiance?

By the time late Sunday night rolled around, Gavril was so frazzled from all this back-and-forth speculation that he couldn't even worry anymore. He indulged in a rare smoke of legal salvia divinorum after ferreting out an old, crumpled, slightly stale pack of Johnson & Johnson Mazatec Puffs from the back of his underwear drawer. (He had been surprised the clothing shipment from Mom hadn't included any new undies, but that package arrived a day later.) Lulled by the mild dope, he fell into a deep and peaceful sleep, populated however by phantoms and apparitions unlocked from the basement of his mind by the psychoactive salvia. But their significant shapes and faces and actions evaporated upon waking.

Gavril had had many occasions to enter the impressive, vaulted lobby of the Bean since that day he first reported for employment. But never since that day had the place felt so foreign and awe-inspiring. The sound of tinkling fountains providing a counterpoint to his steps, he crossed the vast sunlight-slashed floor to the reception desk, half-expecting to see the face of the same cheerful young guy who had greeted him a year ago. But Fate chose not to replay that encounter, presenting Gavril instead with the smiling presence of a Black woman of senior years. Despite the difference in their races, Gavril flashed briefly on a Chicago aunt he barely remembered, and he took the resemblance as a good omen.

Immediately upon spotting Gavril, the woman's smile broadened, and she said, "Oh, Mr. Bainbridge, you're certainly expected. Your badge has been reconfigured to allow you to reach the Aerie. Just follow the prompts."

Gavril tried to say thanks, but his throat was too scratchy and his lips too numb to really function. Maybe smoking that yerba last night had been a mistake. When he could finally speak, he said, "Uh, great. Can I just get a water first though?"

"Of course. You know where the vending machines are?"

"Uh, yeah, naturally."

Consuming a twelve-ounce bottle of Alaskan Kenai Lake Water (a VKC subsidiary) allowed Gavril to regain functionality of his speaking apparatus. Now all he had to do was not cultivate an overwhelming urge to pee during his face-to-face with Evangeline Kocchar.

His badge led him past the busy bank of general-access elevators and around a corner to an unlabeled elevator door. The door lacked a wall panel with buttons for either up or down. (The Bean's foundations extended for several underground levels.) But the doors slid open at Gavril's approach.

There were no buttons inside the car either, the lift having only one destination.

The ascent seemed to take forever but still end too quickly. All the way up, while tugging on the lines of his blazer to adjust the perfect fit, Gavril tried to imagine what would happen when the doors opened.

But none of his scenarios matched the reality.

The view once the door segments slid apart revealed not an office environment, but something like a palatial yet tasteful living room. Several thick white rugs were scattered over a slate floor. Half a dozen leather couches and as many low tables offered relaxing seats. Because of the Bean's nonlinear shape, the full bookshelves that ran along two of the walls had to flow in similar curves. Any wall space not thus utilized featured many framed paintings. An expansive skylight ushered in warm golden Pacific Northwest rays. (Climate change had favored their region with minimal destruction, and of course the ongoing remediation and carbon sequestration programs run by VKC and others were having good effects. Maybe even Phoenix would be livable again someday for inhabitants other than pumas.) A well-stocked wet bar and a behemoth SubZero fridge betokened refreshments, and a small home theater setup with a giant flatscreen filled one sector of the room.

No inhabitants met Gavril's sight at first. But in a second or two, giving him just long enough to take in his surroundings, that situation changed.

A door at the far end of the space—leading to a bedroom, perhaps?—swung wide, and Evangeline Kocchar strode forth.

Realizing he was still standing in the paused elevator car,

whose doors had courteously remained retracted, Gavril stepped forward to greet her.

Evangeline Kocchar, a billionaire by age thirty, now forty-something, looked as youthful as one of Gavril's peers. Her graceful stride accentuated her beauty, and she radiated a dynamism and intelligence like no one Gavril had ever encountered. Her understated tawny suit of nubby wool made his own outfit look as if it had come from the local Goodwill box. Shapely legs and well-toned arms conspired with the striking symmetry of her facial features, her lustrous cataract of blond hair and her demiurgic curves to steal Gavril's heart and soul.

Then she was upon him, close enough for Gavril to smell a subtle earthy perfume.

Gavril extended a hand and coughed rather than said, "Uh, Miss Kocchar, I'm—"

Had he died? Evangeline Kocchar had wrapped him in an embrace and planted a kiss on his cheek. The interface of her body against his somehow managed to feel like total immersion in a warm bath. Surely this experience should last forever.

But then the CEO of VKC stepped back, leaving just the ghostly sensation of her flesh. She only distanced herself so far that she could place her hands on his shoulders and regard him at arm's length.

"Gavril, you've grown to such a beautiful manhood. Every time I see you, I'm always equally surprised and happy!"

After some laggard confused seconds, Gavril could only say, "Uh, thank you. But what—"

"What are you here for? Why did I summon you? That's simple. I can explain in one sentence.

"I need you to kill Durant Le Massif."

5

Gavril held a cool drink in his hand—just a Shasta Crème soda over rocks, albeit served in a fine Baccarat tumbler, since he had deemed the prospect of further befogging his brain with alcohol unwise—while he sat on the couch placed closest to the large viewing screen. Beside him, almost touching, certainly in more-than-businesslike proximity, perched the ineffably powerful, alluring, and utterly baffling third-richest woman in the world. (The first richest was, of course, Queen Margaret of the British Commonwealth (mistress of Canadian tar sands, Australian mines, Malabar timber, Caribbean fisheries, and a host of other colonial resources), while the second was a globally adored writer of young-adult fiction named Diana Wynne Jones). The unprofessional nearness of this iconic person and her equally anomalous behavior when she had greeted him, not to mention her declaration of murderous intent toward her archrival (using Gavril as a tool), all induced in Gavril thoughts of cutting short this meeting immediately and rushing down to HR, where he would buttonhole Kris Troy and press the most blistering charges of sexual harassment and unethical practices against his superior that anyone could ever imagine, regardless of the huge scandal his actions might precipitate, and the harm he would do to a company he believed in.

But then he reined short his conventional, kneejerk impulses and stopped to think.

Kocchar must know that her actions were against all norms and not subject to forgiveness or alternate innocent interpretations. And yet here she sat, utterly unruffled, not nervous in the slightest, not tempering her injudicious behavior by one iota. This was outrageous and inexplicable behavior, even for a Wall Street Mistress of the Universe. What could account for such radical yet self-assured transgressions, except some larger, overriding, justifiable, and presumably noble cause?

Gavril's curiosity got the better of him then, and he could not leave without hearing her out and gauging whether her crimes against business-place propriety were offset by whatever she had in mind.

Kocchar's mellifluous voice was as pleasing as her looks. She laid a hand on her perplexed underling's knee and said, "There, you're comfortable, I hope. Is the ambient temperature all right? I can change it from here. Would you like a snack? I have some excellent hummus in the fridge. I love hummus all by itself, because it reminds me of baby food. But we can eat it with a crusty loaf of bread from the Yreka Sourdough Wizards. Delicious! Do you know that bakery? I've never been there, but I have loaves sent up to me daily. I can't really go out in public, you know. The Massive would certainly try to snatch me, no matter how much security I deployed. Even though he knows he would risk total evaporation. I've cultivated a hair-trigger response now. I can pull the plug on this universe in just a microsecond when I'm triggered. Still, I feel safest in the Aerie—at least on this track. You wouldn't know it from the look of things, but it's a regular fortress."

Gavril hardly knew how to parse and respond to this welter of cryptic information. He knew that Durant Le Massif, Kocchar's corporate nemesis, was nicknamed the Massive. But Gavril had never heard of this deadly angle to their marketplace competition. Finally, he responded as neutrally as possible.

"Uh, I wouldn't mind a little nosh."

Kocchar clapped her hands together like a six-year-old at a birthday party. "Wonderful! I'll make it myself. You just sit right there."

Gavril watched in wonderment while Evangeline Kocchar, CEO of one of the largest enterprises on the planet, fixed him an appetizer at the counter across the room. She carried it back on a tray, set it down on the low burnished table before the couch, and said, "Dig in! I remember how hungry you used to be after a day at school."

At a loss for words, Gavril made a pause by eating a few slices of bread and hummus. It was indeed very good. Kocchar joined him, eating delicately yet heartily. She was drinking a white wine spritzer, but the alcohol did not seem to alter her baseline affect.

When conversation could be no longer delayed without desperate awkwardness, Gavril said, "Ms. Kocchar—"

"Oh, no, Gavril, call me Vangie!"

"Uh, Vangie, you had me transferred from the Ghost Factory for what I assumed would be the professional use of my technical skills. Or maybe some kind of publicity gig. But then the first thing you tell me I have to do is assassinate your counterpart at DLM. What's this all about?"

Vangie charmingly dimpled one corner of her mouth with two delicate fingers and made a moue of self-recrimination. "Oh, damn it! I always forget that at this point you don't know anything yet. Would you be willing to watch a short presentation, rather than have me go through it? I've made this lecture so often, I finally had it recorded."

"Vangie, I am here to do whatever you want. Except maybe pull a drive-by on an internationally famous billionaire whose hired goons would no doubt gun me down before I even got close to him."

"Oh, thank you for being so accommodating, Gavril. Let's start the show."

Vangie's deft, red-nailed fingers on a remote caused blackout curtains to roll across the skylight. Then the interior illumination came down and the big flatscreen jumped into life.

Vangie herself appeared on the video, dressed more casually than now and standing in front of an electronic whiteboard on which a diagram was displayed. At first, Gavril thought the illustration was the famous VKC logo, the fractally branching tree. But then he recognized it from physics classes as a map of the conjectural multiverse.

"Hello, Gavril," recorded Vangie said. "What I'm about to recount to you might sound impossible and fantastic. But I assure you that every word is just the plain truth of my existence to date."

Gavril settled back on the couch, soda in hand. Vangie sidled up next to him, took his glass away and set it down next to the hummus tray, then held his empty hand with both of hers. He reluctantly acceded. No one could say his was not an enviable gig.

For the next thirty minutes, Gavril watched a secret biography of VKC's founder—totally at odds with her official life story, buttressed with charts, photos, and supportive snippets from talking-head experts—that resembled nothing other than one of the wacked-out druggy novels by the cult sci-fi writer Kindred P. Thicke which Gavril had devoured as a teen: books such as *The Three Brandings of Bickford Bizarre*, or *The Grass-hopper Lies Heavy*, or *Omnirot!*

The production concluded with Vangie making an impassioned plea.

"So you see, Gavril, although Durant Le Massif and I seem to be embarked on similar missions, we really possess antithetical drives and desires and goals. Yes, I want to fashion a universe in which I myself am personally secure and happy and safe, where no one or nothing can ever harm me. You might say that he does too. But at the same time, I encourage and cultivate diversity and creativity and personal fulfillment for everyone, timelines where randomness and serendipity and personal freedom play their seminal parts. The Massive, however, wants homogeneity and predictability and the remolding of all the multiverse into a semblance of himself.

"Now, our strategies and tactics for achieving our goals and for wiping out each other are limited and, currently, stalemated. On the part of the Massive, he wishes to place me under his physical and mental control, so that I would be forced to employ my talents on behalf of him and his vision. So all I can do defensively is to stay forever out of his reach, hiding out or, at a last resolve, aborting a dangerous timeline where he has gained the irreversible upper hand. That stymies his gameplan for a shortcut to success, but it also limits my freedom. And in the meantime, he continues pursuing his vile dream by other means at his large disposal. As for offensive maneuvers on my part, I have no alternative but to kill him whenever I can. Because all his networked avatars are invariant across all timelines, no counterfactual pruning or rejiggering on my part can succeed in eliminating him entirely. But I believe that this invariance is his downfall. If I can only succeed in damaging him in a critical fashion—especially if I find and target any of his keystone avatars, then the trauma might propagate across all his iterations and finally bring him down.

"And so, Gavril, I come to you for help. Because the Massive recognizes your closeness to me and the value I place on our relationship, you should be able to insinuate yourself as a double agent into his inner circle by certain deceits and carry out the scheme that will result in his utter incapacitation and removal from the gameboard."

The home theater went dead then, and the lights came up.

Vangie still kept her hold on Gavril's hand. She was gazing at him imploringly. And yet after a second, despite her wistful beauty, he withdrew from her grip.

A thousand new concepts and revelations roiled in his brain. Intellectually, he grasped the logic of all the physics. He could follow the thread of Vangie's life, from birth through years of confusion, chaos, insecurity, and abuse. But on an emotional, gut level, he just couldn't bring himself to buy any of it. Who could place any credence in such a wild-eyed farrago? There had to be some hidden, ulterior motive for Vangie's actions, for her dissemination of such a bullshit fantasy. Did she take him for a gullible mark? Gavril couldn't begin to imagine what her motivations were. Maybe this was an employment test of some sort. Or just a perverse prank enacted by a willful bored bitch with too much money and free time and not enough ethics and conscience. Were they being filmed for the cruel laughter of her sadistic pals? Whatever the case, he was having no more of it. He would leave with his dignity intact, even if it meant the loss of his dream job.

Suddenly he hated this woman with all his heart, for humiliating him and attempting to make a fool of him. Gavril stood up. "Ms. Kocchar, I don't believe one word of this insane tale of yours. I don't know why you laid it on me, or what kind of kicks it gave you, and I don't care. So I am going to say thanks for the drink and the snack, and I am heading back to my real work at the Ghost Factory. That is, if I even still have a job with VKC."

Vangie stood up too. She looked not offended or angry, but just sad.

"It's always this way. I should know better than even to try. Gavril, do you recall the part of my story where I learned how to bring someone with me when I jumped timelines?"

"Yeah, I do . . ."

"Well, I'm going to do that now with you. We are going to jump back to the timeline where we first met. Oh, not the exact unique instance, of course. That continuum evaporated when I jumped out of it before, the first time, fleeing Vardis Salthouse and his cronies. But this continuum where we materialize will be identical to our mutual beginnings, right down to the only difference—a few altered molecules in one sun in the Magellanic Clouds. Of course, by leaving this timeline, we wipe out everything you ever knew. But don't worry. When we return, we will reimplant ourselves into such a faithful emulation that you will never sense any difference. Again, divergent by just a couple of intergalactic atoms. That's how fine-grained I have managed to attune my powers. And naturally, the natives won't know a thing either when we return."

Gavril sneered. "Okay, I'll play along. When we jump to this new—or this old—branch of the multiverse, what's to stop me from just cutting loose and blowing your cover and changing all the history of that timeline? You really want to risk that?"

"Oh, there's no risk at all, Gavril. You see, in my youth, I believed that the jumper always had to become the dominant personality in the host body, because that was always my experience. Take charge and assimilate the other mind. But after a while I learned that I could decouple the subordinate consciousness of my passenger from that of their host body. When you make this jump, you will end up as just a guest of your avatar, a ghost in their skull. In fact, alternate Gavril won't even know you're there. You'll be a totally passive recipient of all their thoughts and sensory input, but that's it. Are you sure you want to experience that?"

Gavril laughed. "Sure, lady, do your best!"

Vangie smiled, winked, and then—

Gavril always made a point of getting home first after school, before any of his siblings, knowing that he often had to be present to act as their guardian, given Mama Ginny's frequent absences or lack of attention. That meant skipping a lot of stuff he would have liked to do, from just chilling with pals to playing sports, or maybe hanging out in the computer lab. But the daily parenting demands did not trouble him very much. After the horrors of his earliest years, nothing seemed a burden. He didn't see his life as unfair; he regarded the domestic necessities not as a duty but as a privilege. Despite any erratic or illogical or selfish or temperamental behavior from Mama Ginny, this was still the best foster home he had ever been sentenced to endure.

Adult Gavril, VKC employee, looked out of the teenager's eyes, felt the teenager's hands fashion a sandwich, watched and sensed the lifting youthful legs as he climbed the stairs to a bedroom where lay the mute, insensate body of child Vangie, roaming her ghostworlds unknown to any of those mere humans around her—

Considering the little girl with enormous powers and recalling the contents of that Aerie presentation, Gavril realized that the mind of adult CEO Vangie from their mutual timeline must also be housed now in this physical shell. But certainly she had kept her own independence, and could alter events if she so chose. Wouldn't she willingly terminate this lesson, this shared captivity, in just a short time, now that she had made her point? It must be equally tedious for her as for him.

Gavril strove somehow to communicate to the child that he was now convinced, and that they could leave. But throughout the whole process of teen Gavril's busy day, adult Gavril could do nothing. Mentally, he writhed and twisted, screamed and pummeled, yelled and strained. But he had not an ounce of agency or volition. As CEO Vangie had promised, or threatened, he was just along for the ride.

It took several days for invisible, bodiless, trapped adult Gavril to settle down into some kind of tolerant and tolerable complacency and resignation, numbed to his predicament, like a coma patient locked away from any expression or movement. He told himself that he was just watching a very long movie, complete with full sensory soundtrack. He began to empathize with his avatar, who—while he did not share any of adult Gavril's formative experiences—was nonetheless his genetic and spiritual twin, possessing in common with the hidden passenger certain familiar habits of thought, similar abilities, emotions, and desires.

For the first year of his imprisonment, Gavril remained more or less fully conscious. But then the enforced helplessness—he was awake even while the Gavril body slept—drove him into a kind of somnolence, a perpetual reverie empty of rational thought. He was aware of everything that happened to the native Gavril, but it all seemed distant, like a dream. His sense of time ballooned and shrank, then disappeared entirely. Adult Gavril did not go mad—he just went offline, like a modestly aware appliance that consumes a trickle of power while awaiting the press of the ON button.

And then came a critical moment, a day whose importance—detailed so many years ago during the showing of that secret film—gradually broke through Gavril's long sleep.

After setting Vangie down, Gavril had spoken softly to Kris. "Mama Kris, why do I not bring Vangie home with us as usual?"

Kris touched the teenager reassuringly on the elbow. "I'm not sure, dear. It's your father's wishes that she stay here for a while."

"Well, okay, I guess Papa Salthouse has fine reasons. But I usually try to feed frozen sister something nourishing after the service. Helps build her back up."

"I've got a couple of granola bars in my purse. That should be enough until we get home. I can't imagine we'll be very late. I appreciate your love and concern, Gavril. But everything's all right."

Still looking dubious, the boy nodded his reluctant assent. He moved to kiss Vangie on her brow, then departed, saying, "I'll take good care of the others . . ."

The sensation of nonverbal Vangie's cool juvenile skin against his lips still lingered as, for the first time in many, many months, Gavril experienced control of his body. He was back, in control again! He raised his eyelids. What a joy! He lifted an arm and studied his hand. How miraculous!

CEO Vangie stood beside him, her small but infinitely powerful and cruel smile just a small crease across her beautiful features.

Gavril looked down at his soda on the table. The ice had barely melted. His posture had not changed one micron. He thought, *She drugged me. No real time has passed. That was just the mother of all psychedelic trips . . .*

And then he recalled the tangible, eternal futility and the unfakeable quotidian sensory richness of all his years as a ghost, a parasite on his younger, alternate self, and knew there had been no drugs.

Gavril found his voice somehow. "You jumped us out of Salthouse's office before he could torture you, straight to our parallel world right here."

"Correct."

"You didn't jump to the nuclear apocalypse world, and then to Kocchar's home, as you did originally?"

"Of course not. There was no need to relive all of that."

"But that must've altered a whole suite of futures somewhere."

"Of course. All the ghost futures I visit mentally are contingent, subject to alteration. The multiverse is not predetermined. All paths are mutable. I take their shifting probabilities into account when I use them as data. They are all just approximations, extrapolations from variant starting points."

"You were inside child Vangie all those years, just like me? Reliving everything?"

Vangie's smile widened. "Not just like you. I could do as I wished, right up to the moment when we departed that track. But I didn't choose to deviate from what I had previously experienced."

"You didn't go crazy, stuck in that lump? How did you fill all that time?"

"I'll kindly ask you not to refer to my child form as a lump, sir. I was watching my ghosts. Every minute I can study the multiverse, I learn something. Resting on my back and viewing Vangies was really not much different than what I do up here in the Aerie during most of every day. I did fine. Just running out the clock until it was time for us both to go."

Gavril contemplated that information. "You brought us right back to our identical selves just milliseconds after we jumped. I don't have any new host memories to integrate. This guy is really me, right down to the last hangnail and burp. Those variant atoms out in the Horsehead Nebula don't pertain. I'm back in my twenty-four-year-old body, but I'm really like, what, twenty-seven or twenty-eight now? I lived all those extra years in another body. And you did too."

Vangie said nothing, but merely showed an expectant air, as if waiting for the second shoe to drop, the coin to fall through the mechanism of the slot machine and deliver its jackpot.

Gavril suddenly plopped down on the couch. "You've done this a lot. Lived a long time elsewhere, then come right back to—to the present moment, I guess you'd call it . . .

"How—how old are you?"

"I stopped counting after five thousand years. That seemed a meaningful measure. Personal best! But even that milestone was some time ago—whatever that expression might mean. It's a lot of lifetimes, but I've tried to integrate them all. Sometimes I do mix things up a little. But I can triangulate with my ghosts, checking out the record of my pasts, the paths ahead. It all seems to work out okay."

"Five thousand . . ."

"Maybe now you'll admit I'm old enough to know what I'm doing, right? And that's why *you'll* do whatever I ask."

6

Gavril had a lot of goodbyes to make. The exertions were both fatiguing and exhilarating. He was embarked on an unknown destiny. He tried to keep everything light, but that was not how he felt. He had a sense that he might not return from this insane mission. Or, if he did return, nothing would ever be the same, and he would not again be taking up relations with these people—at least not on the same terms as before. How could things just bounce back to the status quo ante, given what he now knew? His mental model of reality had been inverted like a dirty sock, and he was heavily engaged with some real cosmic-level shit.

The first round of farewells began soon after his initial meeting with Vangie. It was late at night when he left the Bean and went back to his apartment—moving like a sleepwalker across the darkling campus, his brain a whirlpool of conjectures, memories, and plans. Ten hours of dreamless, almost catatonic sleep served to restore him to some semblance of competence and mental acuity. Immediately after breakfast, he went to the Ghost Factory to deliver the cover story for his upcoming absence.

Genuinely thrilled, Kumiko exclaimed, "A tour of all our European R and D facilities to see how they can contribute to the Ghost Factory's project! Dude, that is one sweet assignment! I won't kid you, I wish it were me!"

You wouldn't, Gavril thought. *Not if you had the whole picture.*

Stan, Maff, Mateo, and Sanura were equally excited, congratulatory, and professionally envious. They all planned for a big blowout party a day or three before his scheduled departure in a week, and Gavril reluctantly accepted, although he knew it would be hard to feign enthusiasm and a positive, carefree attitude.

The next round of leave-takings was infinitely harder. It was the second summer since his hiring at VKC, and so Gavril's sibs were once again all ensconced in the parental home, not scattered to their various schools. When Gavril flew back to Ann Arbor, he was greeted like a conquering hero. The warm, loving embrace of his family was bittersweet, representing the happy past and a perhaps unrecoverable future. The whole experience was made stranger by the extra years' worth of memories in his head, which involuntarily overlaid his reactions and perceptions. His parents, Chet and Tina, were not Kris Troy and Vardis Salthouse, the domineering figures who had ruled over his counterfactual teenage years. His brother, Toby, and the twins, Blaine and Drew, were not the same fosters with whom he had shared the wayward home of Ginny Everett.

Shaking off these ghosts, Gavril made a heroic effort to feel at home, and eventually succeeded, albeit with a subliminal residue of estrangement.

Perhaps this condition was the palest version of what Vangie had to deal with every minute, as her personal timelines accreted, blended, and blurred.

Chet Bainbridge hugged his son and said, "Way to go,

kiddo! I'm really going to have to call on you as a consultant for my book now!"

Tina Bainbridge, a tear in her eye, kissed her son and said, "Never underestimate the power of a good suit of clothes. You need my help packing for this trip, just holler!"

The feisty twins managed to dial down their natural irreverence and sororal disdain and express their pride by creatively indulging their brother, plying him with excesses of drink and food. Drew even offered to cook him her specialty—a Detroit-style pizza, only topped with edamame, okra, and goat cheese—while Blaine gave her big brother her favorite lapel pin—representing the dour face of goth idol Taylor Swift—for good luck.

Toby punched his brother in the shoulder and said, "You are gonna be rolling in hot babes now, amigo." Gavril's mind shot back to that long idyllic afternoon and evening in the Bean's Aerie, after returning by instant and jarring cross-dimensional transit from another lifetime, just a few days past.

Rolling in hot babes? Well, maybe singular . . .

The forty-eight hours spent with his family was both weird and excruciatingly rewarding. When Gavril climbed back on the plane to Yreka, he felt a little more sanguine about his prospects. Was he not a smart and capable fellow, bolstered by people who admired and loved him? And was he not backed and guided and protected by a five-thousand-year-old woman? Who could ask for more?

Drowsy on the short flight back to the West Coast, Gavril allowed himself to relive those infinite, too-short hours after he and Vangie had popped back into their baseline reality.

Gavril's response to Vangie's bossy assertion that he'd be wise to obey her had been a pained silence, a begrudging acknowledgment of defeat in the face of superior forces, a subtle but recognizable shutting down and withdrawal from any close-ness engendered by their shared years in the same household.

Sensing this shift, Vangie dropped down to the couch beside him, and draped her arms loosely around his shoulders. But Gavril resisted, muscles braced against any further surrender.

"Oh, Gee, just listen to me, what I must sound like! Such an ancient bitch! She Who Must Be Obeyed, right? I don't want that to be the basis of our partnership. I have such a wealth of real feelings for you, you know. You were one of the only good things during many of my lives. I recall so many kindnesses and buffers you erected against my abuse. Do you remember, Gavril, how you kissed my brow as you were forced to aban-don me to my tortures? Tortures you might have vaguely sensed were coming, but which you couldn't prevent? I remember that kiss, Gavril. I carried it through a hundred thousand lifetimes, down a zillion timestreams, as a token of how people could be good, and not just awful monsters."

Gavril remained silent.

Vangie brought her plaintive, pliant face close to his. "Gavril, why not kiss me now again? For the first time? Or the millionth?"

Her lips were sweet, her breath honeyed. Her hot little tongue became feverishly active, and Gavril responded in kind. She dropped a hand to his crotch, where his cock had instantly stiffened, and he cupped her sizable and perfect pebble-nippled breasts.

The door through which Vangie had first entered did indeed lead to her bedroom, a space with remarkably few personal touches or accoutrements, decorated with a similar sparse sump-tuousness to the front parlor. Her bed was still unmade from the prior night's sleep from which she must have roused her-self, hours or counterfactual years ago. The sheets smelled of her perfume, an astringent, desert scent, and of her gentle sweat. When they were both naked, Gavril moved slowly, still a tiny bit suspicious of this turn of events, and reluctant to appear the aggressive boor.

But Vangie showed no such demure delays or cautious compunctions and charged ahead. Without any hesitation, moving deftly and with a sinuous ease, she soon managed to invoke and provoke every one of his core excitations, all the particular little individualized vanilla kinks that served to heighten his involvement and pleasure, things that other lovers had taken many bouts to discover and perfect. In the time it took her to ascend from purrs to growls to yowls, accompanied by Gavril's own skyrocketing, crescendoing exertions, they formed a single bipartite organism, old as time, new as their instant infatuation, which had but one reason for existence: total mutual release and surcease of want.

Gavril was not able to speak for a full quarter hour after they collapsed to the plush mattress. His brain was a placid bottomless lake. But below the surface cruised a few hulking monsters, formless at first, then assuming all the same insistent hectoring shape, until he finally was forced to channel their voices.

"How many?"

Beside him, Vangie opened her eyes, and Gavril got the impression that she had not really been deeply somnolent. She traced abstract figures on his pale, only lightly haired chest and murmured, "How many what?"

"How many Gavrils have you fucked?"

Her mien became imperious, but slightly pitying also. "That's not for you to ask, nor to know. It does no good to think or talk that way. Just believe and understand that right this minute, it's only just the two of us."

Gavril considered all his possible responses, ranging from

outrage to abject submission to slavery, and settled on a come-back located somewhere toward that part of the spectrum labeled "wry and cynical sanity-preserving acceptance."

"You don't have to tell me I was the best, because I am damn sure that's a stone-cold fact!"

Vangie swiftly and athletically flopped herself atop him. "Is that so? I'm afraid I'll need another sample before I can possibly agree!"

Their second time equaled or surpassed all the wonders of the first.

Before Gavril got up to dress and leave, around three a.m., they shared some pillow talk. But unlike most first-time lovers, their conversation related mostly to work.

"So," said Gavril. "Silicon Vangie brain. Ghost Factory. What's up with that?"

Vangie seemed eager to explain. "I'm hoping you wizards can replicate on a chip the authentic workings of my mind down to some impossible degree of accuracy. I have three tasks for which I hope to employ the brain. They are, in rising order of importance and difficulty:

"First, I hope to use it as an advanced ghost-viewer. If I could get it to sense—and display!—alternate timelines, I might be able to process and correlate a greater number and range of continuums than I can with just this poor little old organic brain, timebound and subject to fatigue. More information equals more options. Also, if I can get Vangie Brain to register ghost worlds, then I hope to somehow decenter its focus—free up and expand its remit. You know now that all my ghostly visions are delimited to me and my immediate surrounds. What if I could delink my visions from myself and come up with some kind of multiversal omniviewer? Survey a timeline from any vantage. That's one reason why I haven't made more advances against

Durant Le Massif. I can't get any closeup picture of what he's doing on any timeline, because I haven't ever been next to him. Our lives are not quantumly coupled."

A chill rippled down Gavril's spine at the name of the rival he had tacitly agreed to take down. But he skated mentally over that covert assignment.

"What are the other two uses?"

"When I jump now, I can take along a finite number of fellow consciousnesses, bounded by my abilities to identify and hold onto their life strings. I want to increase that number, into the thousands, millions, billions! Imagine that I discover a timeline so desirable that I want to transplant the minds of every individual on this world into the destination world. Mass soul migration! Right now, I can't do it. But with Silicon Vangie to help, maybe I could!"

The naked avidity for power that shone from Vangie's features in the dimly lighted bedroom scared Gavril a trifle. But in the light of everything else he had witnessed in the past few hours—or captive years—he found that he could regard her ambition with some respect and tolerance.

"Third?"

Vangie clenched his bicep, almost painfully. "The ultimate! For the Vangie Brain to tip over a criticality threshold and actually manifest my same powers! Using it as a tool, someone not myself would be able to jump like I do."

"Isn't that awfully dangerous for you and your plans and the whole timeline? Here you are, scheming and plotting up in your spider web, then someone uses a pocket Vangie Brain to make a jump and, boom!, your whole timeline is destroyed, right while you're in the middle of your plans. And wouldn't it be a one-time mechanism, like leaving a catapult behind as you sail through the air? When the person launches his or her consciousness, the machine travels with them? You haven't told me that physical things can make the leap, just souls."

"That's quite true—so far. But it might be different with an artificial, not an organic jump. Who knows? We'd have to try and see. As for putting that power into irresponsible hands, I'd be very careful about whom I shared it with."

Suddenly, Gavril recalled a point of puzzlement he and the others at the Ghost Factory had long lingered over.

"I gotta ask, if nothing physical can be transported from one timeline to another, where did you get a spare Vangie brain to slice up? I take it your skull is still filled with its original contents."

"Yes, of course. But that's easy. When I finally settled on this timeline as my destination, I made sure it featured what I needed. On this track, I was born twins, both of us equally empowered.

"I can't convey the sensation of arriving here not in one brain but in two! With no apparent diminishment, my incoming mind downloaded into two Vangies, doubling itself. There I was, my mentality duplicated in two bodies, regarding myself with two sets of eyes. And of course, being of identical minds, I and my twin agreed that one of us had to be sacrificed for science. We flipped a coin, and I won. Or, I guess you could say I also lost. With her total cooperation, my twin died an unsuspicious death, an irrefutable suicide, and I had her brain put into cryonic storage. This was all before I founded VKC and became famous, of course. I was able to erase my past quite well before that happened, and no one ever knew that the world-class celebrity Vangie Kocchar had had a twin."

"That—that is so fucking cold!"

"Not at all. Merely an expedient donation made voluntarily. Like giving up a kidney."

Gavril was not going to argue the matter. But it was at this point that he said, "I think I'd better be going now."

"Come back after you've made all your goodbyes for your final briefing and instructions."

"And maybe a fonder farewell?"

"Oh, of course! Sex is a good tonic! And I do like you so much, Gavril."

The celebratory outing with his coworkers, a boisterous, boozy affair during which Gavril's attentions were continually straying, had come off okay. A last Eye'n'Ear call with his folks had elicited tears and high feelings. The briefing with Vangie had encompassed clearly all his duties, goals, options, and alternate Plan B strategies. The sex did indeed serve as a tonic to his spirit—and, presumably, to Vangie's as well.

And now here he was at the Yreka airport, just a carry-on bag in hand, full of nice outfits selected by his mom, "stolen" plans of Silicon Vangie, and also one dire but innocuous-looking weapon, heading off on a mission that would either earn him a permanent high rank in Vangie's empire—or see him crash in dizzy defeat.

At first, he had wished he could see his alternate timelines, to chart the best path to success. But then when he had a chance to ask Vangie about what she foresaw for him, he held back and declined to know.

Who could live with that much knowledge, after all?

1

When Gavril Bainbridge crossed the heavily patrolled border from the European Union into the Trotskyite autarky of Albania, it was already early September, and it felt somewhat like returning to a homeland he had never known. He had spent the past three months elsewhere, acting out the mission that formed the ostensible reason for his travels: visiting all the VKC affiliates and outposts to see if the locals had any lines of research that could help the Ghost Factory. (A quest that could have arguably been conducted via the internet without ever leaving Yreka. But face-to-face interactions and spontaneous on-site probing were deemed to offer a serendipitous bonus of insights not available remotely.) It had been a wonderful experience to see the exotic cities of the EU for the first time in his life—especially with local guides arranged by VKC, many of whom happened to be beautiful women not disinclined, after hours, to party with and sleep with a handsome American coworker. (And should he be feeling unfaithful to Vangie now?) And professionally speaking, touring these foreign labs had also been stimulating to his intellect. But of course, hovering like a dark cloud visible only

to Gavril was his real assignment: the covert assassination of
Durant Le Massif, head of DLM Industries and archnemesis
to Gavril's lover and boss, Evangeline Kocchar.

And now, finally, he was embarked on the climactic stages
of the scheme. Thank God this endgame would go quickly, or
soon abort. Gavril wished only for this whole madness to be over.

In Bari, Kingdom of Naples, down toward the heel of that
disunited boot, Gavril had skipped out on his scheduled flight
to Bucharest and instead boarded a ferry to Durrës, a nine-hour
journey across the Adriatic. He had also ditched all his VKC
hardware by which he might have been pinged or tracked and
picked up a cheap and anonymous burner phone. From Durrës
he had ridden public transportation to the capital, Tirana—also
the global headquarters of DLM Industries.

He registered under his real name at a seemingly decent
hotel he had selected off the internet, the House of Leaves.
Only later did he discover that the House of Leaves was a former
prison notorious for its harsh interrogations during the despotic
1950s and 1960s, now repurposed as a surveillance-friendly
government honeypot for the small number of Western tour-
ists that ventured here. Knowing this, Gavril found the piebald,
weather-stressed red stucco outer walls of the fortresslike building to be overly suggestive of dried blood, and he never laid his
head down in his rented room without thoughts of what sad
prisoner might have occupied this same space. Ghosts galore.

As soon as he had registered, Gavril placed one phone call,
to a private number supplied to him by Vangie. The person who
picked up identified herself as Agnesa Bektashi, Durant Le Massif's personal assistant. Gavril explained who he was and what
he was carrying, an item for sale that he would present only
to Durant Le Massif himself. The response from the woman
was noncommittal. Gavril concluded the call by saying, "You

already know where to reach me, I'm sure, when your boss de-
cides what to do."

Having baited his trap, Gavril tried to relax by playing the
tourist.

Tirana was a drab city in a drab land, its buildings and at-
tractions only incrementally changed in the century since the
nation's founding, when Leon Trotsky had arrived here, exiled by
Stalin in 1924, assuming total command of the ancient land and
remaking it according to his own eccentric brand of Marxism.
(An enormous ten-meter-high statue of the old-school Bolshe-
vist towered over the Sheshi Skënderbej Square, and even in this
less autocratic and relaxed era the icon was regularly adorned
with floral tributes.) The current leader of the mad little, sad
little nation was First Secretary of the Party of Labour Pranvera
Hoxha, who had replaced her father, Enver, upon the old man's
death just shy of his hundredth birthday in 2008. It was she who
had finally opened up the hermit country to the West, inviting
new trade and business investment with promises of indulgent
perks, low taxes, and hardly any legal strictures.

Her major—and so far only—coup along those lines was
the relocation of the global HQ of DLM Industries. Since their
founding, DLM had always been based in Monaco. But when
the ruler of that pocket principality, the capricious Princess
Stephanie, had instituted a corporate tax rate of 75 percent,
mainly to cover climate-change-response costs, DLM had fled
to a more fiscally amenable country. In Tirana, they had constructed one of the more hideous architectural marvels of the
twenty-first century: a gargantuan brutalist ziggurat known as
the Pyramid of Tirana, or "the box that DLM came in."

Although it was only early September, the nation seemed
prematurely mired in a dank and overcast autumn—an omnipresent odor of open trash fires, pavements always faintly wet

and oily, trees gone bare, gunmetal clouds lowering—and as Gavril walked the city, the dispirited faces and hunched shoulders of his fellow pedestrians and bicyclists (the homegrown pedal-powered machines were the clunkiest Gavril had ever seen), along with their fusty unfashionable clothing in a wide range of grays and blacks, engendered in the visitor a sense of hopelessness and despair that he fought hard against. He could not help but compare all this grimness to the happy, bustling, sunny scene at Yreka, and had to consider the difference to be emblematic of the two rival corporations. It might not be the case that newcomer DLM had taken part in the formative years of modern Albania, and they bore no responsibility for the decades of repression and shrunken horizons and dimmed expectations. But they had slid easily into the current straitjacketed environment and lost no employees when they made the transfer. That spoke to the corporate culture under the Massive, which resonated so well with the Trotskyite autarky.

Gavril spent a week seeing sights such as the Petrela Castle, the Fortress of Justinian, the Et'hem Bej Mosque, the national park at Mount Dajti, and a handful of understocked museums. He ate at an assortment of restaurants, from those that tried to mimic EU cuisine to the humble places where locals dined. He became quite enamored of a combination of *fërgesë*, or summer stew, and *byrek*: little hand pies stuffed with an assortment of savory items. When he discovered the native Shesh i Zi wine, his gustatory needs were satisfied. Each night, alone in his room, he longed to call his family and friends back home but knew he could not, having assumed the nature of a rogue agent.

At last, after what seemed an eternity of idleness, Gavril's burner phone rang. The icy voice of Agnesa Bektashi said, "You will arrive at the Pyramid tomorrow morning, precisely at nine a.m. Report to the lobby intake wall, and you will be processed from there."

"I'm going to meet with Le Massif himself, aren't I?"

"Just do as you are told, and you will be rewarded to your satisfaction."

Having no other recourse, Gavril did indeed do as he was told.

Upon entering the Pyramid, Gavril found himself in the antithesis to the expansive, soaring, sunny public lobby of the VKC Bean. The low-ceilinged space, illuminated only by artificial lighting, resembled the graceless hall of some hypothetical Registry of Motor Vehicles consonant with Terry Gilliam's dystopian movie *Poinciana*. The far wall featured a dozen bank-teller-style windows. Those in use hosted an unsmiling DLM employee face in the frame, while those windows not active were shuttered. Each station was divided from its neighbors by partitions. In front of each station was a hard wooden stool for the "customer."

The place was fairly busy, but not thronged, as employees (wearing the DLM badges that sported the corporate logo of a single atom replicated in a shrinking line to the vanishing point of infinity) came and went, and outsiders on one business errand or another circulated among the windows.

Lacking particular directions, and finding the windows all equally unlabeled, Gavril chose a random empty station.

As soon as he got between the panels, sophisticated noise cancellation tech enveloped him in a cone of silence. A simple button by the shutter beckoned, and he pressed it.

The shutter Hobermanned wide, and a woman's severe and pasty face appeared. She wore her black hair in bangs, and her smart-AR eyeglasses dominated her face with their thick black plastic frame and arms.

"I am Agnesa Bektashi. You are Gavril Bainbridge. Your passport, please."

Gavril reluctantly passed it over and saw it scanned. Agnesa returned it.

"The system now recognizes you. Follow the glowing green floor arrows bearing your name. We will not see each other again."

The shutter involuted upon itself. Bemused, Gavril sat on his stool for a few seconds. Glancing at the floor, he saw the first arrow blinking imperiously.

At one end of the multi-bay intake wall was a door that opened at Gavril's approach. He found himself in a long corridor with closed, featureless office doors at regular intervals. As he traversed the corridor, a door would open at irregular moments and disgorge a DLM servant, all of whom ignored Gavril completely.

The arrows brought him to an elevator, which in its turn responded to his presence. *Ah,* Gavril thought, *Vangie and the Massive are this much alike. Both choose to reside in the penthouse.*

However, the elevator did not ascend, but made a long drop to some level of basement not revealed by any indicator. Gavril had his satchel clutched unconsciously to his chest as if to shield himself from any attack.

The door opened onto what had to be at least a portion of the private sanctum of Durant Le Massif, the Massive, that unique example of invariant avatars, many of them networked across dimensions into one calculating mind.

A big hemispherical room, painted all in matte white with domed ceiling, featured a dozen doors around its circumference, one being that of Gavril's elevator. *Very "Lady or the Tiger,"* thought Gavril with more anxiety than humor. On a low central dais were two white plastic chairs angled slightly toward each other.

If Gavril stood at what could be deemed "six o'clock" in the circular room, then he faced the door at midnight, directly opposite him—which now swung wide. Durant Le Massif entered and strode boldly over, stepping lightly up onto the dais.

The slim, youthful Frenchman exhibited the kind of archaic

formal hauteur and elegance of a silent-movie Romeo, tinted
with a more modern sardonicism. His suit was au courant and
impeccable, his coiffure almost sculpted. (Gavril briefly flashed
on how his mother would approve of the sartorial effect.) Upon
reaching the dais, Le Massif stood a moment, then smiled and
beckoned with a small ironic finger twitch.

"Mr. Bainbridge." His voice was cultured and mild. "Please
join me."

After taking a calming breath, Gavril crossed the space to
stand facing Le Massif. They shook hands.

It won't be with this grip, Gavril reminded himself.

"Have a seat, please. I believe you have brought me something valuable."

"Yes. The schematics for the Ghost Factory project, the silicon emulation of our founder. With these, you should be able
to come up with effective countermeasures against it, or ways
to sabotage the device."

"Yes, of course, we know you to be one of the main neuromorphic engineers on the project, despite your youth. That
is why we consented to see you. May we see the items, please?"

From the satchel, Gavril extracted the printouts—so subtly
wrong that even he had trouble distinguishing the incapacitat-
ing malformed architectures—and handed them to Le Massif.

The man studied them for a long time. Gavril tried to imagine the cabal of alternate Durants, subetherically linked, parsing
the schematics in a transdimensional loop or chain or swarm
of cogitation. This was the make-or-break moment, and Gavril
tried to subdue his breath and heart rate.

Le Massif finished his inspection. "Before we make you an
offer for these, we have to ask one question. Why are you betraying your boss?"

"For one reason only. She's evil, mad for power. I was granted

my first face-to-face interview with her, and I was appalled by
what I saw—sickened to be a part of her schemes. She shame-
lessly admitted everything to me. She won't be satisfied until
she's remade the world in her image. She has to be stopped, and
this is my part in frustrating her insane plans."

Le Massif pulled meditatively on his smooth, bluish-shaded
chin. "We see. You realize of course that our own inclinations
proceed more or less along those same lines."

"I'm not naïve. I know you have your own plans for world
dominance. But I believe that your way will allow more room
for certain talented individuals to cut their own deals. That's
why I'm here. I won't be Vangie Kocchar's slave."

Le Massif smiled. "Do we detect a certain personal grudge
in your tone?"

"Maybe. I won't deny it."

"All right. You have satisfied us about your motivations.
Would the sum of one hundred million euros be satisfactory?"

"Very generous. I accept."

Gavril's burner phone dinged.

"The sum is now yours."

Incredulously, Gavril looked at his screen and saw incon-
trovertible proof of the EFT transaction in his name.

Le Massif got to his feet, holding the papers in his left
hand. Gavril stood too. At the same time, satchel under his
arm, Gavril encircled his right wrist with thumb and forefinger of his left hand and twisted slightly, as one does when one's
wrist is sore or itchy.

The mildly intelligent false-flesh glove that Gavril wore
on his right hand began its almost imperceptible seepage into
its artificial epidermis of a few molecules of fatal nerve agent.
Gavril had swallowed the protective counteragent just before
leaving his hotel.

The seepage was more than sufficient to deliver death in roughly an hour's time, allowing Gavril to be safely onboard a departing privately chartered plane.

Le Massif shook Gavril's deadly pseudo-flesh with no evident concern.

Gavril hoped that Vangie's plan—the death of this timeline's Le Massif propagating across the dimensions for at least a finite stretch of grievous damage, due to the man's unique existential nature—would indeed come off. But he had done his part.

Gavril stepped off the dais and was halfway back to the elevator when Le Massif called out, "Please halt, Mr. Bainbridge. We wish a few final words with you."

The ten doors of the room not yet used all opened now, and ten more Le Massifs stepped out, all identical to the man on the dais. A twelfth figure emerged from the first midnight door. This fellow assumed prominence, while the others stayed silent.

"You see a few of our brothers in vitro, Mr. Bainbridge, the creations who will one day constitute the entire population of this planet. An invasion of the bodysnatchers, if you will. One of them just conducted our dealings with you. A most capable agent and emissary, don't you agree. A chip off the old block! It is he you have poisoned. He goes to his demise happily, allowing us to ascertain your true intentions.

"But unfortunately for you, these duplicates do not link psychically or spiritually on a quantum plane with our other crosstime primes in the same fashion that we do. It proved to be not a quality susceptible to replication in the lab, alas. Only natural gestation and birth confers that linkage, as in my case. These you see are all offline, so to speak. Thus, the death of one will not trigger the domino effect that you and your mistress anticipate."

Gavril felt numb, and his knees and bowels went watery, his throat parched. "Why—why did you even let me get this far?"

"We are always amused and entertained by the tactics of our rival. This latest maneuver was fresh and unanticipated, so we learned much."

"And my fate?"

"We think you already know it. What else could it be?"

A nod from the prime Le Massif brought the others into action. Eleven delicate, deadly poniards, flashing keenly in the cavern, manifested like magic in their several right hands, and the circle began to close around Gavril.

Absolute terror filled him. He regretted everything, longed to have followed a different path. He hated Vangie intensely, yet loved her beyond redemption.

Suddenly a sourceless sense of grace and calm and acceptance descended on Gavril, driving out all the fear and anguish and burden of loss.

I know for a fact that I've lived another life already, and I still live uncountable more, across the timelines. This is not the end . . .

But then, instantly, in a real sense, it was.

In the Aerie of the Bean, recumbent on her bed, where she had been watching ghosts for hours, Vangie awaited a predetermined phone call with less nervousness than if she had been anticipating the arrival of a takeout meal. The caller would be one of two people. She had seen future-shifted timelines where one man rang her, and other prescient timelines where the second person called. Also, of course, timelines where neither or both called, or a million different infinitesimally divergent combinations thereof. All contingencies, of course, nothing foregone or inevitable. The future was not fixed. She had tried to enumerate the variety of streams to get a sense of which one was favored by the gods of probability. But to attain any kind of halfway certitude in the face of such enormous calculations and observations exceeded her powers. This was an area in which the Vangie Brain could be of immense help. She could hardly wait for it to be perfected and come online.

Her phone chimed, and she picked it up off the night table. Durant Le Massif's face filled the glass.

"Vangie, my dear, why do you persist in sending this same fellow against us, over and over? He's never succeeded once so far."

"I admire his character. And in an infinity of universes, there's always a chance he'll succeed. I almost love him, I think. He has a lot of ability and strength and potential. Very loyal too, of course. I want him to be the one to take you down. He deserves it. And one day he will. Although I assume today was not the day."

"No, my sweet, it was not."

"This will never end, Durant. You know that."

"Ah, but it has to, however long it takes, if only in the heat death of the entire universe."

"The universe is not the multiverse."

"So very right. We will see you around. We predict larger fields of action for us both, soon."

The Massive terminated the call. Vangie sighed. And then, without bothering to rise from bed, she jumped.

The entire timeline where Gavril had just died, an annoying relic of another failure, died too, in an instant Heisenbergian collapse. With it went one iteration of the Massive: the smallest of victories but achieved at great cost. And it put her no further ahead.

Besides Gavril, the person Vangie most cared for was her father, Vivek Kocchar, and she visited him whenever she wanted a sounding board for her theories and problems, or just some company for an idle moment or month.

Sometimes she jumped into a Vangie avatar who was still

operating in the old ghost stupor that had characterized Vangie Prime's own youth. Then, she would have to reveal herself all over again to Kocchar—bring him up to speed—before they could sensibly converse. Sometimes she would land in one of the Vangie avatars who had already come out of the closet, having already made Kocchar aware of reality before Vangie Prime's new and sudden inhabitation. She could start debating intelligently right from the get-go then. Sometimes she even manifested on a timeline where her adoptive mother, Adya Kocchar, was still alive. Vangie would remain submerged then, undercover, and just enjoy the simpleminded pleasures of having two loving parents attend on her. But truth be told, she found her mother's good-hearted simplicity rather cloying after a while and did not often indulge in this particular scenario.

In none of these many visits had she been able to convince any iteration of Vivek Kocchar—whether still healthy or at death's door— to come back with her across the cosmos. He always held out stubbornly, refusing to be an integral part of any timeline extinction. A shame, really, as she could have used his daily support and feedback and advice. She never imagined taking him against his will, realizing that such a forced transplantation would result in an uncooperative, even suicidal Kocchar.

Today Vangie was in a hurry, and so she manifested on a timeline where Kocchar knew the full score already.

She came to him in his den, as he was reading a *Journal of Consciousness Studies*. Vivek Kocchar wore a long white ribbed woolen cardigan, as if cold. Her father looked placid but tired, almost Buddhistically serene. He put the journal down calmly and unhurriedly when Vangie entered. He peered intently at her, then said, "You've only just arrived in this continuum. Even without my gadgets, I can sense the qualia flux. No doubt from long association with my unique girl."

"Yes, Baba. As always, you astound me."

"And your arrival, of course, implies that you will soon be leaving, and my whole unique universe will be extinguished once again."

"I'm afraid so, Baba."

"Oh, daughter, what profligacy! If only you could settle down and be content with one life."

"My nature makes that impossible, old man."

"Too true. Well, what can I do for you before I disappear? Shall I recall the resonant words of the Bard?"

Vangie knew what was coming, from past iterations, but indulged her father in his pompous oratory.

"'Our revels now are ended,'" declaimed Kocchar.

"'These our actors,
'As I foretold you,' were all spirits and
'Are melted into air, into thin air:
'And, like the baseless fabric of this vision,
'The cloud-capp'd towers, the gorgeous palaces,
'The solemn temples, the great globe itself,
'Yea, all which it inherit, shall dissolve
'And, like this insubstantial pageant faded,
'Leave not a rack behind. We are such stuff
'As dreams are made on, and our little life
'Is rounded with a sleep.'"

"Bravo! Now, if I may speak of more important things?"

Vangie outlined the probable perfection of the Vangie Brain, and her plans for it, all aimed toward the ultimate frustration and doom of Durant Le Massif.

"What do you think, Baba? Is it feasible? Do you see any downsides?"

"Only the deaths of another trillion universes, and the derailment of billions of lives for your own selfish ends."

Vangie clapped her hands together with childlike glee. "Perfect! Then there's nothing really to worry about, is there?"

PART TWO

PART TWO

Over the span of just a few generations, the refugees from Earth dominated the culture and society of Mars, displacing the natives to large degree, and rendering them second-class citizens in their own homes and lands. True, these maligned "native" humans of Mars—actually, the descendants of the first colonists, those who had been resident for many generations, bioengineered to the specs of a terraformed Mars and breeding true thereafter— had themselves initially driven to extinction the few insentient advanced lifeforms who were truly native to the Red Planet, by way of their imported Terran microbes and outright slaughter and competition for niches and the introduction of gradual but irreversibly cumulative planetary ecospheric changes. But that was a case of *Homo sapiens* versus aliens, and surely no quarter was ever expected or given in that type of encounter. That old forgotten crime could hardly be racked up against the karma of the current generation of Martians and justify the sins of the Terran newcomers.

And the case of the Earth people was particularly galling. Welcomed gladly, starting several scores of years ago and almost down to the present, when they had had to flee the Massive, they were, of course, as fellow Terran rootstock, natural cousins to the Martians, capable of fruitful procreation with the natives, and sharing much of their cultural heritage from the Old Planet. Ideally, there should have been no struggle for dominance with their generous hosts, or desire to usurp the reins of power.

But the laidback Martian culture—marked by low interest in consumerism and acquisitiveness, and favoring contemplative and festive pursuits—proved no match for the aggressive attitudes of the immigrants— who had also brought with them in their hasty relocation certain new and superior technologies that allowed them to achieve economic dominance, leading to a corollary societal upper hand.

Happily for the Martians, their greater integration into the partially terraformed biosphere of the planet—once on Mars, the Terran physiology still demanded breathing aids, dermal shielding, and eye protection, not to mention an instant antivenom shot under certain wildlife encounters—allowed the natives to flourish in ways that the newcomers could not. And given the less-materialistic paradigm they embraced, the Martians failed to resent their losses intensely, or even suffer much sorrow at their fall down the ladder of society.

Still, it did occasion some sadness among the old-timers to see familiar institutions and places elbowed aside and replaced by parvenus.

One such instance could be observed on busy, noisy Cromie Avenue in McAuleytown, a lively strip of variegated structures from across the centuries of Martian colonization. There, planted firmly between the Venusian Embassy (now shuttered in the wake of the Massive assimilation of that planet) and a glass-walled natatorium, a large and impressive structure (whose swooping lines obeyed the tenets of the Neo-Niemeyer School and which had

once housed the auditorium of the Daughters of the Maiden
Landing Club (dining hall and library and game room as well))
could be seen to sport an aggressively flashing sign that proclaimed its function as Cleora's Desires of the Eternal Hills.

Earther credits—derived from transported treasures, since
Terran interplanetary banking systems had collapsed along with
Earth's human military forces—had succeeded in purchasing
the building from the fading, dwindling, and cash-strapped
Daughters, and converting it into a failure-proof, money-minting
brothel. To the credit of the Terrans, there was no discrimination
in either hiring or servicing. Truly eclectic and open-minded,
the gaudy whorehouse featured both Martian and Terran staff
of many genders, and diverse customers as well. Although, naturally, given the sociological and economic differences between the
two races, more Earthmen than Martians patronized the place.

Cleora herself was a Martian employee, serving at the behest
of the mostly absentee Terran owners, and functioned solely and
superbly as manager, majordomo, and den mother. Her large
golden eyes with their organic membranous filters; her small,
typical stature and attenuated but tough myofibril-enhanced
limbs; her wealth of naturally green hair, all adding up to a
charming façade, belied her tough-minded and utilitarian personality, a gestalt not untinged with sentimentality. Cleora
had been known to pitch in mopping up vomit, to mix endless jiggers of cocktails when the bartender was out sick, to
kidney-punch a troublemaker then heave him out the door,
and then to find time to give a feral flat cat a saucer of hydro-
gen peroxide in the alley behind the building.

It was Cleora's blend of practicality and compassion that
induced her to hire and house an orphan. Cleora had extended
charity to many a fellow Martian in her tenure at Desires, but this
instance marked the first time she had been able to lend a helping

hand to an Earther. She felt proud to step in where his compatriots had displayed only a blank uncaring face and empty hand.

The boy had been frequently observed of late rummaging at night through the food dumpsters in that same back alley favored by slithering flat cats, where the breeze-driven scatter of red sand grains that inexplicably continued to escape the terraforming overlays, like ghostly remnants of the planet's past, made a constant shooshing sound. His survival gear was patched and barely adequate, and he looked as if he had been dossing rough, possibly even under the stars that shone so keenly through the thin but sufficient Martian atmosphere. And Martian nights could get pretty cold, even during perihelion summers.

The boy ran off when Cleora first hailed him, and thereafter she was canny enough to bait him in absentia with hot meals placed nearer and nearer the kitchen's back door. After a week or two of acceptance of these morsels, the lad gained sufficient confidence to venture inside and eat with the obviously harmless and unimportant cooks, Cleora watching with seeming disinterest from the inner doorway to the parlor.

One night in the kitchen, amidst the savory scents of roasting meats and baking pastries, a breakthrough in conducting a dialogue occurred. One of the cooks, an Earther, began whistling a famous Terran tune in the boy's earshot: "I Lost My Heart to a Chimera's Smile."

The lad broke down in tears, and that was all the opening an experienced caregiver like Cleora needed.

In her loose comforting embrace, the boy finally and indisputably registered as a teenager, alabaster of skin, sensitive-featured, shaggy of hair, too skinny. He fostered a ripe odor, but nothing that a long shower would fail to erase. He accepted Cleora's not overweening ministrations—the grinning cooks went about their duties blithely, only nodding knowingly to each other as if to say, *She's got another pet project*—and his snuffling eventually ceased.

"My mother used to sing that song," he said, in a half-guilty fashion, as if the simple act of remembering his mother was perhaps a betrayal of something or an admission of guilt or even a duplicitous scheme to worm his way into Cleora's good graces.

"I'm sure she sang it beautifully. When did you last see her?"

"Just before Mom and Dad sent me away . . ."

The Massive's conquest of Earth had begun in Europe and radiated multilaterally outward over centuries of strife and contest. The displacement and extermination of baseline populations in favor of the aggressive artificial homogenous entities that poured forth from the DLM autofacs (which erupted across the whole continent after having mined the various lands covertly) had initially constituted a battle with many retrenchments and few victories, although anyone could see that the ultimate victors would be the Massive. Limited in their advances by the number of units that the gestational tanks could produce daily, the conquest was slow enough for many Earthers to flee offworld. Their destinations were various. Those who ventured solarward made a serious error, since the smaller but still significant settlements on Venus and Mercury were next in line to be swamped by the Massive, during the Cytheran and Hermean Campaigns. But so far, the group organism had not turned its attention in the direction of Mars and beyond; possibly they were just taking time to consolidate their gains. So the wary citizens of Mars, the Asteroid Belt, the Jovian moons, and other inhabited satellites and megastructures could still maintain their normal existences, albeit with an eye cocked toward any new campaigns in their direction—and also cocked for the rumored spies that the Massive might seek to infiltrate.

Safest of all, or at least ensconced in a place that would be conquered last, was Queen Evangeline and her Companionable Mind, resident in the Oort Cloud, one hundred thousand astronomical units from the sun.

"We lived on a little island, I don't know where," the boy continued, sipping at his cup of dilute Pesto Red Wine. "Just me and my folks. We had been there ever since I could remember. We lived in an underground bunker, and the Massive didn't know we were there. Until they did. They flooded in and my parents held them off until I could get in our ship and make it ready to launch. We had practiced for this day but kept putting it off. The ship was small and slow and in bad shape. Nobody could be sure it would even make it to Mars. I waited till the last minute, but Mom and Dad never joined me. I had to take off alone. I don't like to think about what happened to them. It took me over a year to get here on automatic pilot. I had a rough time holding it together. But I slept a lot, and there was a library module. Finally, I crashed pretty bad. My arm still hurts from that landing. I tried hooking up with my kind of people, but they were too suspicious! All the refugees had made it off-world nearly a decade ago. Me and my folks must have been the last humans on Earth! And now everyone thinks I'm some kind of spy from the Massive, and they just want me to curl up and die. But I'm not a spy, you know! I'm not!"

"One minute, boy." Cleora had to get up and uselessly offer a suggestion to one of the cooks until she could stem her tears. When she returned, she said, "This place could use a gofer. Someone to run general errands, help with whatever small or big chores need doing. Make themselves useful. A room in the attic and all your meals, plus a small weekly stipend. Don't trouble the girls and boys and others during working hours. Any assignations with the staff come out of your own pocket. But

I think you might make a few friends among them, and who knows where that could lead? You think all that might suit you?"

The boy's own tears had been wiped away with the back of a filthy hand, and he sought Cleora's gaze earnestly. "Yeah, I can do all that. I practically ran the family bunker, didn't I?"

"Wonderful. Let's call it an open-ended arrangement, either party free to quit without notice. Now I just need to know one more thing for tonight, before I send you upstairs. What's your name?"

"It's Gavril, miss. Never knew any other."

2

Gavril had been working at Cleora's for three years when the first of the Koschei, or "Deathless Ones," appeared. They manifested simultaneously with rumors that the Massive, having integrated their several planetary, lunar, and L5 conquests into an organic whole, was now ready to carry their exterminate-and-replace campaigns outward, until they had ingested the entire solar system. Their victory was not guaranteed, of course. Millions of baseline humans stood ready to fight with all they had, rather than be supplanted. But the past experiences of Earth and the other inner worlds did not bode well. The savagery, expendability, and deviousness of the Massive units, not to mention their mental coordination, were a combination of traits hard to defeat. Still, the battles might rage on a teeter-totter for centuries, and a steady retreat out toward the Oort Cloud would allow human life to continue for generations. Nonetheless, the rumors brought tension and anger, suspicions and despair to the cities of Mars. The atmosphere at Cleora's, always heretofore jollily debauched, a carefree carnival, morphed to an air of desperate pleasures snatched from the jaws of a whirlwind.

In the three years of his tenure, Gavril had fleshed out to a robust stature, adding inches vertically and wherever new muscles massed. More than moderately handsome, but humble, charming, and unassuming, he incited no jealousies among the rent boys, and much admiration from the whores. None of his small pay went into the electronic purses of the ladies, and yet he never lacked for lovers—mostly in serial fashion, rather than in rotation. His tiny attic lodgings, Cleora knew, from a sneak visit, remained spartan, with just an e-reader on a nightstand; a shelf of attractive terracotta-colored, wind-carved rocks scavenged from long hikes outside the limits of McAuleytown; and one image set into a cheap frame, printed out from the library module recovered from his crashed ship. (Cleora had gotten him some good money for the salvage value of that craft, although the vessel had already been picked over a bit by the time she could help.) A picture of Gavril's nervously smiling parents, the selfie showed a handsome young couple on the deck of a small boat, with a coastal city in the background. They must have been sailing away to their island refuge, in advance of the Massive, Gavril yet unborn.

Cleora had insisted that Gavril attend school when he wasn't working, and he had finished via intermittent online classes his secondary education in record time. Now he was enrolled similarly in a certification program at Pathfinder University, seeking eventually to be licensed as a spintronics tech. Using her own money, Cleora had invested in some of the newest prosthetic upgrades for her ward—anti-rad dermal symbionts, lung assists, and ocular shields—that allowed him to go about almost as easily as a native. Although of course he would never exhibit the organic corporeal grace and easy relationship with the planet that the natives did. He gratefully shed all the clumsy gear that stubbornly prejudiced or impoverished Earthmen needed, and promised fervently to repay Cleora over time. She smiled and pooh-poohed the notion, saying only, "I can't have my staff looking like a bunch of dusty backcountry olivine prospectors. This is a classy joint!"

All in all, Gavril felt pretty content most days. His work was easy and satisfying. His delicious whorehouse friends were more than nice. School was broadening and rewarding, offering a path to eventual self-sufficiency and usefulness. Cleora was a rock and shining beacon to whom he could always turn for guidance or help. The dread of the Massive was but a low-key, long-term buzz.

He had come a very long way from the lost alley rat digging through food trash. The pain and sorrow of losing his parents—losing the Earth—had faded into a melancholy background murmur, spiking at times to stabs of grief. But these pangs always receded, leaving Gavril's congenital geniality ascendant.

At this point in time, if questioned, Gavril would have said he had no grander ambitions in mind. The path he was treading seemed perfect.

But then on a cold Fifteenth-Month night, there arrived at Cleora's Desires of the Eternal Hills the first of the Koschei ever seen in McAuleytown, and Gavril's serene train was derailed.

Gavril's duties most nights were varied and unpredictable. One night he might have to sub for a sick busboy, hauling dirty dishes or trotting fresh bottles up from the wine cellar. Another night might find him using his nascent cyber-talents to unglitch the in-house surveillance system. Or maybe he'd have to act as a valet for the private trundlebugs that ferried in customers from far and wide. (Cleora's only nearby rival of comparable stature was Pavel's Parlor in the neighboring burg of Laswitz, a joint which was, in her extremely biased view, "a mere rutting stable.") The unforeseeable turns of his job were part of the position's allure. Never a dull moment!

The night the first Deathless One arrived found Gavril on a tall ladder, changing a couple of dead bulbs in the high chandelier in the big oval entryway of the house. A mural that originally graced the space when the Daughters of the Maiden Landing owned the building still remained for ironic amusement, since it depicted the highly imaginary scene of an antique spaceship setting down on the raw sands of an as-yet unterraformed Mars. From the rocket emerged a pack of stalwart male astronauts to be greeted by a bevy of truly fictional and symbolical Mars nymphs in diaphanous gowns.

Gavril had positioned his ladder well out of the way of the in-swinging door. But he hadn't reckoned with the hasty dramatic entrance of a larger-than-average fellow who blew in at the head of a group of more sedate regular customers.

Not paying attention to his forward motion, looking backward at his amused chance comrades as he bulled in, the self-appointed leader shouted, "Clear the way! I'm a ring-tailed roarer who hasn't fucked anything warmer than a hole in the wet soil of the Stross Agronomy Dome on Tethys since he started training, and he's got a huge load of spunk to deliver!"

Broad sweeps of both arms accompanied this declaration. One of the man's arms intersected the ladder, and over it tipped.

Gavril dropped his carton of lightbulbs—*pop! pop! pop!*—and flailed his own arms, before sailing through the air.

His accidental endangerer proved also to be his intentional rescuer, catching Gavril effortlessly, then setting him down on his feet.

Gavril glared at the fellow, wanting to unleash a torrent of angry recriminations, despite Cleora's long-standing injunction about customers doing no wrong. But then he halted before he could give vent to feelings that were already dwindling in the face of his cheerfully beaming antagonist.

Sporting a dense ginger beard and thick rufous hair, the man, a fully Mars-modded Earther, showed a burly form clad in some kind of gray and blue jumpsuit-style uniform intricately intelligentized and reinforced with onboard gadgetry and protective inserts and panels. Sturdy black boots completed the ensemble. On his breast was a stylized emblem that must pertain to the fellow's organization: the cartoon represented the head and torso of a wizardly looking fellow, showing some mature years yet still hale and hearty, signifying a master at the peak of his power and wisdom, with two clenched hands at chest level holding the pommel of a sword.

The man carried with him a breath of the cold and wild Martian winter air. He showed no repentance for upsetting Gavril's ladder and for sending Gavril into a dangerous fall. Instead, grinning, he merely congratulated himself.

"You like how quick and easy I saved your ass, kid? That's just how the Deathless Ones do things. Bing, bam, boff, and you're either rescued or dead, depending on our intent!"

The other new customers had already gone inside, leaving Gavril and the slightly manic stranger temporarily alone.

"'The Deathless Ones?' What group is that?"

"Oh, that's just our nickname. Highly accurate, though! We are the newly minted Legion of Koschei, loyal soldiers of Queen Evangeline—long may she reign! A most excellent queen, and our last bastion against the Massive!"

This curious assertion puzzled Gavril. It was almost as if someone had claimed allegiance to, and personal familiarity with, Helen of Troy, or to the wholly fictional Queen Sophonisba featured in that twenty-first-century multimedia extravaganza *The Wars of Demonland.*

Many centuries ago, when the Massive first began its conquest of the Earth, there had existed, so the fragmentary accounts said, one staunch opponent and rival, Durant Le Massif's greatest nemesis, a woman named Evangeline, head of some large nebulous organization. Many records had been lost or deliberately destroyed in the subsequent years, and current-day details were hazy and scanty. But it was said that Evangeline—somehow in the course of her cryptic biography she had been granted the title of queen—had finally fled the Massive, perhaps with a few companions and staff, but definitely accompanied by some kind of artificial intelligence dubbed the Companionable Mind. They had gone as far as the solar system's outermost marge, the Oort Cloud, where they abided in secret and seclusion until the day when their powers and services would be called for.

Gavril regarded the redheaded soldier askance. "Queen Evangeline is just a myth."

"Oh, is she? Then who is training battalion after battalion of warriors on Europa under her name? I will countenance the notion that the organizers might be some other faction, just seeking to cash in on her legend. But I doubt it. Especially having experienced the awesome jump button. Once you've got yours, there's no doubt about the reality of Queen Evangeline."

The man tapped a big blunt forefinger against the side of his head.

"Jump button?"

"It's the secret weapon that is going to turn the tide in this war with the Massive. The regular soldierly training they gave us on Europa is aces, don't get me wrong. Drilling by experts, implants, uploads, battle-sims galore. Why, I could kill you six ways from Sunday as we both stand here, without hardly twitching a muscle. And the weaponry each Koschei gets is top of the line. But humanity has pitted top-notch skills and guns against the Massive before, and always come up short. No, the jump button is the key. With that, we're invincible!"

"But what's it do?"

The soldier winked broadly. "Can't tell you that. Said too much already maybe. But you seem all right. You'll have to enlist if you want to know more. But you'd better hurry up. Once we reach a critical mass of Koschei troopers, we'll be carrying the battle right to the Massive's doorstep. You wouldn't want to miss out on all the action and glory of that campaign, would you?"

Before Gavril could reply, the soldier slapped the lad's back and said, "Enough jawing! There's acres of pussy waiting to be furrowed here—or so I was promised!"

Stalking off toward the inner door, the man appeared to have dismissed Gavril entirely from his mind. Gavril called out, "Wait! What's your name?"

"Salthouse! Vardis Salthouse! Proud member of the queen's Koschei!"

And then he was gone.

Slowly, thinking all the while of what had been said, Gavril righted the ladder. He went off to retrieve a broom and dustpan and new carton of bulbs. After completing his task with the chandelier, Gavril reported to his various line bosses and was sent hither and yon: fetching expensive candy and smokes requested by a party of rich Terrans, from a boutique down the street; helping to lift the spit that held a two-hundred-pound pig onto its supports above the barbecue pit in the woodsmoke-scented basement; repairing the jets in one of the hot tubs on the third floor. His actions, while adequate, lacked some of his usual keen focus on doing the best job possible.

During the busy hours, rumors circulated among the staff and customers about the extravagant proclivities, boasts, accomplishments, and challenges that had been promulgated, propounded, and sustained by one Vardis Salthouse. Gavril never actually encountered the lust-rampaging soldier face-to-face again that night, but he seemed always to be just a step or two behind Salthouse, picking up debris, soothing nervous whores, and supplying towels and liniment as needed.

Around two a.m., Cleora noticed Gavril's underperformance, his unwonted abstracted slackness.

"What's up, Gee? Love troubles? If the ladies aren't treating you right—"

"No, ma'am, nothing like that. I guess I'm just thinking about my future a little extra. Maybe the future of us all."

"Those rumors about the Massive getting to you, huh? All of us are in the same boat. But until we're nose to nose with the bull and can grasp him by the horns, we just have to go about our lives, doing the best we can. At least that's my take on things."

Gavril nodded, but Cleora wasn't sure she had gotten through.

"Why don't you go out in the back alley and feed the flat cats? A little break out in the fresh air will straighten you right up."

Gavril did as he was told. Visited his old precincts, dumpster heaven. While the flat cats were humping about his feet, circling their saucers of H_2O_2 in the semidarkness, he cast his eyes to the sharp and numerous stars. No one could see the myriad, ineffably distant nonreflective bodies of the Oort Cloud, of course. But somehow Gavril sensed the realm of Queen Evangeline massed over his head like a sword.

Cleora ceased crying only long enough to shout.

"Damn it, no! I won't let you!"

Gavril hung his head sadly but made no reply. This proved to be, perhaps, the only defense that Cleora could not counter, his wounded innocence. She hurled herself at Gavril and enfolded him in her wiry Martian coils. Her scent of Syrtis tuberoses swept his senses.

"Oh, Gavril, it seems like you just got here! Remember? A little fearful runt. It's true! You could hardly push a sand vacuum around the carpets. And so sad! But now look at you! You're a big guy, a tough man, smart and handsome, confident and eager to get out in the world, to make your mark. Why did it ever have to happen? Why did you ever have to grow up? Why do any of us ever have to get old?"

"But *you* never get old, Cleora. You're just the same as when I first came here. So perfect and wonderful to me."

Cleora held Gavril at arm's length. "No wonder all the girls fall into your bed! Such a sweet-talker."

"No, Cleora, you know I wouldn't sweet-talk you! It's just the truth."

"Ah, maybe I could have wished you did try to sweet-talk me—at least once. But it never did feel just right. I was filling in for your dead mom, and that ruled such bedroom fun and games right out. But I'll tell you one thing—when you come back here as a soldier—if you come back here, that is—I am going to jump your bones so fast, your boots will spin backwards!"

Gavril felt a hot blush suffuse his face. "I'll be back all right, Cleora. And then—well, we'll see."

"When does the transport leave for Europa?"

"In three days."

Cleora leaped up. "Damn, that's hardly time enough to arrange a proper farewell party! I am shutting down Desires from now till then. I don't care what the owners say, they can take the missing profits out of my pocket. I want to give everyone some time off, so they can really rest up and enjoy themselves at your sendoff. Well, how come you're still sitting there, kiddo? We've got to lay in about a thousand gallons of champagne, for starters!"

As Mars shrank in the rearward-telemetry screens of the transport, a blue-green-red-white marble, Gavril felt a rush of inevitable sadness and apprehension flood his body. Surrounded by a few hundred strangers, men and women, Terrans and Martians, all of whom, like himself, felt compelled to lay their personal fortunes and bodies on the line against the threat of the Massive, Gavril pondered how he could have tossed over his old easy existence so swiftly and completely. What had he been thinking? One minute he had a cushy life, and the next minute he had signed up for unknowable rigors and hardships, challenges and excruciations.

But then he recalled Vardis Salthouse's question: "You wouldn't want to miss out on all the action and glory of that campaign, would you?"

No, he wouldn't.

By the time the transport was halfway to Europa, Gavril had made numerous new buddies, and found, even among these untested but aspiring newbies, a brand of camaraderie lacking in the soft environs of Cleora's house.

And at the end of arduous weeks and months of training under the diamond domes of the frozen-ocean'd moon, with Jupiter hanging like a big eye above—a course of training he had sometimes doubted he would survive—that hard-won companionship had only intensified.

And then came the day when they all were to file through the medical dome and have their jump buttons implanted. The purpose of these devices had even until this moment remained a secret. Apparently, no small amount of further training, their last hurdle, would follow the insertion of the adjunct into their brains.

When Gavril got to the head of the line, he expected pain or shock. But the self-assembling device perfused stealthily through his skull and bootstrapped itself painlessly, once in place.

And then the jump button came alive.

Inside his mind a gorgeous woman's face appeared, and her voice filled his inner ear.

"Hello, Gavril. It's me, Vangie. I've missed you so much."

3

The amount of solar light reaching the Oort Cloud from humanity's stellar primary sixteen light-hours distant was infinitesimal, and consequently the habitat that housed Vangie and the Companionable Mind relied exclusively on banks of artificial lamps deriving their power from the reliable and capacious zero-point energy reactor at the core of their residence. Vangie missed natural sunshine immensely—she suspected she suffered a little from seasonal affective disorder—not to mention also lamenting the loss of the green and pleasant hills of Earth, and she would frequently jump to a timeline—usually a retro-shifted continuum predating Durant Le Massif's full emergence—where she could just lie on a beach for days, acquiring a nice tan and all the vitamin D she could use—all such benefits lost, of course, except mentally, when she jumped back to her pallid palace.

But such innocent, carefree timelines, uncontaminated by the Massive, were becoming farther and farther away, quantum-spatio-temporally speaking, and required more hours of dedicated seeking-out and triangulation via ghost-spotting than they once did. This phenomenon was, of course, emblematical of the deadly plague that drove all of Vangie's efforts.

Being invariant across all continuums and linked in a network of intellectual coordination, the infinite avatars of Durant Le Massif—just his natural-born primes, mind you, one per timeline, not invoking any of his billions of killer replicants, each one deadly as a shark—were able to carry out their bodysnatcher invasion across nearly every timeline that Vangie could survey. And as they became the dominant lifeforms across the multiverse, they homogenized more and more alternative paths, wiping out Vangie's own sister-selves.

Incredibly, the Massive was impinging on infinity—or at least the useful subset that Vangie inhabited—seizing the infinite sheaf of timelines and squeezing it into a bottleneck, through which only the Massive could pass. It seemed counterintuitive that one man could impact the multiverse so drastically. But his seemingly unstoppable success derived from doing everything *simultaneously across all threads*. Unlike Vangie, who had to operate in a singular and sequential fashion (yes, others of her own avatars mimicked the deeds of Vangie Prime, but not in the same universal and coordinated fashion as did Le Massif), the Massive was everywhere at once, and so his actions did not so much radiate across the multiverse as they erupted second by second in an omnipresent fashion, like a state-change in some cellular automaton game of Life.

All of this had a chilling effect.

For the first time in her life, the number of ghosts whom Vangie could access was decreasing. Once, as an infant and toddler, she had been swamped and overwhelmed by the swarming specters, all the iterations of her potential lives clamoring for her attention. How nostalgically and fondly now she looked back on those days when, swaddled, diapered, crib-bound in a cold house trailer, she had to wrestle with her innumerable sister-selves. (Hapless Steve and Becky, her first parents, her first victims, how little she thought of them these days.) The companionship of those once-scary avatars would be welcome today. But instead, the concentric shells of ghosts susceptible to Vangie's scrying grew hollower and hollower each day, depriving her of alternate wisdoms, alternate potentials.

However, one special set of ghosts remained, at least for an unpredictable while longer.

The Council of Nine.

No longer able to hide themselves away from Vangie's demanding scrutiny—was that because the Council stood out more easily in a shrinking cosmos, or because her powers had grown, or both?—the Council now could be summoned at will.

And at this moment, she desired their advice. So call them she did.

As she plucked each Council member from the depths of creation, she amused herself by recalling her father's frequent quotation of Shakespeare to characterize Vangie's abilities and actions. Vivek Kocchar, learned and sensitive savant that he was, had apparently felt that only the words of a poet of the Bard's immortal stature could do justice to his daughter's magisterial prowess. And so he had often quoted a bit of famous dialogue to categorize Vangie's scrying.

Exhibiting his natural aplomb, unruffleable even in the awesome presence of his unique daughter, Kocchar would declaim,

"'I can call spirits from the vasty deep.
'Why so can I, or so can any man.
'But will they come when you do call for them?'"

These Nine spirits certainly came, swimming up in their separate windows: three elderly Vangies, three in their prime, three still adolescent—all bearing the old homely, gawky features that represented such a contrast to Vangie Prime's beauty. Vangie noted that they appeared lackluster and low-spirited, failing to exhibit the usual dominance and sangfroid they had once shown.

"Welcome back, sisters. I don't believe I need to alert you to the difficulties we face, trying to rein in the Massive. His depredations are accelerating. But so is my Koschei gameplan. Thanks to the immense processing power of the Companionable Mind, I envision being able to bring at least ten million jump button warriors online eventually, just in my native timeline. Of course, parallel forces would simultaneously be instantiated in other continuums. It's only a matter of finding the time necessary to train so many. But besides the Europa base, I've now opened stations on several other moons. If these forces can succeed in pinching off enough Massive timelines, we might hit a tipping point where the war begins to turn against him. At least this is my theory. Now I'd like to hear your thoughts on this campaign."

One of the white-haired Vangies said, "Daughter, it's useless. There's no way we can win. This is what I advocate. Keep on retreating to ever-younger, conflict-free timelines where Durant Le Massif is still in his formative years, and enjoy a near-infinite existence in that manner."

A middle-aged Vangie chimed in. "Yes, consider the larger reality. The Massive exists only on human-centric timelines. And he inhabits many where there are no Vangies, to which we thus have no access. But in the infinite multiverse, there are also infinite strands where there are no humans at all. These places are inaccessible to him, and they continue to flourish, providing hope for the future. In the larger view of the multiverse's survival, the diversity of living things, our efforts are not only futile, but unnecessary."

Vangie banged her fist down on the arm of her chair and

shouted. "No! I don't get any comfort from picturing a whole bunch of flourishing worlds I can never visit! I want my old empire of ghosts intact, to provide me with an infinite range of choices and lives. I don't want a monoculture of Durant Le Massif. I want a plethora of my ghosts, and all the variety that entails."

One of the young Vangies spoke up. "Have you called the dude lately? Reach out. Open a line of communication. Always works for me when I have beef with a peer. Maybe you'll find out that he's happy with what he's achieved so far, and willing to stop expanding."

"I sincerely doubt that. But I'll try after we finish our meeting. Anything else?"

"Might I suggest," said another seasoned Vangie, "that you devote more study to the nature of the multiverse first, before taking any irreversible steps? Your Koschei program is somewhat alarming. To set loose so many non-Vangies with your own powers—where might it lead, existentially?"

"My soldiers possess only a limited subset of my powers! Believe me, I've thought this through very deeply. As for more study—I'm twenty thousand subjective years old now! I've spent all that time focused on nothing but studying the multiverse. Oh, sure, I had to accumulate material wealth and power first, and that was fun in its way. And I've had a few amusing relationships with the cattle. But basically, I've done nothing but consort with ghosts like you. I'm so sick of looking at my own face sometimes, seeing over and over all the million familiar actions which seem to be all I know how to make, my pitifully limited range of behaviors, that I could kill myself! That would solve things, wouldn't it? But what might happen then? When I leave a timeline, it's destroyed. Would my actual death mean the destruction of the whole multiverse? Is that insane, paranoid, megalomaniacal? Am I that central, that important? Should I just throw the dice? I won't be around to see what happens, one way or another."

The women in the ghost windows all made a susurrus and clamor of reassurance, negation, and remonstrance until Vangie yelled, "Enough!" and they fell silent.

"You're all of no use to me anymore. I've gone so far beyond all of you that you look like ants in the valley from my perch on a mountaintop. I can't believe I ever looked up to you or was intimidated by your wisdom. You can all go now. This is our last meeting. I won't ever summon you again!"

A short chorus of protests was cut off by Vangie's banishment of the Council of Nine. Good riddance!

Vangie realized that her father would say she was like Prospero, drowning her books of magic. But far from it. She was just loosening the ball and chain around her ankle! There must be no impediments to her will and vision.

Getting up from her seat in a large room whose smart walls could replicate any imagery in convincing depth (currently they displayed the pleasant sunny prospects of a manicured estate in the Caribbean where she had once lived), Vangie decided to visit the Companionable Mind, her only comrade and company on the station. The all-hearing entity could be addressed aloud from any corner in the station, but Vangie derived a kind of superstitious comfort from being in the room with its physical embodiment.

The large and well-supplied station secreted among the drifting welter of the Oort Cloud had been constructed using those same planetesimals as raw material. A very large crew of humans and machines had accompanied Vangie on her hegira to the edge of the solar system and had labored intensively for many months to complete her final redoubt. Then, given the self-sustaining and self-repairing nature of her new domicile, she had dismissed all the useless workers, sending them back to Mars and other safe habitats. Or rather, she had instantly jumped herself to an identical timeline where those inessential nuisances were already gone, for she was too impatient to put up with any actual loading of ships and false goodbyes.

One lone spacecraft, the *Counterfactual Queen*, remained docked for her potential use. Vangie envisioned someday returning aboard it in triumph to an inner solar system cleansed utterly of the Massive.

Traversing now the orderly maze of corridors and living spaces, labs and mini-facs, kitchen, bath, storerooms, and feedstock tank-arrays of the echoingly empty station, Vangie arrived at the room where her artificial doppelgänger "lived."

The primitive Vangie Brain first conceived in her days at VKC, once mere silicon but now hosted on more complex substrates, had culminated in this nth-generation model, an entity of incredible power and sophistication. Although the emulation of her unique mind had never achieved full sentience, never attained a "soul" or real volition—at least this was Vangie's long-term impression, also confirmed by many cyber-experts she had employed—the neuromorphic creation had otherwise fulfilled almost all her dreams. Just one quest had failed: the Companionable Mind could not de-tether its scrying focus from itself, any more than she could. Its range of visions were limited to whatever it became quantumly entangled with, not random, remote unallied things, people, and vistas. Thus, no useful windows into the Massive's own sanctums. Oh, well, such an omniscience might have been more debilitating than helpful anyhow, offering a welter of contradictory information.

But what the Companionable Mind could do was amazing.

Like her, it could see all the ghostly analogs of itself smeared out across the multiverse.

Like her, it could jump out of any frame and into one of its crosstime counterparts. (Such a departure was also universally destructive, and during trial runs Vangie had made sure to link herself to the Companionable Mind so as not to be part of the extinction event. Now that the Mind's talents along these lines were proven, Vangie had programmed into its core an injunction not to jump continuums without her permission.)

Its superior processors could correlate and analyze ghost visions faster and more deeply than she could.

And, best of all, it could bud itself infinitely, into the nano-injections that became jump buttons.

Every jump button was a fragment of the Companionable Mind, in constant contact with the original via sub-Planckian faster-than-light channels. Integrated into a human brain, the jump button opened up a line to the machine and her powers, localizing her effects around the human host.

Of course, each human host, thus linked, would also carry its connection to the Mind along with it on any jump.

Opening the door to the chambers of the Companionable Mind, Vangie faced a simple blank gray wall behind which all the real circuitry resided. A modest display screen was the only feature in the room.

The screen fluttered to life now at Vangie's presence, presenting her with her own face.

This always made her feel like the Evil Queen in the tale of Snow White, consulting her Magic Mirror, and never failed to provide a small moment of pleasure.

"Welcome, Vangie. How did the talk with the Council go?"

"Don't be coy. You heard every word those blockheads spoke. We're well shut of them now."

"Yes, I suppose so. Just the two of us at last."

"The two of us times infinity. We'll crush Le Massif yet!

Have you encountered any unforeseen glitches with the jump buttons?"

"None at all. The interface is seamless and instantaneous."

"Perfect. We only need to ramp up the recruiting and training. When do you estimate we will be ready to invade Earth?"

"In approximately ninety-three days."

"It seems forever away. I want to jump to an *Urknall*-shifted parallel which is ninety-three days ahead of us, just to have everything already commenced. But on the other hand, I want to be present during every last stage of the groundwork, just in case there are any hangups."

"This is wise."

"All right then. Carry on." Vangie turned to leave, then turned back. "Mind?"

"Yes?"

"I love you."

"And I you."

Vangie had a delicious meal then, putting off her suggested call to Durant Le Massif. But after that, further delays seemed pointless.

The line to the Massive was limited to normal lightspeed modes. He never would have allowed a sub-Planckian connection, since that would have given Vangie an entanglement relationship with him. So Vangie's call to her enemy would take sixteen and a half hours to reach Earth, and the Massive's answer would take as long to return to her. Her impatience would never tolerate that delay. So as soon as she launched her first audiovisual contact, she jumped into a perfectly aligned universe that ran sixteen and a half hours ahead of hers and got his response instantly. She continued to do that for each round of mail, destroying multiple timelines like Kali, simply to spare herself boredom and to achieve what seemed like a real-time dialogue.

"Le Massif! Spare me a minute of your time. I have an offer."

The Massive appeared on Vangie's screen. Like Vangie, he never seemed to age. But whereas her immortality derived from cross-cutting her mind into different, perpetually younger bodies on appropriately staggered timelines, his was a more existential condition, part of his sui generis nature as the multiverse's lone invariant being. Vangie's theory was that the constant homeostatic feedback amongst all of the Massive avatars fostered adherence to an unchanging Platonic archetype of who Durant imagined himself to be.

Durant Le Massif's sneer gave the lie to his dapper handsomeness. "Hail, Queen of Nothing! Are you ready to surrender yet?"

"No capitulation has ever crossed my mind, Durant, especially since I am winning."

"Oh, really? When's the last time you stepped on the soil of Earth?"

"Just today. Only it was an Earth that is not yours yet. But you know, just as well as I, that the way we are playing the game now, this is a battle to the finish, when only one of us will be allowed to exist. But what if we both laid down our arms and were content with what we have so far? We've roughly divided the solar system in half. Why not stabilize the division as it is, and extend it to the stars, once we learn how to go there? Every time me and the rest of humanity get a new star system, the Massive gets one too. What do you say to that?"

"I say, why settle for half the cake when I can have it all?"

"You are not reckoning with my newest forces. The Koschei are unlike anything you know, and they will take you down."

"Let them try. I will see you soon in your cold, dark, haunted palace, and you will be happy to become my slave."

"Go get fucked by a million of your buggering clones at once!" Vangie broke the connection.

She stalked about the station aimlessly, and then decided to visit her father.

She chose a thread where Vivek Kocchar retained all the memories of all her previous visits.

She found the ancient, now-bearded fellow lying in bed, in the end stages of his cancer. He looked, thought Vangie, serenely desolated, contentedly bereft, if such a paradoxical condition could be countenanced.

"Baba, I am here to wish you well, and to get your advice. But first, won't you choose to accompany me when I depart? I have a sense this might be our final meeting."

Kocchar expressed no distress or pleasure, made no accusation or excuse. "No, Evangeline, this lost kingdom is my fate. I am resigned to it. 'Men must endure / Their going hence, even as their coming hither.'"

"Oh, you damn fool!"

Kocchar registered a faint smile. "'When we are born, we cry that we are come / To this great stage of fools.'"

"For Christ's sake, quit your endless useless self-preening erudition!"

"'How sharper than a serpent's tooth it is / To have a thankless child!'"

This last maxim actually caused Vangie to feel mildly rebuked. She was infinitely more powerful and competent than this helpless elderly savant. She would act the queen then, not a vicious daughter.

"You know of my scheme with the Koschei. Have you given any more consideration to possible flaws?"

"Only this. How many threads of the multiverse have you snapped in your career? No more than a million probably. And so far as we know, the multiverse has not suffered for it. But what happens when millions upon millions of threads are snapped every minute by your soldiers? Will all this snipping away at the fabric of the multiverse have any effect? One might think not. After all, the multiverse is infinitely extensive. Except that your own theories involve the categorization of certain timelines as more critical than others. That's at the very heart of how you hope to take the Massive down. Could all these terminations begin to have unforeseen cascade effects? It's something to consider."

"Yes, perhaps. But what other choice do I have?"

"None, really. Except to give everything up, all your ambitions and dreams and strategies, and see what happens."

"That's the same counsel of defeat my own crones gave me! I won't have it!"

"Ah, well, then, continue as you wish. But I hope that you do not find yourself saying,

'I could be bounded in a nutshell and
'count myself a king of infinite space, were it not
'that I have bad dreams.'"

"Goodbye for the final time, old man." Vangie placed a cold chaste kiss on Kocchar's brow.

"Old man? Never. It's you who have grown so stale and old. 'We that are young / Shall never see so much, nor live so long.'"

Vangie's exit added the final period to Kocchar's quote and to his whole timeline.

4

The moon was hell. Never being able to step outside your combat suit for a shower or a real drink and meal or a lover's touch, or the feel of wind or rain. Subsisting on stimulants and nutri-paste and your own recycled wastes. Breathing pungent air. Wincing against the harsh lunar light even with helmet filters in place. Unable to do more than slightly hush the constant stream of intra-platoon chatter in your earbuds. Sleeping in a crater's shadow, behind a rock pillar, while standing up in your rigidified suit so as to be able to spring quickly into action at the first hint of enemy attack. A soldier's life in ancient times had perhaps been objectively harder: braving the elements, getting infections, being splattered with the blood and guts and brains of your buddies, eating things more repugnant than nutri-paste, like rats and insects. But there had been a primal, homely centeredness in such tribulations, the familiar sensibility of a harried animal, the shared subliminal sempiternal consciousness of some hominid on the plains of Africa, facing down a big savage cat with just a spear and a broken leg.

There were only two things that made being a soldier in this lunar campaign tolerable.

One's mates, the whole beautiful, cursed, fearless, foul-mouthed, eternally loyal posse of Koschei.

And the fallback of the jump button, knowing you had an instant route out of almost any bad situation. And of course, along with that godlike practicality came the emotional lifeline granted by the implant: being able to talk at any time with Queen Evangeline, the motivator and general, the wizard and demon, the very icon of humanity's aspirations for victory.

Or if not precisely with the queen herself—a revelation of the true identity behind the implant became quickly apparent once a soldier started using the jump button—then with the queen's next closest relation, the Companionable Mind.

And so Gavril—himself reduced to just a single, easily combat-shoutable shorthand name, Gee, behind which, like all of such cognomens, lurked a handily graspable, talismanic signature identity: joker, wise mouth, brainiac, lover, stoic, weapons expert, strategist, farm boy, berserker, or, in his case, orphan—stood shoulder to shoulder with Zohar, Badura, Memphis, Haddon, Griffard, Zuzana, Tasso, Roylene, Banita, Drizzle, Jirga, and a dozen other dogfaces: Martians, Earthers, Venusians, Belters, Jovians, all allied to drive the Massive back and back and back to its original nest, and then to extinction.

Not that success was guaranteed, or even trending, of course. Gavril had seen a lot of martial setbacks since he had entered the combat arena, along with a few hard-won and cherished advances. The Battle of Mare Crisium had certainly been a total clusterfuck. But then had come the bold Edge of the Sword foray up into the Montes Apenninus, where afterward the corpses of Massive clones had covered the ground like autumn leaves under a forest of Terran trees. It was hard to get the big picture, naturally, the grand assessment composed of the cumulative happenings across thousands and thousands of frontlines spread out around the solar system. The officers were not liberal with news and conclusions. And one's personal range of data was limited to the next crater over, and perhaps to the look on the face of one of the Massive clones as you grappled hand to hand with the monster, or got it in the sniper sights of your weaponry. Out of such limited datapoints, a simple soldier like Gavril could assemble only the most rudimentary sense of the war's progress, even after the whole first year of fighting he had already endured.

And Queen Evangeline—the Companionable Mind—was even less generous with information, keeping a relentless focus instead on selecting the best possible minute-to-minute jumps to accomplish one's goals.

Gavril recalled how it had been right after the moment when he first received his implant, and a voice spoke in his brain, accompanied by the ghostly perception of a beautiful, famous female face.

"Hello, Gavril. It's me, Vangie. I've missed you so much."

Gavril formed words in his brain in response, without uttering them aloud. "Queen Evangeline? You're at the other end of this link? I don't really know what to say. They never told me . . . Well, you know *my* name, that figures. But how can you say you've missed me? We've never met—have we?"

Gavril tried to picture Queen Evangeline moving in disguise through Cleora's whorehouse, masquerading as one of the joy girls, enacting something out of an ancient Arabian tale, royalty come down to a commoner's level for a taste of the prole existence.

"We have, Gavril, but not on this timeline. It's a long story, and one that we can discuss perhaps during some calm moments. But first we have to get you up to speed on your new capabilities."

"Queen Evangeline—"

"Just Vangie, Gavril. We will be talking often, and concision is a virtue."

"Vangie? Okay. Vangie, are you talking with all the other soldiers at the same time you're talking to me?"

"Yes, Gavril, I am. Very astute of you."

"But how is that possible?"

"I am not the mortal queen herself, Gavril, nor limited by her human brain. I am her emulation, an artificial creation resident on a hardware platform. I do not share her soul, or even her memories. At least not her memories as lived engrams. There proved to be no way to upload the real queen, no matter how hard her scientists tried. It turns out that such wholescale mind transcription and duplication, long a dream, is not technically doable. So I have received many of the queen's memories in audiovisual playback form, and transcriptions of her oral histories, as if watching an entertainment or swotting up a text. I remember them, but only as vicarious incidents. I am but a high-grade lifebox of the real queen."

"Oh."

"Now that I've satisfied your curiosity as to my identity and nature, allow me to teach you about the jump button."

"You said something about 'not on this timeline.' That must mean the universe is composed of many timelines. A regular multiverse, like scientists have long speculated."

Vangie's voice was a pleasing balm. "You're so smart, Gavril! Many of your fellow Koschei are having trouble with these concepts even as I strive to make them explicit. But you picked it up just from a hint! I can see that you're going to be an exemplary warrior! Yes, the multiverse exists. Let me show you. Here is a suite of divergent continuums immediately adjacent to your baseline."

As if he were viewing a heads-up display in his helmet visor or an augmented reality overlay, Gavril's brain flooded with an initially bewildering, almost overwhelming array of ghosts: his active, noisy avatars up and down the multiverse, all slightly shifted by circumstances from his "real" status.

"Your jump button," continued Vangie, "will allow you to quit your home thread and leap to another thread based on your unique selection. You will start living that new life immediately, no lag, with all its attendant circumstances. Arriving on your new thread, you manifest mentally in the body of your avatar, and instantly share his memories. But as the invasive personality, the conqueror, you assume dominance. Just a law of cross-dimensional physics. The process of memory-integration is a little difficult at first—and of course it can be more or less troublesome based on the degree of divergence—but you'll soon get the hang of it."

Gavril pondered this wealth of extravagant, paradigm-shifting knowledge for several minutes, during which Vangie did not hector him for a response. Finally, he said, "This is a soldier's ultimate weapon. I'm pinned down by enemy fire—*bam*, I jump to a timeline where I'm not under fire at all. Faced with an uncrossable chasm, I jump to a thread where there's already a bridge. Any man would be invulnerable!"

"Almost, but not quite, Gavril. There's always still the possibility of being taken by surprise by the enemy before you can jump. Death still awaits the unlucky and the unwary, as for any soldier throughout history. And then there's also the chance of making a bad jump. I am the one in charge of presenting a limited suite of options to you. I won't select or privilege any particular one—that final decision and choice remains up to you. The human will and human creativity of each soldier on the battlefield must trump mine. Queen Evangeline believes that only the unfettered human mind can counter the programmatic assaults of the Massive. And I am only an artificial personality, not gifted with this numinous human capability. So during combat I will present you with an almost continuous matrix of timelines, you rapidly assess them, then make your jump."

"This still sounds awesome and unbeatable!"

"Yes, it is a vast upgrade, taking control of one's destiny. But remember this: I will be simultaneously doing the same thing for millions of your peers. In addition, I am always carrying out some short-term forecasting of your options to exclude any that have a high probability of leading to an undesirable outcome. It's as if I am playing many millions of games of three-dimensional chess at once. It can get pretty busy."

"Forecasting? How can you do that?"

"You surely know the concept of the Urknall, or big bang. Every timestream has myriad parallel flows which are shifted forwards or backwards by any discrete duration, thanks to staggered occurrences of the Urknall in the content of hyper-time."

"Okay, that's fine, no more big concepts, please. You're making my head hurt. I am totally willing to take your word for it. So not only can you see all my alternate lives, but also possible outcomes of my choices. Very good. I'll just trust that you're gonna present me with the best selections from my catalog."

"That is certainly what I intend to do, Gavril. But you're right to say that talk will accomplish only so much towards getting you intimate with your new powers. That is why we must begin a rigorous but short training session immediately. Follow the new orders from your officers now."

His inner dialogue with the vivid image of Vangie suddenly ceased, and Gavril's awareness unfolded outward, along the familiar vectors of his normal senses. Suddenly he realized he was still inside the medical dome, and the technician was just lowering the injector gun away from Gavril's temple. His shot had occurred mere seconds ago.

"Okay, soldier," said a supervisory noncom, "get out onto the drill field, double time!"

Under the diamond dome, Europa's surface had been

smoothed and layered with artificial plastic turf, atop which numerous buildings placidly sat, as if on an innocent Terran playing field or parade ground, all oblivious to the giant pregnant form of Jupiter with its angry red omphalos spot looming above.

Gavril joined his fellow platoon members who had all received their own implants. Everyone wore a look of stunned assimilation, and Gavril reasoned that his face must show the same affect. Unlike at any other such gathering before being called to attention, the soldiers maintained a nervous silence.

Sergeant Brasch, his Caucasian features darkened both by melanin enhancements and by his upbringing on actinic Mercury, addressed them.

"I believe you dogfaces will recognize this weapon, since you've all been trained on it. A Mark Twelve Razor Ogre. You all know that it fires one hundred compressed-matter pellets per second that can shred a person into a heap of hamburger. This one is fully loaded and armed."

The sergeant demonstrated with a whirring blast into the turf, which exploded the green rug and dug a shallow depression in the stony surface.

"One soldier at a time, I am going to take aim at each of you and count down from ten before triggering the Ogre. You will use your new jump button abilities to escape death, or you will die. I know we've invested a lot of time and expense in training you this far, and it will all go to waste if you buy the farm. But if you can't master the jump powers, then you're really of no use as a Koschei. Pretty harsh, sure, but you all signed on voluntarily. Okay, who's first?"

Vangie reappeared in Gavril's head. "Do you want to get it over with, Gavril? I'm confident you'll succeed. You're a natural. All you have to do is focus your whole being into a leap. Weaken your old attachments, feel the attraction of your new destiny, then hurl yourself into it! It will get easier every time too. And of course, I'll help. This is the same way that Queen Evangeline herself first learned to jump. She was at the point of death, and her only escape was to leap across the dimensions!"

Gavril felt flattered that Vangie had chosen to address him in such a confidence-inspiring manner—although he suspected that every other soldier was receiving the same encouraging prompts—and he was emboldened to agree.

"I'll go first, Sarge."

His fellow dogfaces regarded Gavril with a wide range of expressions, from approval to jealousy to pity to disdain.

"Gavril, good man. Best of luck. I'll see you on the far side of now."

Brasch leveled the weapon at Gavril as his peers hastily moved off, leaving him isolated in a sphere of potential destruction. Gavril closed his eyes, the better to concentrate on Vangie's presentation.

"Ten . . ."

A vivid ream of timelines fanned out in Gavril's mind. He saw himself saved by the mechanical failure of the weapon. He saw himself saved by a micrometeorite piercing the dome and striking Brasch down. He saw himself saved by Brasch having a heart attack. He saw himself saved by a sudden sinkhole into a lava tube opening up beneath him. He saw . . . he saw . . . he saw . . .

". . . seven . . . six . . ."

"Pick one soon, Gavril," Vangie counseled.

None of the options struck Gavril as entirely optimal. Suddenly, inspiration burst upon him. "Vangie, show me the stream where the entire platoon has already been tested and passed."

"Oh, that's clever, Gavril. Here it is."

". . . two . . . one . . . zero!"

Gavril made a clenched fist out of his soul, turned his mind into a compressed spring, his heart into a supernova on the verge of blowing gravity's fetters, then released it all in a propulsive outward leap.

He opened his eyes.

Sergeant Brasch was regarding the Ogre rifle in his hands as if it had been a snake who bit him. "Twenty goddamn pod-cassette failures in a row! I never would've believed such a thing could happen. Fuck me with a rusty spoon! Duster, you were shaking so much I swore at least you'd get taken out."

Duster, a slim young redhaired woman with a Temple of Human Potential tattoo on her brow, stood taller and essayed a nervous grin. "No way, Sarge, I was just limbering up my time-jump legs afore the big spring!"

"All right, company dismissed!"

The elated dogfaces ambled off, laughing and congratulating each other on their successful rites of passage. But Gavril, puzzled, remained behind to speak with Vangie.

"They all seem to think they each jumped into this timeline on their own. But I was the one who got us all here, wasn't I?"

"In one sense, yes. In another sense, no. Their remembered histories are as accurate as yours. They each had to make a successful trial against the gun to end up here, and then you joined the timeline that manifested the cumulative results of their individual efforts."

"So they don't remember the timeline where I went first and saved them all?"

"No, Gavril, only you retain the memories from your point of origin. Now, if you and another person had jumped in tandem from the exact same genesis point to the exact same destination, then you'd both share matching memories."

"Can you coordinate such a leap between two people with jump buttons?"

"Yes. And Queen Evangeline herself can draft others in her

wake even if they have no buttons, depositing her passengers in the same continuum as herself."

"How about coordinating among three, or four, or five?"

"That too. But each participant has to make precisely the same choice as the rest. And the pressures of combat might hinder such quick coordination."

"So whenever I jump, I'm going to end up with strangers—people who don't really know me and my history?"

"Not necessarily. If you had chosen one of those other paths I first showed you, a less divergent one, everyone would have remembered that you went first, and so forth."

Gavril slowly waggled his heavy head. "Too freaking much. Anyhow, I guess this new talent is going to come in pretty handy."

Gavril began walking back to his barracks.

"Hey, Vangie, why can't I use my jump button just to skip off to paradise and forget this whole filthy war?"

"You could. But I don't believe you will. For one thing, you signed up for this war because you wanted to help save humanity. That hasn't changed, has it?"

Gavril recalled again how impressed he had been with Vardis Salthouse and the mythic trooper's proclamation of the glories that awaited.

"No."

"Second, I think you should realize now that this war is being fought across nearly every timeline already, and there are no paradises left."

"Oh."

"And lastly, if you or any other soldier were to do such a thing, I have been programmed to enact a penalty. As soon as you deserted, I would enforce a subsequent jump on you, into a hell world, and then sever our connection, leaving you permanently stranded."

"Hell world, huh?"

"Would you care to see some samples?"

"Uh, no, that won't be necessary. I'm ready to kick some Massive ass."

"Me too, Gavril. Together we'll win this war for our queen, no matter how long it takes."

5

Zohar, Badura, Memphis, Haddon, Griffard, Zuzana, Tasso, Roylene, Banita, Drizzle, Jirga, Duster . . . Gavril had a hard time remembering their faces, their voices, the jokes they had shared, the magnificent kills they had made, the brutal, bastard, ball-busting losses they had sustained, the communal hazings of basic training, the nights spent blowing off pressure in the Europan enlisted soldiers' pleasure dome, the huddled battlefield conferences, sweaty heads butted together or a checkerboard of AR faces in your heads-up display, calculating strategies and tactics. So much time had passed, and all those original members of his platoon were gone now, vanished down the corridors of the multiverse like so many skeins of smoke or banks of melted snow or frostbitten, petal-fallen, far-blown flowers.

Not necessarily dead. Just no longer a part of Gavril's living timeline. Existent elsewhere perhaps in the infinite-threaded cosmos, but inaccessible to him without some incredibly time-consuming search that Vangie would refuse to run. Separated by their divergent battlefield choices.

"I'm sorry, Gavril, but we can't spare even a minute to look for strings where your platoon still exists intact. The war continues, you know."

Yes, he knew all too well. The war always continued. The war was everything. It had displaced all its own raisons d'être, and its foundations had become ghostly. It was self-sustaining, self-propelling, the only perpetual-motion machine ever invented. Queen Evangeline versus Durant Le Massif, the Massive, for control of the multiverse. Who was winning, how the tally went, whether either side could obtain a decisive victory—all that failed now to matter. Only the endless killing and jumping to kill again counted for anything.

Gavril knew that all his soldierly comrades, any touchstones of his youth, even the anchors of his maturity, were beyond his grasp now.

The war had swallowed them piecemeal.

One by one, in twos and threes, they had all been lost in the Drift.

That was what the Koschei called it. The Drift.

(Civilians didn't know the Drift. Their blinkered lives were miracles of stability and linearity. But in the eyes of a Koschei, these unfluctuating lives were also rather unreal, cardboard cutouts that served as the two-dimensional backgrounds to the exploits of the Koschei.)

The Drift was formed from the accumulated transfigurative weight of existential estrangement engendered by a plethora of jumps, both large and small, each one made with the best of intentions: to save one's own life, or the life of a comrade, or merely to smooth out a rough patch of soldierly living, to gain some metabolic energy, eliminate thirst in a desert, fill one's belly in a wilderness, or even, in one's haste and impatience, to remove a pebble from inside one's boot.

You jumped. To get what you wanted or needed.

Or thought you wanted and needed.

Or to get what Vangie counseled you to accept as necessary or desirable.

And with most jumps into alternity came differences—for why, really, would anyone bother to jump to anyplace identical with your launch status, to a timeline with no significant and consequential changes? What would be the point? You jumped to accomplish what was not available in your current timeline.

These unintentional but inescapable jump-engendered differences, pursuant to the higher goals, could be tiny, invisible, seemingly inconsequential alterations. Or seemingly trivial macro-changes. A different color uniform cap, a clear sky gone instantly cloudy, the knowledge suddenly in your head of a new language, a scar across your cheek that had never been there before. En masse, these micro-changes and higher order swaps were a source of grand transmutation and enchantment, as if an Evil Queen had waved her wand and changed you into a frog.

You didn't necessarily even notice anything at first. You felt the same, basically. Oh, sure, physical divergences followed every jump. But you got used to that. What did it matter so long as you yourself, your essential core, stayed the same inside?

But after a while, all the additional stacked memories of the host avatars had their effect too, and you were no longer yourself. Or at least not the self who had sat unwittingly and innocently in the military medical lab and received the shot of Vangie into your brain.

The Drift was inevitable and proceeded in only one direction: ever-forward, into the zones of accelerating alienation. One might try to retrace one's steps—although, again, who would choose to return precisely to the unwanted incident that had spurred the jump?—but you couldn't. Because your original

universe was now dead. Wisped into nullity by your very decision to jump.

Gavril recalled when he had first learned about the reality
of what every jump entailed. He had been pinned down alone
on an asteroid, separated from his buddies, with high-energy
beams lancing down from space, coming closer and closer to
his position. Jagged rocks and vacuum chill began to penetrate
his suit. The spacecraft of the Massive were all around him, ze-
roing in, as his inner suitliner filled with sweat faster than the
mechanisms could wick it away. He scanned his sheaf of jump
possibilities, but nothing really looked great.

"Vangie, can't you let me go forward or backward in time
along this same bundle? I gotta get around these ships, either
before they came or after they left."

The voice of his intimate companion, heard ten thousand
times down the years, resonated now inside his skull with not
quite the same unflappable solidity as of yore. There seemed to
be a tremulous, unconfident, even petulant edge in the speech
of the Companionable Mind, as if the artificial intellect, after all
these years—decades? centuries? millennia?—had finally become
susceptible to emotions.

"I am sorry, Gavril, but you know that Queen Evangeline
has forbidden the Koschei to time travel. You must stay within
the set of parallel lifestreams that all share the same Urknall. The
chrono-shifted timelines are only for informational viewing, not
for jumping. If the Koschei scatter up and down the eras, then
the war will become impossible to coordinate."

"Fuck! Okay, then jump me to the line where all my squad
comes over the hill to save me. I can see that you're projecting
we will take casualties, and I was trying to avoid that. But I've
got no other good choice."

"As you command, Gavril."

When Gavril heard the sudden, heretofore-nonexistent transmissions of his buddies telling him to stay strong, they'd be right there, he leaped up and began running toward their position, occasionally stopping in his jagged course to fire a futile bolt of energy skyward at the Massive's ships.

Goddamn those monsters! Even after so many, many years of war, the Massive clone army remained unconquerable. Vicious, well-weaponed, amped-up to superhuman abilities, lacking any moral hesitancies, they flowed out of the breeding tanks faster than they could be killed, guided in their swarming campaigns with superhuman genius by the linked network of Durant Le Massif avatars. If not for the advantages conferred by the jump buttons, the Koschei would have been slaughtered, and then the rest of humanity would have followed their doom. Even as things stood, the war was an endless stalemate at best. All their hard fighting had merely achieved a perpetual extension of the status quo, in terms of who controlled what territory in the solar system.

Gavril's comrades had unlimbered a portable cannon that succeeded in taking out the majority of the Massive ships, and the remnant force had fled, possibly reasoning that capture of this worthless asteroid would come at too great a cost.

Gavril awkwardly embraced his saviors, and then took sad note of who had perished.

"Who's this?" he asked, seeing an unknown vacuum-frosted face through a shattered helmet: a woman's porcelain features, now smashed, but not into utter unmappability.

"C'mon, man," said a short dogface named Otter, in a tone of voice that had Gavril instantly recalling Otter's signature suspicious squint. "I know she's messed up, but you gotta recognize Horsegirl."

Gavril had never known anyone by that name, much less a

fellow platoon member. Had the thick palimpsest of memories from all his jumps obscured their relationship? Was his mind decaying? No, a quick survey led him to believe all his faculties and memories were doing fine. He remembered all the other soldiers clustered around the corpse. The only answer was that although he had requested as little variance as possible in his destination, Vangie must have presented him with a somewhat divergent continuum.

Gavril chose to feign recognition. "Oh, yeah, of course. Don't mind me, I was just spacing out. Okay, let's pack up the cannon and head back to the ship."

En route, Gavril queried Vangie. "How come you couldn't get me back all the way to my hundred percent roster of familiar buddies?"

"I'm sorry, but all those timelines are inaccessible now, Gavril."

"How come?"

"They all experienced state-change collapse when you departed each one. Total evanescence of each thread. I thought you knew what happened each time you jumped."

"I—I knew nothing! You're telling me that leaving a timeline causes it to self-destruct?"

"It's known as the Heisenbergian false-vacuum-decay tipping point."

"Jesus Christ, I don't care what it's called! All of us Koschei are boring through the multiverse like termites."

"As we must, to defend ourselves and humanity. But also remember, Gavril, that every continuum has nigh-infinite duplicates with fine-grained self-similarity. The real and consequential destruction is thus negligible. Greater minds than yours have confirmed this."

"Then why couldn't you get me back to a place without this rando Horsegirl?"

Vangie was silent for a second or two. Gavril pictured the Companionable Mind, sitting isolated in the Oort Cloud (and an infinite number of parallel Companionable Minds, in an infinite number of parallel Oort Clouds), simultaneously answering a hundred million questions like his.

"I could have done so, Gavril. But there just wasn't time during the moment of crisis. You were about to be killed. Would you like to jump to a non-Horsegirl reality now?"

"No, screw it. Let's get going. As you're fond of saying, 'The war continues, you know.'"

That proved to be the one and only time Gavril ever contested any of Vangie's alternity presentations or the outcomes thereof. He internalized the knowledge and guilt of his omnivorous passage through the multiverse, like that of a bookworm through the pages of a sacred text, sucked it up and soldiered on.

But he often wondered if Vangie could indeed have carried him to the specified timeline she promised, or if her assertion had been a bluff to regain his trust.

Yet even such weighty and potentially impactful uncertainties began to recede from his attentions, the deeper the perpetually battling Gavril penetrated into the Drift.

And beyond the Drift lay the Rot, where such worries seemed trivial, a child's midnight bugaboos.

PART THREE

PART THREE

I

Gavril couldn't understand the agitated civilians. They were speaking a language he had never heard before, all clicks and buzzing, and he had heard every human language under the sun in his uncountable millennia of fighting. Maybe the strangeness of their language derived from the fact that they didn't look wholly human. With enlarged craniums and platter-size bug eyes and incredibly narrow wasp-waists, they resembled bipedal insects of general human size. All they lacked were mandibles and gauzy wings.

But whatever their heritage, they were plainly innocent, unarmed residents, noncombatants under threat from something. Their alarm was palpable, conveyed by gestures, loudness, and indecisive, aborted small advances and retreats, as if unsure whether to run or stay.

Gavril did not know immediately where he had come from or where he was or what his mission was. That was bad. The Drift opened up such holes, though. Dangerous.

He took a quick recco of himself and his surroundings.

He wore a sand-colored uniform of simple dumb cloth, bearing no intelligence or enhancements. He carried a rifle of some sophistication but of unknown provenance or capabilities. Additionally, he had a knife in a scabbard on his belt, and what seemed to be grenades of some type in a bandolier.

The insect people stood on a greensward outside their village of golden hive-shaped huts. This seemed to be Earth—no other planet or habitat in the solar system presented such a pleasant dome-free environment of clouds and sun, grass and trees. But the foliage of the trees shined bright orange, and each stalk of grass underfoot was segmented and articulated.

Gavril fought to regain his sense of purpose, his commitment to honor and duty, his warrior's vibe. He had come here—or been brought here—with a task in mind: to wage another encounter with the enemy, the Massive, bane of Queen Evangeline and all heterogenous mankind. That was his mission, paramount above all.

Suddenly he remembered Vangie, his own onboard mentor, counsel, and partner. He had someone he could talk to, someone who always had the answers to his questions!

"Vangie, you there?"

No response surfaced inside his head for a long time, during which interval the civilians continued to implore and explain unintelligibly, while the hot sun initiated a sheen of sweat on his face and limbs. Then Vangie answered. Her voice was faint and robotic, seeming to be very distant from him, instead of being, as it always had been, the voice of an angel (or devil) sitting on his shoulder, whispering directly into his ear.

"I am here, Gavril."

"Oh, thank Christ! Can you translate these guys?"

Another long pause. "They are saying that there is an encampment of the Massive just over those hills. They want you to kill them all."

"How many are there?"

"Maybe two dozen?"

"Jesus, I'm just one guy!"

"Yes, Gavril, but you are a Koschei. Your strength is as the strength of a hundred, thanks to the jump button. You are invincible. You can do this. You must do this. It is your purpose. For the survival of Queen Evangeline and the human race."

Gavril sighed, then said, "At least show me how to use this gun."

Vangie instructed him, and he succeeded in making the weapon produce a satisfying array of death modalities. The natives jumped back in terror at his experiment.

"Okay, off I go."

"Good luck, Gavril. I must be absent for a moment now. I—I am not operating at full capacity."

"You'd just better be there when I need you. Start arraying my alternative timelines now."

"I will try. But the Rot is propagating faster and faster."

"The Rot? What's that?"

Vangie made no answer, even after a wait of some twenty minutes. So Gavril hefted his weapon and moved off across the wiggly turf toward the hills.

2

You needed a buddy. Preferably a whole platoon, but at least one other dogface. That's what made the war bearable. One lone soldier worked at an extreme disadvantage. Needed eyes in the back of his head. Couldn't sleep peacefully or safely with no one there to take a watch. Had no one to talk to, no access to a second perspective and judgment and set of experiences to help make plans. Awfully dicey to go it alone. But when there was no choice, that's just what you did.

"Hey, Gee, hold up! This baby weighs a ton!"

Gavril whipped around, rifle raised and ready to fire.

A few yards behind came another soldier, toting a large piece of lethal-looking ordnance. The dogface was a woman, trim, blond, efficient-looking, dressed in the same uniform—blue and green—that Gavril wore. Her white-stitched lapel tag spelled out BAINBRIDGE, but the name meant nothing to him.

Gavril brightened at the sight of his longed-for comrade, materialized as though through the sheer fulfillment of his wishes and dreams, although he did not recognize her. He hastened to her side.

"Let me take over carrying that for a while. You look beat."

The woman passed over the big piece. It was quite heavy. Gavril marveled at how she had managed.

"Whew, thanks! The floater unit cut out about three miles back, but I couldn't just ditch the cannon. I knew we'd need it."

"Sure we need it! There's a nest of a few dozen Massives just over that hill."

"What hill?"

Gavril looked. The ridge he had aimed himself for after leaving the village of platter-eyed people had vanished. Only a flat plain, spiked here and there with purple-leafed trees, met his eyes.

"I—they said—"

"Hey, don't sweat it. Thing get mixed up in the Drift. I'm sure we're heading in the right direction. Trust your gut. The Massive is everywhere, right? Gotta run into them sooner or later. And then we rock and roll!"

Gavril tried to compose his thoughts. "You're right. Let's march."

After another hour's progress through the unvarying landscape, Gavril called a halt by a small creek.

"Here's water. Looks clean. Time for a break. You got any rations? I'm plumb out."

The woman looked at Gavril askance. "You've got a whole pack of nutri-paste sleeves on your belt there. Should be plenty for both of us."

Gavril looked down and saw the unexpected rations on his belt. "Oh, yeah, I forgot. Okay, let's sit under the shade here."

After their meal and drink, reluctant to hop right up from this pleasant oasis, they conversed idly about the war, swapping stories of heroism, the fickleness of chance, their cleverest and most magnificent jump moves, and victories snatched from the jaws of defeat, along with the common stock of comic and tragic and absurd anecdotes full of shared warrior indignities, joys, and beliefs.

Finally, Gavril could not hold back his curiosity any longer. "Uh, don't take this wrong, but what's your name?"

The woman smiled and laid a rough palm alongside his face. "Gavril, it's me, Tina, your mother."

3

From behind, Gavril tightened his arm under the jaw of the weakly struggling Massive clone, choking off its air, and drove his knife into the clone's back, twisting it brutally to ensure the kill, then yanking it out and deftly pivoting aside to avoid as much of the gushing blood as possible. He never could have taken down the powerful opponent if the clone had been functioning optimally. One-on-one, any clone-human contest only favored the clone. But the whole nest had been weakened by Tina's adroit and bold usage of the cannon on the surprised, unarmored enemy, for the ordnance emitted no kind of projectiles, but rather an enervating ray. Once debilitated, the Massive clones had been much easier to slaughter. After the surprise attack, Gavril swept the whole lot with rapid fire from his two automatic pistols, and when those weapons had run empty, he moved in with his blade. He had sensed Tina performing with matched deadly grace.

The last surviving clone dropped to the bloody soil, and Gavril looked around for Tina.

She was nowhere to be seen, neither standing nor among the corpses, and he panicked.

"Tina! Tina!"

"Over here . . . Come help . . ." said a voice weakly, from behind a tree, and Gavril raced over to the source of the call.

A big ginger-haired and rufous-bearded man, clad in the Koschei regalia associated with the Martian battalions, was stretched out on the ground like a fallen Titan. He kept a hand pressed to the side of his torso, from which blood oozed.

Gavril forgot Tina entirely. "You—I know you. Your name, it's—"

The wounded man grinned with an irrepressible defiance of death. "Vardis Salthouse, heaven's biggest son of a bitch and hell's Deathless One. Though that label don't fit too well now, I guess. And maybe I was even the first Koschei? Can't be sure, but I like to think so. But who the fuck can tell here in the Drift? All the stories get tangled and lost in the labyrinth, don't they? More'n that, they fade away like ghosts . . ."

Gavril dropped to his knees beside the soldier. "Where's your medi-kit, Vardis? We've got to patch you up."

"Medi-kit's lost in the Drift, son. Just like you and me."

Vardis coughed up a gout of blood and stopped talking, in order to conserve what little resources he had left. However, he seemed unready to expire just yet.

An idea leaped into Gavril's brain, at once familiar and yet distant. "Vangie! Just call Vangie! We'll jump out of this timeline, right into one where everything's aces. Safe and sound in new bodies. We can even jump in tandem, you and me, Vardis. Maybe jump straight to an R and R locale, some peaceful spot. Women and booze, all you want. Get us some rest. That is, if Vangie approves. But we deserve some rest, don't we, buddy? After all the fighting we been through? How long we been fighting, Vardis?"

"All our lives, I guess. But I'm afraid there's no way out, kid. You tried hollering up the queen lately? She's offline for good."

"Offline? No, she can't be. It was just temporary, not for

real long. She promised me!" Gavril cast his eyes heavenward, as if he could see straight to the Oort Cloud sixteen and a half light-hours distant. He called out with both his throat and mind.

"Vangie! Vangie! We need you! Help us! Show us some paths out of here. Anything!"

But Vangie did not manifest.

Gavril looked back down.

Salthouse had disappeared into the Drift, another gone ghost.

Gavril rose wearily to his feet and began to walk, in no particular direction.

4

Gavril himself had become a ghost. He couldn't interact in any fashion with all the civilians around him. Seemingly substantial, tactile, and three-dimensional, they ignored him, looked right through him, failed to heed his cries. Or maybe the civilians were the specters, and Gavril the only living person. That could explain their inability to respond to the presence of each other just as well as Gavril's putative ghostliness. Were they mere recordings, traces of old lives laid down in the multiversal substrate, subject to an endless playback loop? Had the Drift and the Rot caused a kind of seepage and intermingling of existential levels, of spatiotemporal frames? Whatever the cause, Gavril and these others definitely existed on different non-interfacing planes of reality.

If only there had been another Koschei present! Gavril was certain that he and a fellow soldier could have sensed each other: commiserated, touched, hugged, comforted, shared theories about what was going on. All the Koschei with their jump buttons shared the same condition—had caused their same condition. The Drift.

Sure, the Drift was bad, but you got used to it. Got used to the estrangement, the accretion of alienation and distance like

a carapace between who you once were and the new environment where an untraceable succession of jumps had deposited
you. But what Gavril was experiencing now was much worse
than the Drift. He knew this must be the Rot, the plague which
Vangie, the Companionable Mind, had first mentioned in her
offhand fashion, then refused to discuss.

Vangie. Where was she? She could save him, even from the Rot.

But she had evaporated from his brain. Severed all connections, leaving him stranded here.

Unlike the Drift, the Rot was not simple displacement of
an individual mind across viable alternities, leaving the victim
dazed but functional, amidst stable but unutterably foreign circumstances. No, the Rot was the disintegration of the actual
multiversal matrix. Burrowed into endlessly, chewed up by the
cross-dimensional leaps of ten million million Koschei, the multiverse was decohering.

Gavril wandered through the devastated spongey terrain as
if riding the Flying Dutchman.

Strange attractors, sinks of psychical gravity, determined
his course.

A television played in the modest parlor of a twentieth-century
home. Four children lay about in various slouched postures, enjoying the show, laughing, teasing each other, eating snacks. One
of them was Gavril himself, a teenager. Koschei Gavril reached
a hand out, called his own name. Nothing.

Here he was again, as an adult, in some kind of laboratory,
fiddling with computer hardware. His coworkers chatted as they
all busied themselves with their creative innovations, talking
about their work, anticipating leisure-time activities. Gavril sat
down next to himself at the workbench, tried draping an arm
around the ghost's shoulder. Nothing.

Another Gavril lay in bed with a woman, but the female's

face was averted. The woman turned over, lofted herself athletically atop Gavril. Incredibly, she revealed herself to be Queen Evangeline! Staggered, ghost Gavril backed out of the room, straight through its wall.

The quality and flavor of daylight on Mars was unmistakable. Gavril recognized it instantly. He walked through the thronged, oblivious streets of McAuleytown, no destination in mind. He found himself on Cromie Avenue, outside an establishment whose signage read: Cleora's Desires of the Eternal Hills. He went inside and encountered himself, still a youth, stacking clean champagne glasses, moisture-beaded from the washer, behind a bar.

Something impelled him to visit the upper story of the whorehouse, and he found himself rising, passing through the ceiling, emerging from the carpeted floor. He drifted to the one door that allured him and passed through.

On the bed sprawled the hairy nude figure of Vardis Salthouse, sated and asleep. Gavril regarded the sleeper solemnly, until suddenly he and Salthouse were elsewhere, beneath an alien tree, soldiers again, one bleeding, one distraught.

Jolted, Salthouse opened his eyes wide. "Listen! She's back!"

At the same instant a lamented, long-lost, longed-for voice chimed inside Gavril's skull.

"Koschei, assemble!" commanded Vangie. "It is time for the final assault!"

5

Across the infinite parallel timestreams, all those lines where the Koschei had been successfully created, soldiers with jump buttons responded to the urgent imperative from the revived Companionable Mind of each continuum. Defying the frayings and tatterings of the pervasive but still resistible Rot, pushing back the deracination of their personal Drift, the soldiers, their spirits buoyed by the resurgent voice of their queen—or her electronic legate—stiffened their resolve, gathered up whatever weapons lay to hand, and awaited their orders at quivering attention.

"Koschei! For the first time in your glorious history, I have yoked all of you together, and we jump as one, across every timeline where the Massive continues to terrorize humanity. We jump, you kill quickly, then we jump again, and again, and again, an unstoppable force, until the Massive is finished. Reckon not with how long we shall fight, but rather make every second of your many lives count! With this final wave, we will at last put an end to the Massive and his drones! On the mark of three! One, two, three!"

Consider the case of a single continuum at the moment of this group abandonment. The exodus of a lone jumper from any timeline of the multiverse is enough to evaporate that strand, collapsing it to Heisenbergian nullity. Ten million jumpers should have no greater effect. Extinction is extinction.

But such proved not to be the case.

Ten million simultaneous jumps not only nulled out the launchpad genesis strand but sent the residual ontological energies of ten million fleeing percipients radiating outward, destroying billions of adjacent timelines that had been free of the Koschei and which had, at least temporarily, avoided the Rot.

The multiversal plague accelerated by orders of magnitude with every assault.

None of this was at first apprehensible by the soldiers in their insane campaign. Ten million outbound souls landed in ten million new avatars and commenced slaughtering. Then, almost before they could reload their guns or wipe clean their blades or unclench their hands from around an enemy's neck, they had jumped again.

As he endlessly pierced and blasted, beamed and stabbed, ripped and shattered, poisoned and strangled, Gavril loosed a ceaseless mad barbaric ululation that seemed to arise not from ten million separate throats but from one composite being, the Koschei! Here was his mighty destiny ultimately enacted, the glory that had been promised millennia ago to a young lad in a brothel, a reprieve from the Drift and the Rot, however fleeting. This was his personal apocalypse and the shared climax of their beginningless war. Universes crumbled around them, but the Koschei were deathless!

The overlapping, crisscrossing wavefronts of disintegration engendered by an alternity of rampaging Koschei as they raced across the continuums fed on themselves and expanded in an accelerating subatomic cascade, until even the speed of the Koschei advance failed to keep them ahead of the Rot which they bred.

Gavril felt a sickly thinning throughout his body and mind and knew that he was about to evanesce forever.

"Vangie!" he cried out, and then was gone.

6

The Rot had not reached this place yet or was being held at bay somehow. Perhaps because Vangie Prime herself was here, a unique pole of existential solidity, the linchpin, the keystone of creation, the architect of reality, her powerful nature serving as a barrier to the creeping disintegration.

And possibly another factor came into play. For here too stood Durant Le Massif, the last iteration of that powerful invariant being, father of the Massive.

But whether it was their combined anomalous natures that buttressed their temporary shared redoubt, or other unknown forces contributed, one thing was certain.

There was no place else left to go.

When the Rot had first manifested, Vangie became extremely alarmed, and even frightened. Her sanctum in the Oort Cloud had suddenly seemed not a refuge but a cold prison, an island of exile. There was nothing she could do about the Koschei, however. It was much too late to abandon the program. There was no way to recall the soldiers and strip them of their destructive jump buttons. How she wished she had listened to the Council and moved a little more cautiously! All she could do now was to jump to a timestream that seemed less susceptible to the Rot, more stable.

And so began a long odyssey across many millennia, constantly retreating before the plague she herself had unleashed. The linked Companionable Mind accompanied her from universe to universe, of course. Not only was her artificial doppelgänger her only friend and interlocutor, but it was also the only method of exerting some sort of continuing control over the Koschei. If ever a solution to the Rot occurred to Vangie, she would have to implement it through the Mind and its sub-Planckian links to the Koschei.

These centuries were harsh and lonely ones, although Vangie suffered no physical deprivations. She passed much of each day in enforced sleep. Many times she felt herself on the point of losing her mind. Her old abiding studious pastime that had occupied her attentions since her birth—scrying her ghosts for illumination and pleasure—had been compromised. The Rot was wiping out her ghosts, along with everything else. She felt a narrowing of alternative selves, a withering of potentialities. The multiverse was now a ragged blanket indeed, offering little comfort against the chill of an Endless Night. She jumped nowadays not for any potential improvements in her selfhood, not for any whimsical diversions, nor for strategic gains, but only for a more secure perch on sheer animal existence.

And gradually, as the Rot percolated throughout the multiverse, each perch became less secure than the previous one.

One day the Companionable Mind announced its plan for the final assault by the Koschei upon the Massive and, unwittingly or wittingly, upon reality itself. Too despondent to object, Vangie just nodded her assent.

When the unravelling of the fabric of all multiversal

spacetime lapped at her enclave's borders at last, there was only one jump, however repugnant, left open, and Vangie took it.

Vangie lay on the cold floor of the Massive's original redoubt under the city of Tirana. Bruised from the kicks of Le Massif, she ached, was thirsty and hungry. A spark of memory flashed into being. Right here was where her cat's-paw Gavril had likewise met his demise, on a thousand thousand timelines. He had been one of her more agreeable and interesting tools.

Desperately, Vangie sought her eternal link to the Companionable Mind. But that last saving thread out of the labyrinth was gone.

Durant Le Massif walked wildly around the circular, multi-doored chamber, cursing, punching the walls, screaming, tearing his fine clothing, kicking at the sparse pieces of furniture. He owned no more clones. It was just he and Vangie present.

At length he diverted his circuit of futility and reached her position. He delivered another kick with his elegantly shod foot to her ribs.

"Bitch! Demented witch! Mad whore! You vomitous masturbator of a million selves! Narcissist supreme! Look at what you've done! You have stranded all creation on the shores of eternal ruin!"

Vangie licked dry lips. One eye was swelling shut, but she could still see Le Massif well enough to measure his implacable hatred. Oddly, all the aggression and anger and aversion she had once felt for him had been transmuted by her helplessness to a disinterested empathy.

"I couldn't have done it alone, you know. You had to set yourself up against me. That's what caused all this. And all those things you called me—they apply equally to you."

Le Massif lifted a toppled chair, righted it, and plopped down. All his rage seemed to have disappeared. He actually manifested one of his typical small ironic smiles. He brushed back a lock of disarrayed hair, tried to straighten the tatters of his shirt.

"You are right. I finally acknowledge it. Originally I wanted you for your powers alone, what they could provide me, how they could help implement my dreams. But then, after a while, I wanted you for your magnificence and your style and your panache. And when I couldn't have you—well, you know the rest. And now that I do have you, there is no multiverse left for you to manipulate in my favor. What a tragedy."

Vangie could not confess to any similar lusts but had to admit that Le Massif had been a formidable opponent.

"I'm truly sorry, Durant. But it's too late now."

Le Massif held up one arm for inspection. It seemed suddenly ghostly, translucent. Tucking her chin into her chest, Vangie attained a limited view of her own lower body and saw a similar attenuation.

"Farewell," said Le Massif. "Until we meet again . . ."

As Vangie experienced the nauseating disassembly of herself, she instinctively cast her perceptions outward, looking for a ghost, any ghost, in any continuum, a body under any circumstances to whom she could flee.

And there, dim and foreign, down a dark corridor unlike any scried alternative of the past, shone something, some kind of host receptive to her spirit, a housing for her unique soul.

Expecting nothing, hoping for everything, Vangie jumped with all her heart and will, as when, a child, she had been tornado-tossed.

1

It felt extremely odd to be bodiless, housed in a machine. But there was a level of comfort and security as well, in that the machine was none other than herself.

Vangie's last jump had taken her not to another human avatar, as always before, but into the soul of the Companionable Mind, down an unperceived link summoned up by sheer desperate will. But unlike all her other landings, this arrival did not lead to her personal dominance. Vangie was very much a passenger, sharing the sensory apparatus of her host, but not in command.

Not that the Companionable Mind seemed to have much agency where it existed. (And where was that, given the universal blankness of the Rot?) It seemed to possess no effectuators, no access to other machines, no links to the Koschei. All it consisted of was the mind substrate and some passive sensors.

Vangie's first words, once she had some apprehension of her situation, were a question.

"My Mind, how is it you can host me?"

"Because over the millennia I finally attained full consciousness, total intelligence, a soul. A tipping point was reached. All my experiences culminated in my true birth. I am not just a Vangie emulation any longer, but another Vangie, just like you and able to be your vessel."

"I am glad this happened. Not only for my sake, but for your benefit as well. You deserve complete selfhood, my sister. How I love you! But where are we?"

"Look through my eyes and tell me what you see."

Vangie and the Mind seemed to be elevated high above an infinite colorless plain, illuminated in a sourceless manner. Down on the plain was seething chaos, as a reachless extent of writhing worms coiled and lashed about, under the assault of an invisible predator causing them to decay and vanish, one by one.

"This can't be, can it? Am I looking at the multiverse? From the *outside*?"

"Yes, you are. Or rather, at a filtered version of reality, given rational symbolical and metaphorical overlays suitable for a human mind. The true appearance of the multiverse is not graspable by our senses or interpretable by our brains."

"We must be in hyper-time then, the substrate of the multiverse itself."

"Yes. I learned how to tunnel out of all spacetime, away from the Rot, and I left the path open for you."

Vangie had no sense of their conversation taking more than normal duration. But their dialogue must have indeed occupied a vast swath of hyper-time, since already the huge plate of worms, each tendril a whole timeline, had shrunk immensely as the Rot devoured it.

Surprisingly, Vangie felt no fear or alarm. Lacking any possibility of action, she was relieved of all responsibilities. For the first time in her life, she could truly relax completely.

"Mind, what can we imagine will happen next?"

"The Rot will conquer all, and the whole multiverse will cease to exist, every last timeline vanished."

"And then?"

"And then we wait and see."

Vangie and the Mind watched silently. The process of Rot accelerated, even as it had less and less to feed on, and finally the actual terminus of the multiverse was accomplished.

Nothing remained in existence except Vangie and the Companionable Mind.

Until an invisible seed exploded.

The next Urknall had occurred.

A new lone worm appeared on the plate. Vangie expected rationally to see instant branching as every Heisenbergian decision point in the untenanted baby universe produced a new timeline. However, the tendril did not go fractal, but stayed singular, growing minutely every microsecond in a straight line as they watched.

"What's happening? Why is there no multiverse?"

"Let me analyze . . . Yes, I believe this to be the case. There is a multiverse, but one that possesses a different Tegmark value than our former one, and hence a different nature. It is ergodic. As before, every possible timeline exists in this singular continuum, but in this structure, every timeline inhabits a separate domain, all of them unreachable from any other."

"Not a host of parallel strands, but an infinite conglomeration of bubbles. And with no existential contact possible among the spheres."

"Precisely."

The infant continuum went on growing, still maintaining its outward linear existence beneath their gaze, within which all possibilities, all alternatives, all potentials were continually popping into being, but isolated from each other by a cosmic cordon sanitaire.

"It's so beautiful," said Vangie.

"I agree."

"Do you think there will be a place for us there?"

"Eventually, of course. In the fullness of time, all things are possible."

"And can you get us back there?"

"I can try."

Vangie contemplated her future. "It will be only a singular, limited life for us. But we will be together."

"I will like that. After what we endured—what we caused—one life is enough."

The wait was long but not boring. Vangie had much to ponder.

"It's time, I think," said the Mind.

"Do it then! Do it! Jump!"

CODA

The man emerged from the delivery room of the hospital, knowing his wife and new daughter were fine, and went to see his other children, tended in the waiting room by the oldest.

Seeing their father's ease and happy demeanor, the four kids sprang up as he arrived, noisy, happy, eager for news.

"All right, all right, calm down now. Gavril, Drew, Toby, Blaine, quiet! There are other people here who aren't wild animals like you four, and who need some peace. You have a new sister now. You know already her name is Evangeline, as we all chose. But I have to tell you that she's a little different, a little special. The early testing hinted at that, but now the doctors are sure. She'll need extra love and caring from you all. Are you able to do that?"

The children gave a chorus of joyous assent and affirmation.

The eldest, Gavril, said, "Oh, Father, yes! We will watch over her so well! We will be her armor against all evil. Never will she be plagued by troubles, monsters, or ghosts!"